ALMA UNDERWOOD IS NOT A KLEPTOMANIAC

LACEY DAILEY

Published by: Lacey Dailey

Editing: Bookfully Yours

Proofreading: All Encompassing Books

For Tristan—
Because every time I look at you, I feel the butterfly kisses
and hear the tiny violins.
You're my Ace.

1

KLEPTOMANIAC

ALMA

My brother says I'm a kleptomaniac. I'm not. I don't steal things. I take things.

A lot of the stuff I attain is lame everyday junk that will never make it to my interesting items list. These are the dull things like various electronic chargers, packs of gum, or half empty tubes of chapstick.

On a lucky day, I find something that's actually worth taking. My collection consists of— but is not limited to— one left shoe, pink post-it notes, a keychain from the Detroit airport, three screwdrivers of various sizes, a novelty concert tee, a handful of pixie sticks, toenail clippers, a three-hole punch, and a bright pink scrunchie. This afternoon, I'm adding a Polaroid camera with no photo paper.

Plopping my new camera on top of a pile of dirty towels, I grip my maid cart with two hands and slowly push it out of room six. The heavy door latches behind me with a click. I have to stop and give the left front wheel a good swift kick before I'm able to continue down the sidewalk. The thing is broken and doesn't manually turn as the other three do.

Pushing a pair of sunglasses up my nose, I start down the sidewalk. My muscles pulse with the hefty shove I give my cart. Jumping on the edge of my new rocket, I struggle to steer and pretend my job title isn't just *maid*. My rocket launching skills aren't as good as they used to be. Take me back to the days when I was a kid racing Walmart shopping carts with my brothers and sisters.

But this hunk of plastic will have to do. Last week, I created a pamphlet in an attempt to persuade my dad to get me some turbo blasters. Turns out, they don't exist.

Lame.

Mumbling under my breath, I curse my sudden boob sweat. No matter how much I love my worn-out overalls, they are not appropriate for a regular workday in the dead of August.

Checking the weather every morning in Michigan is like shaking a magic eight ball. You're never sure what you'll get and half the time you'll wish you never shook the thing in the first place. Today, the sun is hot and beating on my neck harshly, no doubt turning me into a lobster. Despite the sweat in my denim, I plaster a smile on my face anyway. Scorching sun is a hell of a lot better than an ice storm.

Mother Nature is kind of a moody bitch.

I push into the motel's main office and don't bother stopping myself from doing a little happy dance when I feel the cool air. The air conditioner here is as unreliable as a local cable company. But today, bless its little motor, it's working and cranked up on high. Flipping my sunglasses on the top of my head, I ditch my cart and walk right up to the unit. A little hum of happiness leaves my lips while I stand only inches away, letting stray pieces of my bangs flap with the blast.

Standing this close to the air conditioner reminds me of

the days my sister and I used to sit in front of a fan and sing 'Grand Funk Railroad'. Locomotion never sounded better.

Ding!

My blast from the past is interrupted when the call bell sounds and echoes off the old walls. Rolling my head, I find Reginald behind the front desk, his shaky hand hovering over the silver desk bell. He's got a smirk creeping up his wrinkly face and a glint in his eye.

"Young lady, when you stand in front of the air conditioner like that, it prevents the air from getting into the rest of the building."

He makes a fair point, so I step back, but only a small fraction. It isn't like there is anyone else in the building. It's just Reginald and me.

Typical for a Tuesday.

"What'd you find today?"

I reach for my newest treasure. "Polaroid camera. No film."

"I would suggest buying some film and putting it to good use, but that would be a waste of the breaths I've got left."

I never use any of the items I find. I take my lost treasures and keep them just as they are.

"You're right," I say, lifting my gaze to Reginald. "You wouldn't want to waste your breath. Who knows how many you have left."

"Was that an old man joke? You can do better than that."

"Of course I can, but I don't want to hurt your feelings. We're besties."

His blink is as slow as his walk. "I don't know what that word is."

"It means best friends. We've been over that one

before."

"Ah. Forgive me for forgetting. You've crammed hundreds of nonsense words into my head."

"Lingo, Reginald. It's considered lingo."

"It's an excuse to talk like hooligans is what it is."

"Time is changing." Leaning against my cart, I fiddle with the strap on my new camera. "You need to keep up."

"I have no plans to keep up with anything. Certainly not if it means language goes from full sentences to acronyms and made up words."

"Bestie is not a made up word. It's in the dictionary now."

"For Pete's sake."

I can't help my smirk. The way his hand flexes against the top of the counter and his wrinkles become more pronounced, I know he's getting agitated. Not that it takes much. At first glance, Reginald is a snippy old fart with a no-nonsense attitude and a better work ethic than people half his age. Underneath his breath-filled mumbles, usually telling me I'm full of piss and vinegar, lies the kindest soul to ever house a human body.

But *please* don't tell him I said so.

"Are you finished for the afternoon?"

I salute him. "Yes, Sir."

"Then put away that cart. Good gravy, how do you think that looks to any guest that walks in? You've got dirty towels in a heap on top of rolls of toilet paper."

My gaze is flat. "I think we both know nobody is going to come in."

Guests are few and far between at Great Lakes Motel. Probably because we aren't located anywhere near an actual bay of water. Guests look us up online believing their room is going to come with a view of one of the five Great Lakes when they really get a live action play by play of everything that's happening in Flat Rock's freight yard.

"Now that you've said that, somebody will come in. I'm not going to be pleased if they have to stare at that eyesore."

Though it sounds like it, Reginald isn't my boss. His only job is to head the front desk. Great Lakes Motel is actually owned and operated by an overzealous middle-aged couple. Together, they decided building a motel ten miles from downtown directly next to a freight yard was a good business decision. Their hearts were in the right place. Truly. They wanted a quaint and quiet place couples and families could use to escape the hustle and bustle of city life. It was shortly after marriage they decided to take the plunge and become small business owners.

The brave couple is Harrison and Clare Underwood. My parents.

I've heard the story of how Great Lakes Motel went from an idea on a hot dog napkin to a fully functional operation two thousand and forty-two times. My siblings and I have a tally going on the back of the twin's closet door. The love and thought my parents put into each nook and cranny of this motel is only one of the reasons I love it so much. It's decades old but cherished beyond belief. Take care of the things you love and they will last forever. This motel and its employee are a true testament to that.

Reginald is Great Lakes Motel's only employee. He was hired years ago after my parents put out a Senior Internship ad in the newspaper. Reggie was the only one who applied. Not exactly the type of senior they were looking for, but he does one hell of a job for a seventy-five-year-old.

So we kept him.

When he clears his throat, gesturing at my cart with a crooked finger, I abandon ship. After a kick to the faulty wheel, I set my camera aside and drag the oversized cart into the laundry room. I place the sheets and towels in the washer. The loud clunk followed by an obnoxious hum tells me the machine is running. After restocking my cart with toilet paper, clean towels, and fancy bars of soap, I hop up on the washing machine to get a closer look at my new toy.

With my body rocking like I'm stuck inside a storm simulator at the mall, I run my finger across the small crack marring the edge of the camera. After holding it up to my eye as if I'm about to take a photo of the dull laundry room, I find the crack doesn't hinder the quality of the photo at all.

So why was it left behind?

It's a question I ask every time I find an item, and an answer I create all on my own. For each item I take, there's a story in my journal on how it got there. I call it: *A Book of Unwanted Treasures by Alma Underwood*.

That book is proof I'm not a kleptomaniac, despite how often Shepherd expresses his concern. Everything I take was left behind.

Ditched.

Dumped.

Forgotten about.

I'm the one who saves them. If anything, I should get a handshake and a peace medal, not a push towards therapy from my siblings. Out of the five Underwood children, I'm the only one who works at the motel. Of course, we've all been stuck working here at some point but I'm the only kid who works on a regular basis.

And you can bet the last slice in the pizza box this blue polaroid camera is one of the reasons why.

Everything has to come from somewhere. My favorite thing in the world is creating somewheres. Especially for the things that look a little broken.

Those are always the most remarkable.

2

THE UNDERWOODS

ALMA

Sometimes people like to ask me what my favorite treasure is. Which is a completely unfair, absurd question. That's like asking a parent who their favorite child is. The answer is an impossible one.

When my mom gets asked to give the proverbial favorite child trophy to one of her five children, she declares one of two things:

1. She doesn't like any of us because we trash her house and are seemingly incapable of putting dishes in the dishwasher even though it's only two feet from the sink.

2. She loves us all equally and could never choose between her five greatest blessings.

The second one sounds like it was a bit rehearsed, but it's the answer I've chosen to give when my friends ask me to choose an item as my favorite.

I love them all equally.

It's a cheesy, cliche answer. But it's my answer, and I'm sticking to it.

"Hey." Lenox cocks her hip, leaning against my old

wooden doorframe, her nose to the ceiling. "Mom said dinner is ready."

My doorframe is bright green and from where I'm perched on my bed, it should really be the most questionable thing in sight. But it's my sister and the deli meat she has on her face. "Why is there a piece of bologna on your face?"

"It's not bologna. It's a face mask." Her fingertips flutter across her meat mask, smoothing out any wrinkles. "It's supposed to be rejuvenating."

Rotating my upper body, I let my journal fall to my lap. "What exactly is being rejuvenated?"

"I literally have no idea. It was in the dollar bin at Target and it had a llama on it."

"You bought a bologna mask because it had a llama on it?"

"Yep." She takes the few steps that are needed to make it to the edge of my bed and flops backward, slapping her palm against her forehead to prevent her mask from slipping off. Turning her head, her round eyes peer at me out of little slits cut into her creepy mask. "I have an extra one if you want to try."

"What? A bologna mask? No, thanks." I stand up, tucking my journal beneath my pillow where it will be safe, and kick her in the foot. "Come on. We need food before the twins take it up to their rooms and experiment on it."

With a quick bounce, she's off my bed and leading me out of my room in the attic. "The twins are weird."

"Says the girl with bologna on her face."

"Touché, little sister."

I roll my eyes and push past her, barreling down the narrow flight of stairs. Lenox is only ten and a half months older than me. Irish twins is what we're called. Despite not sharing a fetus and being actual twins, people mistake us for what we aren't all the time. Rightfully so considering Lenox and I share a face. Beneath the bologna mask lies a face the shape of a perfect oval, sprinkled with a dainty nose, saucer-sized green eyes, and a slight flush on her pale cheeks. Each and every characteristic an exact copy of mine.

After watching 'It Takes Two', we took a nod from the Olsen Twins and tried to switch places in the fourth grade. Blake Miller wouldn't stop bullying me and Lenox thought it'd be a brilliant idea to be me for a day so she could kick him in the nuts.

It worked until she, well I, got recess detention for a week. I refused to be punished for what she did, so I made a colossal mistake and told the truth. My parents were so pissed we didn't have the balls to switch ever again.

The greatest thing to come out of our Olsen Twin moment was Blake quit acting like human vermin after my sister busted his chops.

By the time we stopped being afraid of our parents, puberty had hit and we missed our chance. Lenox is now a foot taller than me with boobs the size of my butt cheeks.

The small kitchen is in its typical state of natural disaster mode when Lenox and I make an appearance. My mother is standing at the stove, stirring something with a wooden spoon while simultaneously punching numbers into the microwave above her head. Jackson, one of the twins—actual twins, not Irish—is standing directly behind Mom, his chest to her back while he peers over her shoulder.

"Jackson, sit down before I burn you with something. Oh, Alma! Can you grab some plates? Lenox, honey, what is on your face?"

"Looks like bologna," Jackson murmurs.

I give him a fist pound on the way to the silverware drawer.

"It's a rejuvenating face mask," she says, taking two fingers and pinching the mask at her nose. Slowly, *disgustingly so*, she pulls the bologna away from her face. The liquid drips off the slimy mask and onto the tile.

She holds it up proudly. "How do I look?"

Mom barely spares her glance. "Rejuvenated, honey. Now, would you throw that away and help your sister set the table?"

Lenox tosses her wet bologna into the trashcan at the edge of the cracked counter and glides across the floor to grab some plates.

"I'll get them." Jackson hip checks her out of the way. "I don't want to eat off a plate you touched."

Her nose wrinkles with offense. "What's wrong with my hands?"

"Bologna hands," I blurt, snagging a stack of napkins from the holder beside the sink.

"Leave your sister's deli hands alone." Flipping off the burner, my mom lifts the pot from the stovetop and spins around. "Everybody move before you get Chicken Alfredo dumped down your front."

Holland, the other half of Jackson's twindom and the only person sitting at the table, lets out a loud battle cry and barrels from her chair as if Mom is wielding a torch rather than boxed pasta.

Mom drops it in the center of the table with a huff. Brushing an errant lock of hair behind her ear, she steadies the table as it sways. "Why are all my children so strange?"

Holland chokes on a laugh. "Mom, for real?"

"What?" She feigns confusion, looking around the

kitchen while wiping her hands on an apron covered in dancing hot dogs.

Lenox blinks once. "*Mom.*"

"What?" she asks, standing in the center of our yellow kitchen donning a sweater with a flying unicorn beneath her wiener apron, looking totally oblivious to the notion that she and our father are the strangest people in this state.

"Nothing." I laugh, taking my seat across from the one Holland just abandoned. Plopping the silverware and napkins in the center of the table, I grab a plate. "Let's eat."

Lenox follows my lead, sliding into the chair next to mine while the twins sit across from us. Lenox and I are practically rubbing thighs, same as we always do when our whole family is wedged around a dining room table not much bigger than a card table.

I still remember when my mom bought the table at a flea market. My father argued with her that it was meant for outdoor use.

"Pish posh!" she'd said.

And that was how we ended up with an old cast iron table fit with matching chairs heavier than both of my parents combined. Mom covered the top with a linen cloth the color of a daffodil after our silverware kept falling through the ornate cracks in the top.

It's an odd furniture piece, but it has character, so I can't say I hate it. Anything much bigger wouldn't have fit inside this kitchen anyway.

Beep!

"Oh! The garlic bread is done." With a flick of her hand, Mom pops open the door.

Jackson's nose wrinkles, his hand frozen on the tongs wedged inside the pasta. "You put the garlic bread in the microwave?"

"The oven is still broken. I had no choice." Clearing her throat, she drops the plate of bread on the table and stomps into the hall. "Harrison! Dinner. Now!"

"I can't eat that bread." Jackson drops noodles onto his plate.

"And why not?" Mom asks, coming back into the kitchen and untying her apron. "There's nothing wrong with it."

"You put it in the microwave, Mom. Radiation waves can be harmful. Some studies show that electromagnetic radiation changes the DNA structure of humans."

"One piece of bread will not change your DNA structure, Jackson."

"I can't take any chances, Mom. I have to think about my future."

"You're fifteen, honey."

"Exactly," he mumbles around a forkful of pasta. "Too young to die."

"For the love of Lucy." Pinching the bridge of her nose, she takes a few deep breaths before sitting at the end of the table. "More for me then."

"I'll eat the tainted bread." I reach for a slice.

"Same," Lenox agrees, and I grab a slice for her too.

"Don't say he didn't warn you." Holland shakes her head and looks at me in mock horror when I shove the entire slice in my mouth.

"I'm sorry. I'm here." Dad rushes into the kitchen, stopping only to press a kiss to the top of Mom's head before continuing his journey to the other end of the table. He sits down, staring longingly at the empty chair next to me that used to belong to Shepherd. His eyes dim like Shepherd's dead and not just forty-five minutes away studying mathematics at the University of Michigan.

"Dad, can you please fix the oven?" Holland stabs at a piece of chicken. "Mom is feeding us radioactive garlic bread."

He lifts a piece and inspects it, even going as far as to lick the edge of it with the tip of his tongue. "Seems fine to me. Eat up."

"See, Dad, but it's not fine." Jackson's fork hits his plate with a clank. "Studies show that—"

"Just eat, son."

"I'll eat the pasta, but you can't expect me to eat radioactive carbohydrates."

"I would never expect such a thing." Reaching across the table, Dad snags two more slices of bread. "If I croak in my sleep, I want Elton John to sing Rocketman at my funeral."

"Harrison, good grief. Stop talking like that at the table." Mom stabs her fork into the air. "The bread is fine."

"Yeah, we'll see," Holland mumbles.

With a sigh, Mom gives up and we resume wolfing down piles of Chicken Alfredo until the pot is nearly empty. Jackson refrains from launching into a lecture each time Lenox or I take a bite of the bread, but that doesn't mean he'll let the topic drop. Before the sun goes down, my sister and I will each have received a two-page essay slid under our bedroom doors arguing why radiation waves are bad for your insides.

We're an odd bunch, my family and I.

Despite my mom's inability to see it, all of our quirks came from our creators. Our quirks, our looks, and deep hatred for Michigan State were all inherited from the two of them.

Harrison and Clare Underwood are the kind of people to dress themselves and all five of their children in full denim and then proceed to position each person in a straddle position on a large tree branch in a city park. I'm not sure which one of them thought that'd make a good family photo, but I'm positive if you search *'worst family photos'* on Google, you'll find the Underwoods.

The idea that we look like we were created in a lab doesn't bode well when trying to appear not so strange. All seven of us have the same locks on our head, the color of nutmeg. Our eyes are all forest green, the only exception being Jackson and Holland who sport azure eyes. Thankfully, we all have slightly different facial features and drastically different haircuts that keep us from looking like a complete family of cloned robots.

When my dad starts choking, grasping at his neck and flailing in his chair like a fish in one of those asthma commercials, my lips begin to tremble with the need to laugh.

He starts howling, sobbing that his sudden death must be the cause of the tainted bread, and I lose my shit. Alfredo sauce burns my nostrils while I fight to keep it in. Lenox's eyes are lined with laughter when she looks at me. Her long hair falls into a heap around her shaking shoulders, a big contrast to the grown-out pixie cut I have on the top of my head.

Brushing the hair from her face, she mouths, "what is our life?"

I shrug because I honestly don't know. But I like it.

3

A TRAIN CALLED MO

ALMA

My favorite part about giving my treasures a *somewhere* is the idea that no theory is too crazy or unrealistic. It's my favorite line from Mean Girls come to life.

The limit does not exist.

When writing short stories about inanimate objects that people treated like trash, there is no limit I can't surpass, no line I must halt at. The possibilities are endless, and I often allow my brain to continuously function on a loop of the most outrageous backstories one can create.

For the cracked Polaroid camera, I'm getting some sad, heroic vibes. I'm thinking *Brave Little Toaster* meets *Toy Story 2*.

I tuck my Hufflepuff pen in the front pocket of my overalls and slide each of my feet into an old flip flop. They don't match. In fact, I think the right one belongs to Lenox and the left one belongs to my mom. I don't care much that it looks like I fished them out of a dumpster. Not for where I am headed.

As much as I love being part of the Underwood clan, I don't spend a ton of time inside of my house. It's too small for our family of seven. Even with Shepherd living on campus now, it still feels like we're a bunch of sardines crammed into a foil can. I don't enjoy feeling like a salty fish.

My desire to feel more like a human launched me into a wondrous world of begging. I'm *very* good at begging. It only took me twelve days and a Powerpoint presentation to convince my parents to let me move out of the room I shared with Lenox and Holland and into the attic. With the demise of an uncountable number of dust bunnies and a yard sale to rid the boxes of junk, it was made livable.

My personal paradise has a lack of windows that doesn't do much for my daily dose of Vitamin D and creaky floor-boards that make it hard to be sneaky. What it does have is privacy, a place to sleep, and a place to store my treasures. I don't need much else.

The small attic space was never meant to be a bedroom, so it's a smidge cramped. But it's *my* cramped space, some-thing special just for *me*. In the attic, there are no arguments over who gets to decorate what wall or how many dresser drawers we each get.

No, Sir.

My only two walls come to a point directly above my bed. I strung fairy lights on each of them and clothes-pinned some of my favorite photos in between the lights. My twin bed has a mattress older than Reginald and a sky blue down comforter with prints of big fluffy clouds. I bought it brand new for this room. Sometimes at night, when I'm lying in bed in the highest room of the house, I like to think about what's up there with clouds.

Are there more treasures to be found, spinning with the wind alongside airplanes and birds? Or is there nothing to discover? I'm not sure which would disappoint me more, that there are miles and miles of a lonely sky, or that there are lost treasures that may never be found.

A boxcar I dutifully named Mo was my first lost treasure and currently holds the title for the longest backstory. Mo has forty-four handwritten pages outlining his role as a troop transport in World War II. Mo is where I go when I need solace and a place to write about lost treasures.

He lives in the freight yard behind our house. It takes me exactly five hundred and twenty-eight steps to get from my back porch to him. With my mix-matched flip flops and mind full of ideas, I leave the sardine can behind, step off the porch, and start my steps.

My boxcar of choice has been parked inside the yard for as long as I can remember. It's a rusted bronze color marred with the effects of somebody's vandalism. *Free The Pigeons* is scrawled on the side facing my house in big purple bubble letters. I'm not sure what pigeons need to be freed but if anything, it just makes the boxcar more unique.

Three hundred and twelve steps into my trek, I turn around and peer at our property. Its close proximity is the only reason I was ever allowed to venture out here as a kid. With the motel and my house door to door, my parents were able to peer out a window no matter which building they were in and ensure I was tucked safely inside of Mo.

It made it easy for Mom to get me to come home when it became too dark and I was lost in a world of words. She'd just step outside with a pot and a wooden spoon and start banging until I came running. Now that I'm older and the freight yard is used less and less, her check-ups aren't so frequent.

Completing my steps, I toss my journal inside of Mo and hoist my body into the boxcar. It gets pretty dark and damp in here so I typically leave the cargo door open and always make sure I have a flashlight stashed so I can still use my journal after the sunset.

With a quick swipe of my sandy hands down my overalls, I snatch my journal off the old ground and make my way to the right side of the boxcar—my preferred side. I've just made it to the Big Joe I keep in my corner when I hear the sound of shuffling behind me.

Shit.

Keeping my sigh internal, I spin around. "Look, Ralph, I'll—you're not Ralph."

No. The guy standing in front of me is definitely not the overweight man who's been working in this freight yard longer than I've been alive.

"Do you work here?" I pop my hip and start my inspection of the stranger who is *not* Ralph. He's missing the pair of boots with the toe blown out and the gray bread that goes to his belly button. In its place is the fresh face of a young guy I've never seen around here before. His eyes are hooded and a muscle quivers at his jaw.

"Well?" I prompt when he says nothing.

He stares blankly at me, and I hold my position until he says, "No. I don't work here."

"I didn't think so." The way he's dressed is enough of an indicator. In cropped jeans and a baggy sweatshirt with sleeves so long they hide his hands, he hardly looks like he's been engaging in the taxing work that is loading and unloading train cars.

"Look—"

I hold up my hand. "You're gonna have to find another one."

"Another one?"

"Another boxcar. Mo is mine."

"Who is Mo?"

"The boxcar."

Amusement flickers in the dark eyes that meet mine. "You named this old boxcar?"

"I did, yes." I lift my chin. "I've been coming here for a decade. He's mine and I don't intend on sharing him. You'll have to find your own."

A few seconds go by, the stranger and I engaging in a world-class stare down before his lips twitch with the makings of a smile. A low chuckle fills the air around us. "You're kicking me out of a rusty train?"

"It's not rusty, it's well-loved. But yes, I am, there is a lovely one a few feet down."

"You saying you can't share this one with me?"

There's a glint in his eye that makes me feel like he's challenging me. I don't like challenges. Not when it comes to my treasures.

"Why would I share my boxcar with you when you could move next door?"

"Because I'm already moved into Jo."

"It's *Mo,* and you could move out as easily as you moved in."

"Oh come on. This thing is huge. You take that side, I'll take this side. We can be neighbors."

Neighbors? No. Terrible plan.

He pivots around, his slightly shadowed frame retreating back towards the left side of the car before I'm able to argue my point further. I'm left standing in the center of Mo, unsure of what to do. I can't very well force him to leave. It's a free country, and something tells me scaring him away won't work. He's bigger than me. He's got the height I don't and broad shoulders beneath the fabric of his sweatshirt that look perfect for body slamming me off this rig. There's no doubt his muscle mass percentage is much higher than mine.

I'm left with no choice.

"Fine," I huff. "I'll share with you."

"Thanks, neighbor." He doesn't even glance over his shoulder.

Sure, Mo is fifty feet long, plenty of space for two people, but that doesn't mean I am happy about these sudden arrangements.

I stomp back over to my side of Mo. The Styrofoam beans inside of my Big Joe squeal when I drop down. "What's your name?"

He looks up from where he's now sitting, back against the wall of the car, knees pulled tight into his chest. "Rumor. What's yours?"

"Alma."

He bobs his head in what I think is supposed to be an alternative gesture for a wave. "So, what brings you here for the last, what did you say, decade?"

"Yes, decade." I use my pen to gesture outside. "My house is the one right across the field. Mo is my place to gain peace and quiet." I let my eyes flicker back to him. "What are you doing here?"

"Freeing the pigeons."

A beat goes by. Then, a laugh loud and boisterous rips from deep in the pit of my stomach. I clutch my middle and toss my head back, my cackle ricocheting off the walls. He's staring at me, sporting a smirk that could win awards.

"Well," I say, once I can breathe again. "It's about damn time somebody showed up and saved them."

His chuckle comes with a snort he quickly covers up by throwing one hand over his mouth. He doesn't cover everything though, and I notice the laughter shining in a pair of eyes that remind me of cinnamon. It's a shame his hair is hiding a large chunk of his face.

My new neighbor has locks Lenox would be jealous of. The color of a dark chocolate truffle, thick hair brushes the tops of his shoulders. There's a wave to it that makes me think he's been stuck outside in the humidity for far too long.

That could be why he tried to commandeer Mo.

Turning my attention back to my journal, I prepare to pen the next greatest hero. Except I can't concentrate. Not when there is a stranger eating a sandwich he got from somewhere inside his sweatshirt. Closing my journal, I study him from the corner of my eye. He's taking small tentative bites of what I believe to be peanut butter, if the smell is anything to go by.

His body language warns me not to come any closer, with the way he's hunched in on himself, one arm wedged between his legs and his torso, and his chin dipped low. I'm just about to ask him where he pulled that sandwich from when I notice the overstuffed duffel bag beside him and a thick quilt spread out across the cold ground.

A thought strikes me— one that turns my stomach into knots.

I sit up straighter. "Hey, Rumor?"

He lifts his gaze, chewing. "Yeah?"

"Can I ask you something?"

"You just did."

I ignore his lame joke. "Are you sleeping here?"

He takes a bite of his sandwich. I hold his gaze while he chews slowly and his throat bobs with a swallow. "And if I am?"

"Well, I guess I'd ask why."

"Because I like it here." He pushes the rest of his sandwich into his mouth and lets his head fall back against the wall, talking with his mouth full. "And the mosquitos aren't so bad."

I'm not sure how to respond, so I don't say anything. I must look like I'm curious about something because he clears his throat and says, "this is temporary."

"So, you are? Sleeping here, I mean."

He runs his hand down his face, a low, rumbling sound escaping his throat. "Yeah, neighbor. I'm sleeping here. I'd appreciate it a whole lot if you could keep that between us."

I'm too startled by his request to offer any sort of objection. I attempt to dim the shock on my face but I'm not sure I'm successful in masking the way my body stiffens in shock. The questioning glance I give him isn't enough for him to willingly offer an explanation as to why he wants to keep his living arrangements a secret. I can't quite grasp why he'd rather stay and live here than in a home equipped with running water and air conditioning.

I try to sympathize, put myself in his white tennis shoes, and come up with a reason as to why he'd want to be homeless, but I can't. I don't *want* to.

What the hell kind of good Samaritan will I be if I keep quiet about a guy who doesn't look much older than me living inside an old boxcar?

"Alright, look." He pushes to his feet and pins me with a hard look. "I said this is temporary, and I meant it. If you want me to move to the next car so you can have this one to yourself, whatever, but don't go running to all your community friends that there is homeless teenager shacking up in your extended backyard, cool?"

Teenager.

My chest deflates just a little, and I want to give him a hug. I refrain for obvious reasons. "You're a teenager."

His previously smooth face is now restless and irritable. "Listen, Alma, if you tell anybody about this, I'll torch Mo."

I gasp. "You evil, homeless bastard."

"I won't be here forever. I have something in the works, and I want to make it there without a bunch of complications."

"When you say you have something in the works, you mean what exactly?"

"Not that it's any of your business, but I've got a place."

Relief fills me in gallons. "Cool. So, you just have to get there? I can give you a ride."

"No. I have to find it."

"Excuse me?"

He shakes his head, hair swaying back and forth. "I don't exactly know where I'm headed quite yet. I'll be here until I figure it out."

"Here? As in sleeping in an old train called Mo?" Looking toward Rumor's belongings, I shiver thinking of myself sleeping there in the cold without a pillow to lay my head on. The faint buzz of mosquitos around me has me feeling itchy, and I can almost picture Rumor fighting them off as he tries to sleep. My heart really dislikes the image.

"I don't have any other options, Alma. I could get a hotel but I'd rather save my money for food."

"Come home with me." The offer flies out of my mouth before I gather how absurd it sounds.

His face twists. "Absolutely not."

"Why not?" *Shut up, Alma. Shut up. Shut up. Shut up.* "I have a nice house."

"I'm sure your house is great, but you're a stranger. Hell. *I'm* a stranger."

"No. You're a kid living in a rundown tin can."

He scoffs. "Kid? I'll be eighteen in five months."

"You're seventeen? Cool. So am I. We're practically peers." I jump to my feet, journal in tow. "Let's go, roomie."

"You're insane."

Probably.

"I'm not insane. I'm a person offering you a place to shower." I look around. "Where do you even go to the bathroom? The woods? Do you want to poop in the woods, Rumor? I have a perfectly fine toilet across the field."

He laughs richly. "Who *are* you?"

"Alma Underwood." I stick out my hand. "Your new roommate."

He peers at my hand, making no effort to shake it. "I'm not your roommate. Your offer was nice, a little crazy, but nice. So, thanks, but no thanks."

"Why is my offer crazy?" I drop my hand. "I'm doing the right thing."

He scans me from my head to my toes, probably assessing if I'm a grade A psycho or not. "I could rob your family."

"There is nothing in my house worth taking."

"I could strangle you in your sleep."

"I'll sleep with a steak knife under my pillow."

His right eyebrow raises. "I could murder your whole family and kidnap your baby sister."

"My youngest sister is fifteen, and we have a dog that hates strangers. If you escape my attic room somehow, you'll be attacked."

Okay, so Charlevoix isn't exactly a guard dog. She's a Chinese crested dog that is more creepy than frightening, but he doesn't need to know that.

Rumor inclines his head and studies me, a bewildered expression on his face. "You don't even know me. Why is this so important to you?"

I have no idea.

I widen my stance, my sudden determination like a rock inside of me. "Because you have nowhere else to go. Because your lack of a home tells me you probably need a friend." I flail my arms, gesturing wildly with each word. "Because there's something inside of me that can't leave tonight knowing you're in here battling train monsters."

"Train monsters." He muses.

"It's a thing."

"Somehow I doubt that."

"Come on, Rumor, let me give me you a place to stay that doesn't smell like mildew."

He puts one hand on his hip and lets his other arm dangle by his side like dead weight. "Didn't you say you live in an attic?"

"I have a good assortment of air fresheners." I nod toward the door. "Let's go. If you hate it, you can leave. I'm not trying to kidnap you."

"Really? This feels a lot like kidnapping."

"Okay, fine."

With my journal tucked under my arm, I turn to retreat. Despite how terribly I want to, I can't force him to come stay with me. I probably shouldn't have even offered in the first place. It was a crazy person thing to do.

I'm a crazy person.

But I know, *I just know,* I will get next to no sleep tonight knowing there is a kid my own age five hundred and twenty-eight steps away from me with no place to call home. I'm risking a lot, my life possibly, if he does turn out to be a murderer, but I can't shake the feeling that he's not the next Ted Bundy.

There's something about being in Rumor's presence that brings on a feeling I can't quite explain. It's new. A subtle but persistent feeling that's gnawing at the inside of me, telling me that this small unit of human connection being exchanged by teenage strangers means something.

My natural habit of turning nothing into something is the only reason I hop down from the train car and start walking, abandoning that feeling and what seems like good moral values.

The crunch of gravel sounds behind me. "What about your parents?"

A surge of energy replaces the knot in my stomach. It sails up through my lungs and sparks into a spontaneous smile. I peer at him over my shoulder. "You let me worry about that."

He steps up beside me and together, we walk five hundred and twenty-eight steps back to my house. With each step, I refuse to wonder if I'm making a massive mistake.

4

STRANGER DANGER

RUMOR

I'm making a massive mistake. It's as if every video chronicling kidnapping I was forced to suffer through as a child is screaming at me.

Stranger danger! Stranger danger!

Though I must admit Alma Underwood doesn't look like she even knows the meaning of the word danger. If I took a big enough breath, I could blow her away. She has a slim, willowy frame, and sharp cheekbones hidden inside of a soft face. In all the minutes I've known Alma Underwood, the corners of her mouth have been positioned upward more so than they've been downward. She has an air of determination surrounding her, a spark of defiance humming low in her stomach and ready to break free when she believes deeply in something.

Less than an hour of being in her presence and I'm positive of that. Alma is a passionate girl. Whether it has to do with taking in homeless people, or something to do with the journal that is clutched in her fists in a death grip, I know that for a fact.

I'm more than a little taken back by her offer. Actually,

I'm astonished by the way she's treated me since the second she met me. I'm a stranger, squatting inside of a train, with hair I haven't washed in six days, giving off a rotten smell. Still, she doesn't act scared that I'll try to jump her, or totally grossed out that I clearly need to bathe. Nope. She puffs out her chest with all the confidence in the world and calls me a bastard. Maybe that's why I decide to follow her home.

Not because she called me a bastard, but because she had a whisper of a smile on her face when she said it.

So, despite some strong inclinations telling me I've lost my damn mind, I follow Alma up an old wooden staircase, dimly lit and creaky. I know we've reached her bedroom when we halt on a small landing and she turns us to face a narrow door, slathered in lime green paint. Putting her finger to her lips, gesturing for me to walk lightly, her fingers wrap around the doorknob and she leads me inside.

The first thing I notice is the lack of windows or an additional escape route. Once I get over that, I take a second to appreciate how homey she's made this place look for what it used to be. It's small, less than ten feet from wall to wall is my guess, but it's clear she's done all she can to make it feel big.

There are dainty lights dangling from the wall that comes to a peak above her bed. They remind me of the lights my dad and I used to string up on our Christmas tree each year, and they give this place the light it desperately needs. Her bed is small and clearly meant for one person, but the way she has it decorated with all those little clouds is kind of endearing. I can easily picture Alma Underwood as a girl who finds peace alongside something suspended in the atmosphere.

"So, this is it." She spreads her arms and flashes me a

crooked smile. "I hope you weren't expecting the royal treatment."

"This is great, Alma. Thank you."

Looking around, my lips daring to form into a smile, I allow myself to recognize how great it is. Alma has a short bookcase opposite her bed. Instead of overflowing with well-loved, worn novels, it holds the greatest collection of Funko Pops of all time. There's a tall, white dresser taking up residence beside the door, decorated with dozens of handprints and footprints of all sizes and colors. I gaze at it in wonder, pondering which ones belong to her.

"You can sleep on the floor beside my bed. I don't own an air mattress but I do have a pool float shaped like a slice of pizza I could blow up for you."

Who *is* this girl?

There isn't a force of nature strong enough to help me hold back the spout of laughter that bursts from my lips. I glance over my shoulder to find her sitting crossed legged in the center of her bed, staring at me with an expression laced with seriousness.

"A pool float?"

She nods. "Sleeping on this floor is going to be like sleeping on concrete."

"My other option is sleeping on a pizza slice made of plastic?"

"Better than concrete."

"Nah, it's cool. Don't go through the trouble."

Her eyebrows shoot up to her hairline. "Rumor, it will take like five minutes."

I shrug and leave it at that. Sleeping on the floor isn't anything new to me and asking her to pump air into an old pool toy feels like too much. This stranger put a roof over my head. She's done more for me in sixty minutes than half of my family members have in seventeen years.

I hold no plans to push my luck. My new plan is to lay low, stay out of the way, and find what I came here to find.

I walk across the room, flinching with each creak of the floorboards, and set my duffle bag down beside her bookcase. "Do you think it'd be okay if I used your shower?"

"Sure, that's no problem, but we should wait until my siblings fall asleep so they don't spot you. Cool?"

"Cool." Lowering myself to the floor, I drag my quilt over my legs and rest my left arm to the side, using my five fingers to brush out my wild hair. "What about your parents?"

"They are a non-issue."

"I find that hard to believe."

"No, they are. Promise." Her bed rocks when she turns to face me. "You know that motel next door?"

"Great Lakes or something? Yeah. I was going to stay there but decided to save my money. Why?"

"My parents own it."

"No shit?"

"For real." Setting her journal in her lap, she flips it open and starts to fiddle with the corners of the cover. "They work the midnight shifts together. There's no chance of them stumbling upon you in the middle of the night."

"How did the owners get stuck working the graveyard shift? That kind of blows."

She laughs gently, speaking in a low, warm tone. "They don't have much of a choice. There's not a lot of people who want to work at a motel seven miles from town. Besides my parents, the motel has two employees." She holds up her fingers, ticking them off as she speaks. "One is me and I clean rooms. The other is Reginald, an old man who works at the front desk. Since I have school and Reggie's pushing eighty, they work the late shift. They leave after we all have dinner together and come back to see us off to school."

I nod with understanding. "So I should leave during the day? To avoid them seeing me?"

"I mean, you could, but they sleep most of the day. I don't start school for a couple of weeks so we'll figure something out."

Pushing her journal beneath her pillow, she stretches out on her bed and regards me with two of the biggest eyes I've ever seen. They sort of shine the same way the grass does after it's just got done raining. Her red lips haven't drooped since I've been in here, and I chalk her up to be one of those people who is always joyous. Somebody who is friends with everybody, even the homeless freaks who live inside trains and poop in bushes.

"What about you?" She ponders, brushing long bangs off her cheek. Her shiny hair is short, much shorter than mine. Cropped all around her head, the front pieces are longer and swept to the side in a lazy fashion that works well for her. If I had to describe it as anything, I'd say it's cute.

"Rumor?"

I blink, trying to conjure up the question she was just asking. "What about me?"

"School." She elaborates. "Have you graduated already?"

"No." I fix my gaze on the loose thread of my quilt and wrap my pointer finger around it, only letting up when the tip starts to turn purple. "I'm going to wait until I turn eighteen, get my GED, and then apply to college."

"What will you study?"

I sigh outwardly, letting my lips flap, not bothering to

hide my annoyance with not knowing. "I have no clue."

"Me either. My older brother is at the University of Michigan studying mathematics."

My focus snaps to her, the skin around my face tightening in horror. "Oh God, that's awful."

"Right?" She laughs. "I didn't inherit the genius gene. Clearly, since you know—" she gestures between us. "—I brought home a stranger."

My cheeks rise with a chuckle. "Yeah, I doubt you'll be winning any awards for that decision."

Still giggling, she tucks her hands beneath her head and adjusts herself so she's lying on her side. "Is your real name Rumor?"

If I earned a penny for every time somebody asked me that, I would have never spent a night in a train named Mo.

"Yes. It is," I tell her, trying not to look exasperated.

"You must get asked that a lot, huh?"

I let my head fall back against her paneled wall. "Like you wouldn't believe."

"It is a unique name."

"So is Alma." I grin. "Is that *your* real name?"

"Yes. I'm named after the town."

"What town?"

"Alma." Laughter swims in her eyes. "Did you grow up in Michigan?"

"Chicago."

"Well, that explains it."

Thankful she doesn't ask me how or why I ended up in Flat Rock, I don't think before I ask, "Were you conceived there or something?"

"No. Well... " Her eyes glaze over while she considers my bizarre question. "No, I don't think so. My parents are just obsessed with this state. Everybody in my family is named after a town in Michigan."

"Come again?"

With a twitch in her lips, she holds up her hand, palm facing me. "Okay, Chicago kid, this here is the mitten. And by mitten, I mean Michigan."

My eyes roll like a couple of bowling balls. "Yes, Professor Alma, I got that."

"Anyway, here–" She uses the tip of her finger to stab the center of her palm. "—are my parents. Harrison and Clare. Over here is my brother Shepherd. Down toward the thumb is my sister Lenox. This is me, Alma, of course. Last but not least are the twins. Holland is here, and Jackson is at the bottom." She stops moving her finger around and goes to drop her hands before suddenly flipping them back into position and stabbing the top of her hand. "Oh! Way up here is our dog Charlevoix."

I blink.

She smacks her hands together with a satisfied smile and tucks them back under her head. "It's a shame our last name isn't Michigan. Wouldn't that be wild?"

The bubble of laughter that bursts from my chest is uncontrollable. I roar without restraint, trying to remember to breathe all while trying to shut the hell up. Alma is laughing with me, tears brimming in her eyes and a finger slamming over her lips to remind me to cool it.

I shove my face in my quilt until I can get a grip. When I'm sure I can behave, I drag my face from the fabric to look at her.

Her face is glowing. "Silly, huh? Being named after a town? My siblings and I count our blessings. There are some pretty whack names in Michigan. I thank the universe every day I wasn't named Pigeon, Colon, or Dowagiac."

That sets me off like a firecracker, and I let my hysterics out into my quilt again, wiping my tears with the end of my sweatshirt sleeve. I laugh like I haven't in a really long time, praying Alma doesn't think I'm laughing at her or making fun of her family.

I'm not. Not even a little bit. I'm laughing simply because it's silly– completely and utterly nutty that it almost doesn't seem real. It kind of makes me wish I was named Pigeon so I could be part of the family full of people that must be just as strange as the daughter who took in a stray teen.

Her contagious, airy giggle keeps me laughing, all while something in my chest starts to warm me from the inside out. For the first time since I packed my bag and hopped on a bus, I feel grounded. Almost like I can stop running and catch my breath a little because this kooky girl with the kooky family has given me a pit stop in my race.

I believe the feeling that warmed me is gratitude. Gratitude towards Alma Underwood and her little attic room.

"Ya know, I just thought of something." She smacks her palm against her forehead. "I let you into my house and I don't even know your last name."

"Rawlings." I smile. "Rumor Rawlings."

She beams. "That's a badass name. Sounds like an announcer at a sporting event."

"Well, damn, looks like I just figured out my future career."

She laughs again, shifting a little closer to the edge of the bed, towards the side of the room I chose. We stare at each other for a beat or two, sitting in a silence that feels comfortable and not at all awkward for two people who just met.

I stay slumped against her wall, pulling my knees to my

chest, only straightening when I see the light in her eyes start to dim. "Is anyone looking for you?"

"What?"

She sits up and averts her gaze. "Is anyone looking for you, Rumor?"

A hell-like mixture of anger and hurt swell up in my gut and threaten to bubble up in my throat. Insecurity and rage ricochet off the inner walls of my stomach and fight to break free. I swallow lead and ignore all the emotions I can't make sense of, mumbling a simple, "No."

Her lips turn down into the first frown I've seen all day, contributing to the anger stirring inside of me.

"It's fine, Alma."

"But... what about your parents?"

"My dad is dead," I say harshly, my eyes stabbing her with a look that says drop it.

She does, but only long enough for me to shut my eyes and get a handle on the quell of emotions I don't like dealing with.

It isn't long after I've shut my eyes and start to breathe through my nose like a boxer coming down from a fight that I hear her soft whisper.

"What about your mother? Is she dead too?"

"No."

"She might be looking for you." She offers, her voice so low I almost don't hear her.

"She's not."

"How do you know?"

I open my eyes. "Because, Alma, I'm looking for her."

5

AN UNEVEN RATIO
RUMOR

I'm beginning to understand that Alma Underwood is a girl who likes answers. When I look into her eyes, I see a war inside of them, an internal need to put all of my pieces together. I am the kind of puzzle that takes days to complete. The kind of challenge that comes with turmoil, frustration, and the idea that giving up would be easier than finishing.

Dread snakes under my skin while I wait for her onslaught of questions to continue, and I neutralize my face. Except, she doesn't ask about my mother like I expect her to. For many long moments, she offers me nothing but silence and a sad smile. I wonder if I should feel guilty about the relief I feel.

"Hey, can I borrow your limbs?" She blurts quickly, catapulting herself from her bed with a bounce.

"My limbs?"

"Your feet, most specifically." Her hands fall into place at her hips while she waits for me to answer.

I struggle to form words and bring my bottom lip between my teeth, only slightly weirded out that her gaze is now solely fixed on the feet poking out from the edge of my quilt.

"What's wrong with your own feet?" I gesture towards her bare, tiny toes painted with blue polish.

"Nothing, but I already used mine." Her lips pull into a leisurely smile. "What if I say please?"

"What if I say no?" I tease.

She sticks her bottom lip out so far a plane could use it as a landing strip. Her wide eyes become cartoon-like and she cups her hands together, shaking them as she speaks. "Pretty please, Rumor?"

I pretend to think it over by cupping my chin and letting my eyes roam around her room. When they catch sight of her oddly decorated dresser, it dawns on me what she needs my feet for, and I stop stalling for time. "Alright, fine." I concede. "But then I get to use the shower."

Her head bobs eagerly, eyes shining so fiercely, they remind me of the first sun rays pushing through a window in the morning.

She drops to her knees and wedges half of her petite body underneath her bed.

My brows arch while I study her thrashing legs and listen to sounds of a struggle. She must've moved too harshly, and I flinch when I hear a loud clunk and see the bed jerk. "Uh, Alma? You okay?"

"One second!" Is her muffled her reply. There are a few more sounds I don't have time to decipher before she's wiggling her way free. She emerges unscathed with three small tubes of paint and a sponge looking thing. She sits back on her heels, blowing wild bangs from her face.

Shuffling over to me on her knees, she extends her hands. "Would you prefer brilliant blue, burnt orange, or forest green?"

"Forest green."

"Good choice." She sets her paints down and taps the top of my foot. "I'm going to need you to take off your socks and shoes," she says, and then she's spinning around and reaching back under her bed.

I hesitate. "I haven't showered in almost a week."

With a quick glance over her shoulder, she inclines her head and purses her lips. "I grew up with four siblings and no personal space." She leaves it at that and produces a section of newspaper that's seen better days. Placing it under my feet, her dark eyebrows rise mischievously and she clears her throat, waiting.

With a resigned sigh, I push my quilt aside and start untying my shoe. My eyes flutter closed and I quickly say a pray to whoever's listening that I'm not about to unleash an atomic bomb. I changed my socks every day I could until I ran out of clean pairs. It could be toe-jam central beneath my socks and I'd have no idea.

When the first shoe is off, I pinch the top of my sock and start to drag it off my dirty foot. I wince slightly when it comes free and spread my toes, holding my breath. My chest expands in a big whoosh when I discover I am toe-jam free.

Thank you.

I hurry to undo my other shoe, yanking the sock off and shoving both socks and shoes as far from Alma as I can. Just because I am toe-jam free does not mean there isn't something growing inside those soiled socks.

Gross.

Extending my legs, I rest my feet on the wrinkled newspaper covered in slashes of dried paint and wiggle my toes. "Alright, go for it."

She doesn't move right away. "Are you sure this is cool?"

I jerk my gaze to hers and find the skin around her eyes wrinkled. "What do you mean? I said yes, my feet are bare, I chose forest green, what more confirmation do you need?"

"Well, you took forever taking off your shoes."

"I was making sure we didn't both need gas masks to handle the fumes."

The side of her mouth twitches. "I think we'll be fine."

I poke her knee with my big toe. "Then get to it, slowpoke."

"Me?" She laughs, reaching for the green paint and popping the cap. "You're the slowpoke. It would've gone much faster if you would've used both hands to take off your shoes."

"Probably." She's right, but that isn't an option for me. It never has been.

The paint makes a noise resembling a weak fart when she squeezes it onto the porous surface. I watch her slender fingers wrap around my wide ankle and start to lift, positioning the wet sponge.

"Wait!"

She drops my ankle.

Gesturing towards the dresser across the room, I ask her, "Shouldn't we be doing this process over there? What am I supposed to do once you get the paint on my feet? Stand up and walk?"

"Of course not." She grips my ankle again. Before I have a chance to plead my case, thick, cold liquid is slathered up the bottom of my foot. It twitches and Alma tightens her fingers. "You'll butt scooch."

"I'll— what?"

"Butt scooch," she says again, the tip of her tongue poking out from between her lips. I shiver when she massages the paint into my heel, the strange sensation unfamiliar.

"Butt scooch." I am amused by this. "Are you implying you'd like me to use the muscles in my ass to hightail myself over to that dresser?"

"Exactly, yes." Setting down my right foot, she reaches for the left one after squeezing more paint onto her sponge. "Haven't you ever butt scooched before?"

"I can't say that I have." I bite the inside of my cheek and tense my muscles so I don't kick her in the chin when paint oozes between my toes. "That tickles."

I regret admitting that the moment her head lifts and I spot mischief spinning in her eyes. "Your ticklish?"

"No."

"You just said you were."

"I lied."

Her cheeks pink with her laugh. Setting the sponge aside, she clicks the cap back in place and smacks me on the calf. "Alright, butt scooch. Hurry up before the paint starts to dry."

Because I know she's completely serious, I squeeze my butt cheeks together and propel my hips forward. I feel like a total nut job.

"You're not very good at this." Her voice bounces off my back. "Didn't you ever have butt scooch races with your siblings?"

"I don't have any siblings," I say over my shoulder, using my right hand to speed up the butt scooching process. It doesn't exactly feel great on my tailbone.

"That explains it." She's suddenly right next to me, butt scooching like a proud Olympian.

Fascinated with this girl, my smile is cranked up a small notch. We make it to the dresser at the same time, and I lift my feet, pressing them gently against an open spot on the face of the fourth drawer. I let them sit for a moment, rolling them around gently so the paint will stay.

My feet leave the piece of furniture with a sticky sound. "There you go." Looking at her dresser, I find that I positioned one foot a little higher than the other but all the paint seemed to transfer so I consider my first foot painting and butt scooch race a success.

Carefully resting my heels against her floor, I pick a piece of unwashed hair from my mouth. "Can I shower now?"

"Not yet." Propelling herself across the room, she quickly snatches the paint tube. "We have to do your hands."

"No."

She spins around. "No?"

"No. You said you needed to borrow my feet. I let you borrow my feet, now I get to shower."

"But..." She rolls her head and gazes longingly at her dresser. "Everybody has always done both their feet *and* their hands."

"Not me." I decide. "Besides, who even is going to notice?"

"Anybody with at least one fully functioning eyeball will notice the ratio of feet to hands is off." She forces her lips into a stiff smile and acknowledges me with a sense of determination I now know to be part of her character. "I'm not above begging. In fact, I'm kind of a professional at it."

"A professional at begging, huh? I'll bet you're pretty stubborn too."

"Stubborn as a mule. So give me your hand, Rumor Rawlings." She orders, voice thick with new authority. "I must make my ratio even."

"Well, Alma Underwood, I'm sorry to burst your bubble but your ratio will never be even."

She lifts her chin and sniffles, holding up the wet sponge like a weapon, challenging me. "And why is that?"

I lean forward, close enough to invade her personal space. She stiffens but shows no signs of relenting. Running my tongue across my teeth, I look at her with hard-pressed defiance. "Because it's physically impossible."

"I beg to differ." She rolls her shoulders back, propelling her confidence upward. "All you have to do is give me your other hand."

With a smirk on my lips, I sit back and throw her a curveball. "I don't have another hand."

The long lashes that rest against her cheeks fly up. "I'm sorry?"

Feeling smug, I raise my left arm. The end of my sweat-shirt sleeve hangs limp, flopping over my wrist without anything poking out of the end.

Her limbs jerk as though someone slapped her awake, and she merely gawks at me, tongue-tied with a slack jaw.

I chuckle gently. For the first time since meeting Alma Underwood, she is silent. I can't say I blame her. Most people aren't sure what to say when they discover what's under my sleeve, or rather, what's not under my sleeve.

I stopped letting my skin crawl with embarrassment about ten years ago. By the time middle school had rolled around, I was fed up with the mockery and feeling ashamed of something I had no say in. Eventually, humiliation turned into raw fury and I started sticking up for myself. Not long after that, I was left alone. Now, I don't find it awkward to wear short sleeve shirts in public, and I don't hesitate to make cracks about my missing limb. People still stare and say rude things every once in a while, but people say rude things to people who do have both hands, so I try not to let it bother me.

Alma's throat bobs harshly like she's trying to swallow her tongue but her throat is too dry for it to make it down the passageway. When her cheeks start to drain of color, I wonder if she's choking on lack of air.

"It's okay, Alma. You didn't know."

She snaps out of it with a shake of her head. "I feel like I just shoved your stinky, green foot in my mouth."

I bark a laugh. "You didn't know."

"Because you didn't tell me!" She accuses, her agitated state making me smile. "Why didn't you tell me? You need to tell me these things, Rumor, or I risk being totally insensitive."

"You aren't insensitive. It's fine. I'm wearing long sleeves. How could you have known?"

"You still should've said something. I would've told you if I was missing a hand." Her tone is laced with a heavy dose of impatience and frustration. Grabbing the used sponge, she steals my only hand and starts painting it. "We will just use this hand twice."

I nod. It sounds like a fine compromise to me.

I feel an odd sense of joy at the little huffs of irritation she's making as she thickens the layer of paint on my palm. It's kind of adorable the way her slight nose is wrinkled at the top and she's struggling to keep her bright eyes dark with false anger.

"Are you mad at me, Alma Underwood?"

"I don't know." She slams my hand against her dresser, putting extra pressure on my fingers to ensure the stick. "I guess I feel like a doofus. Here I am, barking at you to give me a hand you don't have."

"Don't feel like a doofus, Alma. You couldn't have

known. I was just messing with you." I let her flip my hand palm side up and apply more paint. "It's not something I normally hide, or even really *can* hide, but the last thing I wanted to do when you kidnapped me was admit I was a homeless teen who needs a shower, a haircut, *and* another hand."

Also, I wanted to proceed with caution. As reluctant as I was to follow her home, now that I'm here, I'm excited to shower and wake up with walls surrounding me. I didn't want to be hasty, show off my nub, and then have to leave or be forced to room with a judgmental twat waffle.

Though if I'm being fully honest with myself, I knew after ten-seconds of being inside this bedroom that Alma Underwood is not a twat waffle. There is nothing about her that has my alarm bells ringing. The spirit that exudes her is carefully colored in a mixture of neon and soft shades. She's a vibrant girl with a gentle heart, who feels both anger toward me for not telling her about my missing hand and sympathy while she wonders how it became that way.

There must be something cautioning her not to ask. I can see her from the corner of my eye, staring at me warily and sheathing the words on the tip of her tongue the same way she did when she brought up my mother.

But unlike the woman that gave birth to me, my lack of a hand is something I don't mind talking about. "It's called congenital amputation," I tell her, my hand falling against the dresser for the second time. "I was born missing my left hand."

She nods gently, pressing my hand to the drawer of her dresser much softer than before, lost in a sea of thoughts and unfiltered questions. "Is it something that just happens?"

"Basically, yeah. The exact cause isn't really known." With my hand peeling away from its twin print, her ratio is even again. "It isn't genetic or something that's in my DNA, it's something that just *is*."

"Is it uncommon?"

"It's not super uncommon but there also isn't a large number of us homegrown amputees running around."

"Well then, Rumor, I believe that makes you unusual, uncommon, and absolutely remarkable."

She offers me a smile so genuine and friendly, my throat constricts. Dipping my chin, I flick an imaginary speck of lint off my sweatshirt and breathe harshly through my nose. There's a small pull in my chest, a twinge, caused by her warm words and welcoming attitude.

Not once in my seventeen years did my father, or anyone else, describe me as remarkable. My father was not a bad father. Nothing he did ever made me feel embarrassed or ashamed of what I was lacking, but he also never described my arm as anything but a defect or a problem formed before birth.

Alma Underwood is the only person I've ever encountered who has met me and concluded the strangest piece of my being is to be categorized as something remarkable.

I'm not sure why her words hit me like a brick in the chest.

I nibble my lip apprehensively, my body rocking awkwardly while I fight with my mouth to say something to break me out of this thick fog of thanks.

She reaches out and places her hand on my shoulder, giving it a gentle squeeze. When I sweep my head up and I'm greeted by her easy smile, my reaction toward her immediate acceptance doesn't feel so strange.

"How about I show you the bathroom so you can finally take a shower?"

"That'd be fantastic." I look down at my painted hand. "You'll have to get the door for me."

She pushes her long fingers through her hair and stands up with a muted laugh. I push off the floor, standing flat on my feet now that the paint between my toes has dried. Gathering my duffle bag, I follow her out of her room and back down the narrow staircase. The creaking is so loud, I wince with every step and cross my fingers one of her siblings doesn't leave their room to figure out who the second set of footsteps belong to.

I breathe a long, necessary sigh of relief once I'm inside the small bathroom with the door secured shut and lock flipped. I receive strict instructions from Alma to ignore any knocking, as it might be her siblings trying to use the bathroom. She believes they will retreat back into their rooms if I ignore their persistent knocking. I'm not sure that plan is going to work but I want a shower desperately enough to risk it.

I make quick work of jumping under the spray, trying to move fast but also enjoying the smell of soap. I groan at the way the warm water feels on my sore muscles. If they could talk, they'd be scolding me for what I've put them through the last thirty-seven days. Sleeping on buses, in locker rooms, under bridges, and trains called Mo, hasn't been great for my neck and lower lumbar support.

Living as a hobo, showering in truck stops and brushing my teeth in a gas station bathroom, hasn't exactly been glamorous, but there is no shower too disgusting, no alley too damp, and no night too lonely that would ever entice me to return to the place I was before.

After my dad died, I learned firsthand that life is all about choices, some we regret, some we are thankful for, and there are some that stay with us forever. I used to believe I wasn't ready to make choices so grand all by myself.

Drowning in grief and late night pleas to the universe to bring my dad back, I learned quickly how to find solace in making choices alone. It came with freedom and a power I hadn't known before. Clinging to that power and the pain I felt with my dad's absence, I bought a bus ticket. I'm not sure if that choice is one I regret or one I'm thankful for, but I do know it's one that will change me forever.

After cleaning every crack and crevice of my homeless body, I step from the shower, dry off using a towel stamped with unicorns, and dress in a T-shirt and pair of sweats. Trying to channel my inner butterfly, I attempt to float back up the stairs, all while writing a mental note to ask Alma where the nearest laundromat is.

Pushing back into her bedroom, I find her perched on her bed, that mysterious journal in her lap. She's changed into a pair of pink pajamas with rainbows spread out across them. I click the door shut behind me and start to move. My feet falter and I halt, trying to mask the sudden hitch in my breath when I see it. I gulp hard, shocked and slightly embarrassed at the ring of moisture that impulsively forms around my eyes.

There, right beside her bed, is a giant pool float shaped like pizza.

6

THE BEST OF EVERYTHING

ALMA

"Girl, you have lost ya damn mind."

I nibble on my French toast stick, sucking syrup off my bottom lip, not bothering to argue with Arthur. Because he's probably right.

His ginger eyes pop wildly from his face, his mouth opening and closing like he's unsure how to reply to my nonchalant attitude. "You brought home a stranger, Alma." He leans close to me, full lips moving uncomfortably close to the tip of my nose. "A *stranger*."

I dunk my French toast back in my syrup. "I did, yes."

He sits backward, folding his arms over his chest in an annoyed gesture. "What exactly were you thinking?"

"I don't think she was thinking," Echo chimes in, licking blue frosting off the top of a wrinkled doughnut. "I mean, really, what kind of friend are you?"

I choke on my breakfast. "Excuse me? What does bringing home a stranger have to do with my best friend status?"

Frowns form and eyes droop. My two best friends share

a look I'm too tired to decipher. Arthur purses his lips and I know I'm in trouble.

"Friends tell friends when they decide to harbor a runaway teenager with a missing hand. They don't just drop a bomb like that a week before the start of senior year."

"As if I don't have enough shit to worry about this year." Pushing away her plate, Echo lets out a deep, drawn-out groan. "I have to worry about my best friend getting raped right before she gets her throat sliced open and toes chopped off."

I drop my French toast stick. It hits the table with a sad flap. "Thank you for ruining my breakfast with that image." I suck maple syrup off the tips of my fingers. "Look, if he was going to chop off my toes, he would have done it by now."

"That's not true at all, and you know it." Arthur pushes his round sunglasses up his nose and adjusts them once they are in place. Smooth, brown skin warms underneath the harsh rays of the morning sun, and his thin mustache wrinkles when he scowls at me. "There are plenty of serial killers who wait to kill their victims."

"It's totally true." Cradling her head in her hands, long red hair falls around Echo's shoulders, masking her face. "You need to be more careful."

"I need new friends," I mumble, using a flimsy restaurant napkin to wipe the sweat pooling on the back of my neck. It's not even ten in the morning and the sun has already decided its mission is to roast the earth's patrons like a couple of wieners over a campfire. "How could you even suggest I kick out Rumor? He literally doesn't have anywhere else to go."

Reaching across the table, Arthur places a hand on my arm, his thumb whispering across my wrist. "A, we aren't suggesting you kick him to the curb. It's obvious he needs help but bringing him into your house? *Your bedroom?* Wouldn't it have been a smarter choice to put him up in a room at the motel?"

Probably.

Giving him a room in the motel would have provided him with an actual bed to sleep in and the chance for more privacy, but truthfully, I didn't even consider that option until the suggestion slipped from Arthur's lips. A week ago, back in the old boxcar I love so much, I hadn't even contemplated taking Rumor somewhere that wasn't home.

When I was a little girl, my parents used to say I suffered from a hero complex. I struggled when my siblings argued or when other kids were injured on the playground. With each situation that needed resolving, a powerful dose of desperation took over my body and I wouldn't rest until it was solved. Perhaps that's why I save my lost treasures and introduce them to a somewhere that's worthy.

I'm not sure.

What I'll never understand is why my parents thought I *suffered* from this so-called hero complex I'm still not sure is a real thing. There is nothing unpleasant or bad about wanting to save or help someone, and I used to say that if I only ever helped one person in life, that'd be okay.

Rumor Rawlings is my one person.

I feel it.

It's almost like I was struck with a calling when I saw him sitting in that train car, duffle bag packed so full it was bursting at the seams, with nothing but a quilt to keep him warm. I felt something at that moment. Something that runs much deeper than sympathy or empathy or even both. It's just *something*. Something I feel in every speck of my body, something that affects each beat inside my chest.

And even though I know the decision wasn't smart, what I feel cannot be pushed aside. It is life's biggest fight, the clash between what you know and what you feel.

I am a girl who follows her feelings. How else would I get to the source of where they're coming from?

"Listen, guys, I get what you're saying. I do." Pushing away from the old picnic table, I gather my trash. "And I'm not trying to dismiss your concern, but there's nothing you can say to me that is going to make me change my mind."

Spinning around, I toss my trash into the slim garbage bin padlocked to a light post. Echo falls into step beside me, letting her half-eaten doughnut drop into the bin. Her silvery, magnetic eyes narrow skeptically. "And if he turns out to be a murderer?"

"I'll die."

"Really, Alma?" She sighs, a smirk betraying the look in her eyes. "Must you be so morbid this early in the morning?"

"It's ten," I remind her, linking my arm with hers. "Besides, you and Arthur started this whole conversation. You have zero faith in my talent of selecting non-threatening homeless teens."

"I'm sorry, is that a talent? Did you take classes for that?" Arthur teases, his right arm linking with my free one.

Together, the three of us leave our favorite doughnut shop and stroll towards the high school, eyes watering and cheeks reddening beneath the fierceness of the sun. It's become a tradition for Echo, Arthur, and I, a pact we made at the end of eighth grade that every year we would brave the day we picked up our books and received our locker assignments together.

It was only intimidating the first year. After we were no longer considered fresh meat, and we stopped floating around the large, unfamiliar building like a couple of my lost treasures, the whole experience became quick and painless. More so with my best friends in tow.

Arthur's head comes to rest on my shoulder as we walk. "Tell me more about your new roommate."

"What is it you'd like to know?"

Echo pokes me in the ribcage with her elbow. "Will we be seeing him in the halls this year?"

"Are you crazy? No. He's homeless with a dead father. How is he supposed to register for school? He's planning to get a GED after he turns eighteen."

"Beauty school dropout, huh?" Arthur's lips smack together. "I want that life."

Echo bends her upper half and peers around my body, assessing Arthur with furrowed brows. "The life of the homeless?"

"No. The life of a person who doesn't have to attend high school anymore."

Patting his head, I wrap my finger around a few of his tight, springy curls. "It's less than a year, Art. You'll be fine."

"Easy for you to say. Your parents are beyond chill and don't give a rip what you do with the rest of your life as long as you're happy. Bleck. My parents are obsessed with me becoming like the first black Jesus or whatever." He stops suddenly, his feet frozen against the pavement. I slow my stride and give him my attention, noticing his eyes are sporting a crazed intensity. "The other night at dinner, my dad asked me what my college plans were and I literally had to pretend to choke on a meatball to get out of answering."

I bite my tongue to muffle my giggle.

Echo isn't as successful at hiding it. Pushing her face into the crook of her elbow, her shoulders shake with silent laughter.

Arthur appears less than amused. "It's not funny. It's tragic."

"It's both." I decide, linking my arms around theirs, making us one unit again. I tug to keep us moving.

Reluctantly, Arthur starts walking, his steps short and stiff. "It's like they want me to become the next big thing, and I'm totally fine with being average."

"Oh, you are not," Echo spits. "You're dressed in cheetah print skinny jeans. There is nothing about you that's average. You just have to find your niche, and you will. I really believe that."

"I feel like everybody knows but me."

"Maybe that's because you spent more time trying to get Spencer to notice you last year than actually looking into career possibilities and college options." I wink at him so he'll know I'm teasing.

He holds up his hand, fingers crossed. "Here's hoping this is the year he realizes I look exactly like Lenny Kravitz during his *Hunger Games* run."

I snort.

"You're number one in our class, there's probably a dozen scholarship options for you." Echo tosses out, pulling a pack of gum from her back pocket.

"There is, but I can't choose a college program until I know what I want to do."

I take two sticks of Juicy Fruit from Echo and pass one to Arthur, shoving the other in my mouth. "Well, what was your favorite class last year?"

"The ones that had Spencer in them."

"You're hopeless." I grin.

"I'm over talking about me." Cocking his head, Arthur flashes me a smile laced in trouble. "Are you working tonight? Let's drive to Ann Arbor and bug Shepherd at college."

"As much as I love forcing Shepherd to drive us around campus, I can't. I promised Rumor I'd help him start studying for the GED."

"Studying for the GED, huh?" He clicks his tongue. "What is that code for?"

"Yeah." Echo nudges me with her hip. "Is that like the new Netflix and chill?"

I slap them both in the gut.

Echo pops her gum. "We need to meet him."

"Agreed," Arthur blurts. "When can we meet him?"

"When you learn how to act."

"That'll be never."

Rolling my eyes, I move ahead with long, purposeful strides. Truth is, I hadn't thought about introducing Rumor to my friends. I wasn't even sure I was going to tell them who he was until I sat down at a picnic table in front of The Donut Hole and the confession just sort of barreled out of my mouth like a spontaneous case of projectile word vomit.

It isn't like me to keep secrets. Not from Echo or Arthur, and especially not from my siblings who remain clueless to the fact that a stranger is living above their heads.

"I'll ask him, okay?" I say after only a few steps. "He can hold his own but I don't want to just bombard him with you two hooligans. Not after I practically kidnapped the dude."

Arthur clutches his stomach, wheezing with sudden laughter. "I can just see you standing inside Mo, hands on your hips and chest puffed out, barking at the poor dude to follow you home."

"That is not how it happened."

"I'll ask him when I meet him."

I groan.

Echo kisses my cheek. "Smile, A. We're just teasing."

"Uh-huh." I tsk, swaying my hips to knock into them both. "You two are trouble."

"You love us for it." Arthur smacks my butt. "Maybe Rumor can join our squad. I need all hands on the wingman deck if I'm going to get Spencer to notice I'm alive."

I nod like I'm on board when I really want to jump ship at his suggestion. It isn't in my nature to be selfish, but his comment ignites a possessive side in me, and I realize I'm reluctant to share Rumor.

I'm unsure why or how I come to this conclusion. In the ten days of Rumor's residency, he has helped me alphabetize my Funko-Pop collection, beat me in twelve million games of thumb war, and let me hold the prosthesis he doesn't wear very often.

Nothing spectacular or overly phenomenal has happened that I must keep covert and all to myself. I actually haven't learned much more about Rumor's past aside from his father's passing and his quest to find his mother.

Rumor Rawlings isn't super keen on talking, especially when it comes to himself, so I try to do all the talking for him.

Sharing him with my friends before I get a chance to really understand how he ended up in my attic irritates me in a way that makes me feel childish. It's almost as though I'm not ready for someone to burst the secret bubble we've created.

Like we're in preschool and we've just become best friends, inseparable and sharing Goldfish crackers at lunch until someone else comes to join our friend group and messes up the whole vibe before there's even a chance to have one.

It's with that thought I realize I'm just as kooky as my best friends.

"I'll talk to him about meeting you."

"Where is he, anyway?" Echo wonders, tucking her thick hair behind her ear. "Just sitting up in your room all alone?"

"No. I dropped him off at the library before meeting you guys this morning. He said he's going to try to find some books on GED prep. I'm supposed to meet him inside Mo later this afternoon. In the meantime, we are one block away from laying the foundation of our senior year."

Out of the three of us, I'm the only one excited. I've never minded school, and my parents have always taught me it's a life-changing stepping stone to everything great that's awaiting me.

I'm ready for greatness.

"I'm just hoping I don't get stuck with a shitty locker assignment again this year," Echo grumbles, kicking a loose pebble. "Next to the bathrooms is the worst."

"We're seniors now, babe." Arthur grins. "We get the best of everything."

We come to a stop in front of Flat Rock Community High School. There's already a steady stream of students filtering in and out of the tall double doors built inside the vast brick building.

Arthur bounces on his toes in anticipation, reaching across me to bop the tip of Echo's nose. Her eyebrows dip and the makings of a silly smile unfold across her pink stained lips.

Soon, I'm grinning too, baring all my teeth and bouncing in time with Arthur.

The best of everything doesn't sound so bad.

7

BUTTERFLY KISSES

ALMA

"So, I told my friends about you today. They want to meet you."

His head is buried in a textbook, and he doesn't bother to look up and acknowledge my confession. "Why?"

"Well, it seems they are both intrigued and frightened by the idea of you. They're worried about the possibility of me getting murdered in my sleep."

Rumor lifts his chin a smidge, eyes finding me through thick eyelashes. "I did try to warn you that might happen. You let me in, anyway."

I lay back, propping myself up on both elbows. "I tried to tell them it's been a lifelong dream of mine to get murdered but they didn't listen. They chalked me up to be a crazy person and demanded to meet you."

"I can't say I disagree with their assessment. You are a crazy person." He begins to gnaw on the tip of his pencil, eyes still cast downward. "Is meeting them really the best idea? I mean, aren't we supposed to be keeping this low-key? What if one of them blabs to their parents about the freak sleeping on a pool float beside your bed?"

"Echo and Arthur know how to keep a secret, but if you don't want to meet them then I won't force you. They're good people."

"If you're friends with them, I don't doubt it."

I throw my hand over my heart and let my lashes flutter playfully. "Rumor Rawlings, are you saying I am a good judge of character?"

A small, lopsided grin moves across his lips. "I'm saying I think you're the best person I've ever met."

My stomach flips.

"And people like you, people who extend kindness to strangers and find more joy receiving a simple smile in return rather than an actual, tangible prize, would never surround themselves with people who don't exude that same type of energy."

My lips part slightly and then close again. Letting my fingertips graze the spot just below my eyes, I feel the heat there, and the way my skin tingles just below the surface. I shiver with each tickle, his words affecting me the same way endless butterfly kisses across my skin would.

I wait until my quickened pulse quiets and my smile turns smug before saying, "I typically make any and all people inquiring to be my friend take a personality quiz before I can say for sure. You were the only exception, and I'm still considering it."

"Well." He regards me with a lively expression, tapping his pencil against his textbook. "You may not approve of my results. In fact, you may just paint over my feet on your dresser drawer."

"Is that so?"

"Sure is. I have a terrible personality. I generally communicate in grunts and avoid eye contact. Also, my favorite past time is stealing candy from children and tipping over old people." He leans forward, inching closer to me but not quite close enough. "You want to know the worst part?"

"Worse than tipping over old people? I'm not sure I can handle it."

He bites his tongue and glances around Mo as if he's making sure we're alone. Then he cups his hand around his mouth and speaks in a hushed, vehement tone. "I never, and I mean *never*, change the toilet paper roll."

"No!" I clutch my chest. "I've brought home a monster."

He shrugs in false resignation. "I tried to tell you when we met but you looked so pleased to be kidnapping me, I didn't have the heart to tell you what an abomination to society I am."

"I can't believe I'm going to have to tell Echo and Arthur they were right about you. What a disappointment you turned out to be." I let my head shake and strain to keep a despondent look upon my face.

It's virtually impossible when he's flashing me a smile so big, it dazzles against his olive skin, enhancing all of his features. His hair is pulled back into a ponytail at the nape of his neck, making me more aware of his bold face. With his chin held high, and laughter carved in kind lines on his face, I find his compelling, dark eyes dominate the rest of his traits. While there is an innate strength in his face, a strong, firm jawline paired with smooth skin pulled tautly over the slight ridges in his cheekbones, it's his eyes I believe to be the most alluring.

There is a story hidden inside of them, a story that isn't sure it wants to be told, but finds distress in the silence.

"I'm deeply sorry I turned out to be such a letdown," Rumor teases. "At least you still have Echo and Arthur. How long have you been friends with them?"

"We met at eighth-grade orientation and have been glued together ever since."

"You didn't know them in grade school?"

"No. Arthur had just moved from Minnesota and Echo went to elementary school a few towns over. I wish I would've known them back then. It definitely would've made the early years more bearable."

He's back to chewing on his pencil. "What about Lenox? I thought you said the two of you were tight."

"We are. She's my number one, but we weren't always in the same classes and we have different interests. It's nice to have Echo and Arthur to share hobbies with but still have Lenox in my corner at the end of the day, ya know?"

"Yeah, I feel you."

As he speaks, the corners of his lips flatten and he gazes into Mo, staring wistfully into the distance as though he's trying to conjure up a memory he previously buried. The more he stares, a film of fog drapes over his eyes, his cheeks hollowing. It makes me wonder who he's thinking about, and what it is about them that has his hand balled into a fist and bones so stiff they look ready to break. He sits unmoving, captivated by a vision that's doing more harm than good.

"Rumor?"

He startles, slowly dragging himself away from the events playing on repeat in front of his eyes. "Hmm?"

"You good?"

"Me? Oh, yeah." He leans back against the steel wall of the train, fiddling with his pencil in a way that tells me he's attempting to look nonchalant.

He's failing.

"Do you have a best friend?" I ask cautiously, studiously

scanning his features to gauge how close I am to hitting the mark.

He snorts, mumbling something I can't make out while looking more uncomfortable than Reginald holding in a fart at church. When his pencil snaps between his fingers, I know I've shot a bullseye.

"What's their name?"

His reply is to flick his broken pencil at the wall and start digging in his bag for a new one.

His silence tells me he's not ready, so I battle with my personal restraint and put a padlock on my mouth. Turning my attention back to one of the dozen textbooks Rumor checked out, I go back to making notes about the GED's registration process in my notebook. I'm making a fourth bullet point with my Hufflepuff pen when I hear it.

A whispered, "Josh" comes from the other side of the train.

I crane my head just a tad, looking at him through my bangs.

He's staring down at his lap. "His name is Josh."

I say nothing.

"We met in second grade when he moved to Chicago from Texas. He made fun of my arm and I made fun of his accent. In some strange way, that made us best friends."

His head finally lifts, the fog in his eyes less prominent.

"After that, we were always a team, beating other kids up each time they made fun of us. He used to knock kids out of their desk if they even snickered at my arm. We spent more time in detention than at recess, but I didn't care. Josh was my Lenox. He was always in my corner."

With the faintest hint of a smile, the fog evaporates entirely, and he can see again.

"He's my best friend, the closest thing I have to a

brother. He was there for me every second when my dad passed. When things went to shit and I took off, I didn't stop to say goodbye or offer an explanation. He's either royally pissed off at me, or I crushed him. Either way, I don't think I'm ready to face him right now."

With a stiffness still present in his shoulders and his smile starting to wobble, I decide Josh is a troubling topic. Similar to his mother and why he's looking for her. Both people he isn't ready to face but never truly wanted to turn his back on.

Focusing my gaze back on the GED prep book Rumor checked out, I change the subject. "It says here you have to be a resident of the state in which you acquire your GED."

"Great. So, I either go back to Illinois or I apply for residency here." He drags his hand down his face and lets his head fall back. "Both expensive options."

"Have you considered getting a job? There are a ton of shops and restaurants downtown. Arthur is a waiter at a burger joint. He could probably put in a good word for you."

"That's really cool of you, but I'm not sure that would work."

"Why not?"

"Well, I don't know what I would do when they give me the tax forms to fill out. I don't have an address, not to mention I'm a homeless minor. As soon as anybody puts my name in a computer system somewhere, I'll get pinged." He slams his textbook shut and clunks it off his forehead. "Maybe I could like mow lawns or something for cash. Do you know any old people who could use some help?"

I point at him. "That's not a bad idea, actually. You could probably make some mad cash in the winter shoveling driveways." A spectacular idea washes over me, and I want to kick myself for not thinking of it earlier. "You could come work at the motel."

"Uhm, what?"

I jump to my feet. "No, it's a perfect solution. My parents are always looking for a handyman, more so since my dad found out he has carpal tunnel in both of his wrists."

Rumor crosses his arms over his chest and lifts his chin, clearly not understanding how magical my solution is. "Define handyman."

"Easy stuff." I bat my hand as I go down the list. "Painting old trim, filling cracks in the wall, replacing the hose on the washer more than you should have to, refilling the ice machine, pulling weeds out of cracks in the cement. Basically, all the extra stuff my parents dread doing when they could be doing book work."

"Alma, I only have one hand."

"So?" My nose wrinkles. "Does that make you incapable?"

"No." He chuckles and climbs to his feet, walking across the car. "It just makes me slow. Even with my prosthesis, I can't get things done as fast. Not to mention, I'm a perfectionist, which makes me even slower."

"Well, my parents are the exact opposite of perfectionists so you'll be good for them." He opens his mouth and I slam my hand over it, ignoring the surprise in his eyes. "Stop making excuses. I've seen you do everything and anything with one hand just as fast as I can with two. Just think about how beneficial it would be if you worked at the motel. You wouldn't have to wait for me to drive you or spend money on bus fare. There is no required uniform to waste money on or a training process to go through, and there's no long commute so you can go right back to studying as soon as you're done."

I drop my hand but continue rambling to heed any protests. "Don't you remember that time I convinced you to follow me home and it turned out fantastic?"

His laugh comes through his nose. "How would we tell them we met?"

"We can say you just moved here and we met at orientation today. My parents have five children and own a small business, they walk through life half asleep and frazzled unless one of their kids is in danger. They aren't going to call the school for confirmation."

He rolls his head, scratching the back of his neck. "And they'd be cool with paying me in cash?"

"Definitely. If things change later on, we will re-assess."

Putting his arms behind his back, he walks around before mumbling a distinct *"what the hell"* and then he looks at me as he says, "Alright, where do I fill out an application?"

I clap my hands and spin around to gather my stuff. "No application needed. Let's go talk to them right now."

He chokes on his tongue. "Right now?"

"Sure, why not? They are probably just about to clock in for the night. We can walk down and wait for them." Tucking books under my arm, I gesture for him to follow me outside.

Throwing his hand up, he retreats back into his dark corner and starts shoving his things into his bag. As I watch him, another realization comes to life and my excitement for this idea grows.

Due to Clare and Harrison's parental inclination to check up on me, Rumor's been keeping himself tucked in Mo's corner, away from the view of the door so my parents are unable to see him if they peer out the window. Once they know of his existence, he won't have to stay so hidden.

"Alright, let's do this." Moving past me, he leaps off Mo and looks over his shoulder. "I'm trusting you, Alma Underwood."

Scoffing, I follow his lead and we start our steps. "Have I steered you wrong yet?"

He halts in the grass, rocking forward on his toes and back down on his heels. Fiddling with the bottom of his T-shirt, he gazes at me with a crooked grin. "No. I guess you haven't."

"See?" I reach out to shove his arm. In the same second, his hand flies upward to block my hit and the tips of our fingers share the faintest touch.

I feel it immediately.

Rumor shivers and studies his fingers, wiggling them as though he no longer knows what to make of them.

I feel his small gasp more than I hear it, and I wonder right then if he can feel the butterfly kisses too.

8

MADNESS, LIES, & TINY VIOLINS

RUMOR

I feel dizzy and slightly levitated as I stare down at the tips of my fingers, and wonder *what the hell was that?*

I was a smart kid. I never once put the tip of my finger in an electrical socket but I assume this is what it would feel like, a lightning bolt being shot straight through my spine while 1,000 tiny violins start to play inside my head somewhere.

It feels a little like madness.

"Are you coming or what?"

I lift my chin to the source of my madness. She has one hand on her cocked hip while she regards me with an animated expression. There's a flush on her pale cheeks that reminds me of when the sunset makes contact with crystal clear water.

When she starts tapping her foot against the grass and checks the watch she's not wearing, I force my feet to move again. "Impatient much?"

"I'm not going to let you stall."

"I'm not stalling."

"You're a liar."

She waits for me to catch up to her before moving again. As the seconds go by, the madness starts to fade. My fingers twitch with indecision and frustration. On one hand, I want to reach out and brush my knuckles against the goosebumps that have risen on her arm. On the other hand, I want to run far, far away from the tiny violins.

My mind is racing when we make it to the enormous glass door stamped with a vinyl sticker of the state of Michigan.

"Welcome to the Great Lakes Motel!" Alma pulls open the door with a proud smile.

I take a tentative step inside, still slightly apprehensive this won't completely blow up and result in the tragic loss of my pizza bed.

"Would it kill you to smile a little? You look like somebody just ripped off all your toenails and made you eat them."

I lift my chin and flash her a noncommittal smile.

"Wow. Okay. A little less terrible school picture and a little more like you're actually excited to get this job."

"Except I don't know if I'm excited to get this job, Alma. What if this backfires?"

She pats my shoulder before shoving me the rest of the way inside of the building, letting the heavy door fall shut behind her. "You worry too much."

"You don't worry enough."

A wrinkle between her eyebrows forms. "I try not to let my mind get tangled in outcomes it can't control. Staying optimistic makes it easier to put one foot in front of the other when walking into unknown territory. You should try it."

I snort.

What an odd pair we make, Alma and I.

Two personalities so contradictory to one another's. She is white, and I am gray. She is the bright, blank canvas ready to be covered with brush strokes of vibrancy. I am muted, the color of a cloud-covered sky. A pessimism chaser because I'm not always prepared for what's behind the clouds.

Alma is more than prepared. She's lively and eager—the type of disposition I normally run from. I can't ever be too sure if what someone is preaching is disingenuous or if their smile is only pretend.

Though I haven't known her for long, I don't believe Alma's permanent smile and pretty words to be pretend, but I do wonder if it's a bandage for any damage that may have been done to her.

"Alright, I'm going to go check the back office for my parents if you're good to chill here?"

I hoist my bag higher on my shoulder. "Yeah, that's fine."

"Cool. Feel free to wander." With that, she drops her books on a long desk and scampers away.

Shoving my hand into the front pocket of my jeans, I move deeper into the building. The walls surrounding me are a deep blue. Not your average beige or other lame, neutral color. Something tells me that's just too mainstream for the leaders of the Underwood clan.

Moving out of the entryway, I find myself greeted by two oversized suede couches. Lying between them is a sheepskin rug, the color you get when mixing chocolate and vanilla ice cream together. It looks so soft, I get an urge to lay on it and wrap myself up like a human burrito with plans to stay a while. Despite its size, it doesn't feel like it's here to be a statement, but rather something for people to enjoy. Nothing about this place feels overly opulent or like it was strategically set up to impress. There are no chandeliers or gold framed stock photos. The furniture pieces aren't carbon copies of one another, and there's not one ugly throw pillow in sight.

It's a welcoming space, built to make guests feel like they are exactly where they belong.

Coming to stand in front of an old stone fireplace, my chest fills and I feel the way I did when I stepped inside Alma's attic for the first time. It's astonishing, really, how a small space can produce such a profound effect.

"Can I help you, son?"

Following the sound of a voice, I turn my head to the right and refocus my gaze on a man. He's parked behind a vast, wooden desk almost comically large in comparison to the slim man who sits behind it.

"Uhm, hi." I lift my hand in a lame wave. "I'm just waiting for Alma."

Clearing his throat, his aged fingers flex against the glass dome acting as a handle on his cane. "Alma doesn't work today."

"Right." I push a stray lock of hair behind my ear. "She's talking to her parents. I'm just waiting."

"Waiting for Alma?"

I nod in confirmation. He says nothing. If it weren't for his finger twitching against the top of the desk, I'd think he's dozing. Slowly, he lifts his hand and starts rubbing at his jaw, the wrinkles in his skin pulling taut while he looks me over.

His gaze is like a bag of bricks. I tug at the collar of my shirt, shuffling around myself and peering at the hallway Alma fled down.

"What's your name, young man?"

I clear my throat. "Rumor."

"Rumor. That's quite a name." His eyelids lower. "Got a last name to go with it?"

"Rawlings."

He cocks a silvery eyebrow and his jaw falls slack. As quickly as I notice it, his reaction is gone and replaced with a tight-lipped smile. "Well, it's nice to meet you Rumor, my name is—"

"Reginald."

His laugh is low and raspy. "Ah, Alma's been telling her friends about me."

I shrug.

He pats himself on the chest. "It's okay, young man, you can tell me all the pleasant things she had to say."

I lift my chin. "She said you're crotchety, have a strong dislike for teenage slang, and should probably retire."

His cheek twitches with the hint of a smile. "All true statements." Rolling his shoulders back, he rises to his full height and starts to hobble around the desk. My tongue stops working when he moves to stand parallel to me and I'm forced to crane my head backward to look up at him.

He points a crooked finger at my head. "You need a haircut. Other than that, you look good. Strong."

I blink. "Uhm, okay."

Pale lips pull into a strange smile. Reaching around me, he pats me on the back a few times. "It's good to finally meet you, Rumor."

With that, he turns and starts to limp away, his cane clicking against the hard floors. "Uh, yeah, you too!" I call, and he disappears through a doorway behind his desk.

I'm left feeling a little amused and a lot puzzled.

Strange dude.

"Rumor!"

I spin on my heels, making eye contact with Alma who's

heading toward me with a spring in her step.

"I found them." She hooks her thumb over her shoulder and directs my attention to her parents.

Two sets of warm eyes observe me as they walk. Alma reaches me first and thrusts her hands at me like I'm a prize to be won. "Mom, Dad, this is Rumor."

Alma's dad chuckles at her eagerness and extends his hand. "Hello, Rumor, it's great to meet you. I'm Harrison."

I grasp his hand and give it a quick shake, attempting to smile the way Alma demanded of me. "It's nice to meet you, too."

Harrison places a loving hand on his wife's shoulder. "This is my wife, Clare."

With gentle hands, she captures my one in both of hers and gives it squeeze. "It's great to meet you, honey. Alma just talked our ear off, I feel like I already know you."

My gaze darts to Alma and I flash her a dubious look.

"I was just telling my parents we met at orientation this afternoon," she says, sliding up next to me. "I told them what you told me about moving from Chicago with your dad."

"Right." I start tapping the edge of my thigh.

"This must be quite a change for you." Clare rests her hand on Harrison's arm, regarding me with a face almost identical to Alma's. She possesses all the same features, exhibiting light wrinkles around her eyes and beside her lips. I imagine them to be the cause of a decade long smile.

"It's different, yes." I force a laugh. "Much smaller than Chicago."

"I'll bet," Harrison chimes in. "Does your dad work around here? Maybe we'll run into him."

Yeah, in the afterlife.

"No. He works in Ann Arbor," I say because it's the

only town I can remember that isn't one of Alma's siblings. "He's in tech support."

"Really? Well, he's a different man than I am. Clare and I still use paper records." His chest quakes with his chuckle. He rubs at his eyes, the skin beneath them heavy, indicating he probably hasn't had a full night's sleep in a few decades. "Alma mentioned you're looking for work here and there."

I stand up straighter. "Yes, Sir."

"Harrison is fine, Rumor." He claps my shoulder. "Clare and I would appreciate any help around here. My muscles don't stretch like they used to."

"I would be happy to help. I'll be honest, I can't work as fast as others but I do a real good job."

I lift my chin with flawed conviction. I don't know the first thing about being Mr. Fix It for a motel older than I am, but I'll be damned if I sleep in their house without their knowledge, lie to them about how I met their daughter, and then be a shitty employee.

I don't like that I'll have to do a top-notch job only to justify the pile of lies I'm burying them beneath, but my options are limited. Each time I try to let my mind forget how shady I'm being, guilt digs up my actions and throws them in my face.

"We'd love to have you lend a hand," Harrison says. "Tell ya what, let's give you the week to get yourself all settled in and ready for school. I'll give you a call next week."

I palm the useless phone in my pocket, dead and without the service I couldn't pay for.

"Rumor's in the process of getting a new phone," Alma blurts, placing her hand on my bicep. "Switching plans and all that. How about I just bring him back here next Monday after school?"

Harrison beams. "Sounds good, kiddo. Mom and I will start a list of some things we need done." He offers me his hand again. "Thank you, Rumor, we appreciate it."

I swallow lead. "Of course. It's my pleasure."

I stay rooted in my spot, watching them retreat back down the hallway I assume leads to their office. My ribs feel tight, and I kind of want to throw up.

Alma's fingers tighten on my arm. "That went great!"

"Yeah, if you consider me being an exceptional liar great." I pick at my fingernails.

"Rumor, it's not that big of a deal."

"Are you kidding me, Ace?" I snap my head up. "I am sleeping in their daughter's room and working at their business under false pretenses. That is mad disrespectful."

"Rumor." Slowly, she wraps her finger around a strand of errant hair and tucks it behind my ear. The madness mixes with the deceit, and I feel like I'm spinning. "You're not just lying."

"Yeah?" My tongue feels dry. "Then what am I doing?"

"Surviving." She seizes my wrist and tugs gently, leading us to the front door. "You called me Ace. Only special people give me nicknames."

"Am I not special? How many homeless, one-handed teens do you know?"

She stops abruptly, our shoulders crashing together. Peering over her shoulder and through two thick pieces of hair she says, "I'm not sure there's anyone quite like you, Rumor Rawlings."

With my heartbeat throbbing harshly in my ears, and tiny violins playing in the background, I fight the shy smile creeping up my face, afraid I'll look stupid.

I smile anyway.

She smiles back.

9

A BENCH BEHIND DOGGY STYLE

ALMA

Doggy Style is the highlight of my week. It doesn't matter how long I have to wait for it, or that I have to stand in a line a dozen people deep just so I can have a hot dog that costs less than five dollars. It's worth it. Doggy Style is the greatest thing to happen to Flat Rock since Krispy Kreme. The little glazed doughnuts used to be my go-to snack, and then I was introduced to Doggy Style. I can't believe what I was missing.

"Next!"

I move up in line, hands stuffed in my back pockets while I wait. The place is packed for a Wednesday afternoon. The handful of tables they have placed throughout the small building are all occupied and piled high with dogs and used napkins. There's a healthy mix of middle-aged people having a late lunch and millennials who need a meal that won't suck the life out of their bank account.

"What is this place?" Rumor asks from beside me, gazing around Doggy Style liked he just stepped into Disneyland.

"Only the greatest restaurant of all time."

"And they only sell hot dogs?"

"Basically." We move up in line, the bottom of my flip flops sticking to the checkerboard floor. "You're from Chicago, don't you have lots of cool places like this?"

"I went to a place similar to this growing up. It was called Top Dog, but much smaller and they sold other things."

"Next!"

"Do you know what you want to order?" I point out the lengthy chalkboard menu above the counter. "I've tried them all but my personal recommendation would be the pizza dog or the mac daddy."

"Mac and cheese on a hot dog? Sold."

"It's too bad you couldn't work here."

"Right? It's always been my dream to wear a hat with a wiener sewn on top."

The corner of his lips twitch but his smile doesn't quite reach his eyes. As we move up to order, I nudge him with my hip and gesture subtly toward the wording printed on the employee's shirt.

"You can't beat our meat but you can touch our buns."

Best. Slogan. Ever.

Rumor sputters and puts his fist to his mouth, holding back his laughter while I order us two mac daddy dogs. He's still chuckling when we step off to the side to wait for our order. The sound gets me hyped enough to run three laps around the building with a pirouette for the big finish.

I abstain, but it's a struggle.

Rumor's laughter is evidence of his happiness, something that dispersed on the walk from the motel back to my bedroom. As soon as he stepped through the doorway, he let his bag slide off his shoulder with a clunk and flopped on his air-filled pizza slice. Tucking his hand behind his head, he gazed at the ceiling with an empty stare and a slack expression. It was a dark contrast to the smile he flashed me outside the motel.

Talk about butterfly kisses.

When I smiled back at him, and his grew wider, I thought my feet might come right off the ground.

Then I blinked, and his whole demeanor changed.

"Order up!"

I spin on my toes and seize our hot dogs from the worker's hands, tugging a few napkins free of its holder. Handing one dog to Rumor, I spot every seat in the building currently in use.

"Outside," I tell him, and then we start weaving through the crowd of eager wiener eaters.

The heat blasts us the moment I pull the door open, and I immediately start leading us behind the building where I know there are some benches and a covered patio.

"Shade. Nice." Rumor makes a beeline for the red bench tucked closest to the building and out of the sun's harsh rays.

I sit beside him, cross-legged, and wait for him to sink his teeth into man's greatest creation.

He groans as the food hits the tip of his tongue. His head falls back against the building behind us, and he props one foot up on the opposing knee. "You were right," he says through a mouthful of meat and cheese. "Best hot dog ever."

"I mean, I'm kind of a wiener expert."

He chokes on his hot dog.

Sizzles streak across my cheekbones and down my neck. I slump into the bench, the tips of my ears smoldering. "That is, uhm, not what I... meant."

Setting his hot dog in his lap, he pounds his chest, sounds ranging from coughs and hysterical cackles rolling from his throat. His other arm is wrapped around his stomach and he hunches over, deathly close to flattening his hot dog. I'm just about to go get him a water when he sits up and wipes beneath his eye.

"Thanks, Ace." He smiles broadly. "I needed that laugh."

"You're welcome. Please let me know the next time you need a laugh and I'll be sure to come up with something as equally as embarrassing."

I take a bite of my hot dog, licking cheese from my lip. He's still smiling as he continues eating, and I almost want to blurt something else heinously humiliating just to keep him laughing. The chuckles and half smiles only serve as a minor distraction from the tragedy he suffered and the feelings he's internalized. Growing up, my mom always told us it's laughter that sets the spirit free. I'm not sure how I know but if there was ever a spirit that needed to be freed, it's Rumor's.

"You're a riot," he says.

"I'll take that as a compliment."

"You should."

A drum pounds in my chest. I look away and finish my food, fiddling with its wrapper. "Typically, the word crazy is used to describe me."

"You say that like it's a bad thing."

"Isn't it?"

He lifts his shoulder in a shrug and shoves the last bite of hot dog into his mouth. He swallows and crumples the wrapping in his fist before saying, "I think you're a good kind of crazy. You have an electrifying absurdity about you that makes the people around you feel like they're entitled to experience whatever emotion they need to, no matter how foolish or sensible it may be."

My chest tightens.

"It's maddening and comforting at the same time." His hand trembles like a bomb getting ready to blow. "And I think it's the only reason I haven't completely lost my mind."

The pressure on my chest increases. I breathe out of my nose slowly and deliberately.

"Rumor... are you..." *Deep breath.* "Are you okay?"

He collapses forward, his shoulders bowing. "I have no freaking idea."

"I'm sorry. About your dad, I mean. I never said it... but I am sorry, Rumor." My throat squeezes. "I'm sorry he's not here anymore."

"Yeah, me too."

Untangling my legs, I place them on the concrete and slide closer to him. "When did he pass?"

"Seventy-three days ago."

Less than 3 months.

"Rumor—"

"You know, it's funny." He sits up, staring blankly in front of him. "It was just a regular day. Dad went to work like he always did. Josh and I spent hours bumming around with our skateboards and a few other guys. When his mom texted him and told him we should come back, we thought it was just because she had dinner ready or something. Never, in a million years, was I expecting a police car to be in his driveway." He clears his throat. "Josh, uhm, he dropped his skateboard and took off running because he thought maybe something had happened to someone in his family. Turns out, it was mine."

I move my hand to his thigh and squeeze.

"He just dropped dead. Right at work. One minute he was fine, and the next he was gone. The doctors said it was an aortic rupture." He sniffs and wipes at his eyes with the heel of his hand. "He said it was heartburn. He went a week popping antacids like candy and then he up and dies on me." A tear escapes and races down his cheek. He swipes at it angrily. "You know, an aortic rupture is one of the rarer cases of death in this country, but that's the kind of family we are. *The rare kind.* The kind that has a kid with one hand and a fifty-six-year-old drop dead at work."

He hiccups and keeps wiping at his cheeks, refusing to let his tears be seen. I slide my hand around his waist and tug him closer.

"I didn't have anywhere to go after that. My dad was an older dad. I wasn't born until he was almost forty. Both of his parents died when I was young, and he didn't have any siblings. I stayed with Josh at first. His parents were filing for guardianship but it had to go to court since I didn't have a parent or anyone to speak for me." He gripped my knee like it was his only source of strength. "They made me leave Josh's house while the paperwork was going through or something. I don't even know. We all tried to fight it."

He straightened, eyes raw and outlined in red. "Four days, Alma. I was in that group home for four days. They didn't even give me a bed. I slept on a mattress in a room with two other guys. One of them smoked and kept a handgun under his pillow! I doubt it was legal but all I got were hard stares and cynical laughs when I tried to bring it up." His lip wobbles and he bites down hard on it to get it to stop. "The first time somebody tried shoving me around, making me out to be an outlet for their frustration, all because I was missing something they all had, I ran."

My heart shatters for him. Like a bullet hitting glass.

"I keep asking myself how all of my dreams turned into

nightmares so quickly." He squeezes his eyes shut. "And when do I wake the hell up?"

My lips quiver and I hold back a sob. Reaching for his hand, I place it back on my knee and leave mine resting on top. I stumble over my words, not knowing what to say or if I should even say anything at all.

So I don't.

I sit there with him, rubbing across his knuckles with my thumb while his heavy, turbulent breaths minimize into ones a bit more even.

"Jesus." He exhales. "I just totally lost my shit behind a restaurant called Doggy Style. What a life."

My laugh is watery. "No better place than the best place on earth."

The smile he flashes me is weak. "Thanks for listening."

I squeeze his hand. *Anytime.*

He blows out a long breath, one that empties his lungs and fills them up again. "I don't regret it, ya know," he says between breaths. "Running, I mean. It sucks that I had to run, but I'm glad I bought that bus ticket."

"To Flat Rock, of all places. I'll bet that was a long ride."

"It wasn't bad."

"Why did you choose Flat Rock?"

"Because it sounded cool, I guess." He sniffs. "No reason."

I let him lie.

Whoever she is, wherever she is, and whatever she's doing is irrelevant until Rumor's ready. So, I take a shallow breath and let him pretend he isn't here for his mother.

"*Gah!*" His shakes his limbs out. "I feel like I just made things so heavy and depressing. My brain feels like lead. Say something else."

My mind races with dorky jokes and ways to bring him out of his head, and then my mouth opens. "I'm a kleptomaniac!"

His jaw drops.

"Well, not really, but kind of. I don't steal from people, I just take their things."

He grunts. "And you thought I was gonna rob you?"

"I'm not a robber! I clean rooms at the motel." I give my head a quick shake. In typical Alma fashion, the babbling begins. "You knew that. Anyway. More times than not, the guests always leave an object behind. I take those items and keep them rather than throw them out. The journal I carry around is filled with little stories about where I think they come from." I smile proudly. "I like to call them my lost treasures."

A beat of silence goes by.

"I think you're a little insane," he blurts. "And I think it's really awesome."

"Yeah?"

"Oh, yeah." Tentatively, he places his hand back on my knee and grants me with a timid smile. "Tell me some of the things you've found."

"Okay." I look up, creating a quick list. "Well, some of the more recent finds include ticket stubs to a blue man group concert, the glue for a toupee, a red feather boa, a studded dog collar, a snow globe of the London skyline, and seven earrings of mismatching pigs."

His smile is quick. "Can I see them?"

"My treasures?" I place my hand over his. "Sure."

"Which one is your favorite?"

"I don't have a favorite. I like to say I love them all equally. Somebody has to, you know? Every treasure I've kept has been left behind. Like, people decide they don't want it anymore, set it down, and walk away. I think a lot of times we treat other people this way. Leave them behind when we decide we're done with them."

Turning his hand over, our palms connect, and slowly—*so slowly*— our fingers link together. "Maybe I'm one of your lost treasures."

"Maybe you are."

Our eyes lock, and I see my reflection in his leftover tears. He squeezes my hand. "I'm glad you found me."

10

SOMEWHERE OUT THERE

RUMOR

"Do you do this often?"

"Draw on my nub? Yeah." I cross my ankles and lean back, my upper body immersed in the pillows on her bed. "Usually when my boredom reaches maximum capacity."

"I'm sorry." The marker against my skin stills. "Did you just call your half-arm a nub?"

"Did *you* just call it a half arm?"

She shrugs. "Half arm sounded medically correct."

"*Medically correct.*" What a dork. "Sorry to break it to ya, Ace, half arm isn't exactly a proper term either. My docs used to call it my stump."

"Like a tree? Weird."

"Right? Dad and I thought so too. It's why we renamed it a nub."

She grins and dips her chin, drawing swirls and uneven lines on my nub with a red washable marker. "I like that better too."

She exchanges her red marker for a pink one, drawing small, circular shapes along her lines. Her chest lifts in even pants while she nibbles on her lip. I watch her with rapt fascination. "What are you drawing?"

She lifts her head just barely, her cheeks now as pink as the marker between her fingers. "The butterfly kisses."

My lips curve. "The... what?"

"Butterfly kisses," she says sheepishly, her eyes fixed ambitiously on her design.

I angle my head, my cheek pillowing against teeny, tiny clouds while I gaze at my artist. As I stare, the lines start to dance against my skin. Circular shapes morph into butterfly wings, getting knotted throughout the strategically woven lines. "I can't tell if the butterflies made the lines or if they're trapped in them."

"Both."

I shiver as the marker drifts across my skin. "How do they get out?"

We finally make steady eye contact. Her pupils large and glossy, I want to submerge myself beneath their surface and get lost.

A soft breath falls from her lips. "If they're lucky, they don't."

My brows dip. "They don't want to get out?"

"No." Right in the crook of my elbow, she fabricates a butterfly much larger than the rest. "The butterflies represent something magnificent, something remarkable we want to hold tight to."

"So we trap them?"

"We try to."

A sea of red and pink oscillate against my skin with the movement of her hand. With each stroke, I become a little less muted, as she carefully replaces my gray with a little touch of her color.

"What's so special about the butterflies?"

"Their kisses give us a little tinge of weightlessness."

My voice lowers. "Have you felt one?"

"I've felt thousands all at once."

"What was it like?"

The tip of her finger whispers across the butterflies in my skin. "Like I'm walking through a dream I'm not sure will end happily but find myself wishing not to wake up anyway." Her finger stills. "Would you like to feel one?"

I can only nod.

She arranges her body so she's on her knees beside me. Swaying forward, she places a tentative hand on either side of my head. The arms holding her upright quiver, the hair spanning them vertical and motionless. Her throat bobs, and she's inclining, her cheek mere centimeters from mine.

Warm breath moves across my cheek, and she's right there, her lips a fraction from my skin.

"Don't move."

I stop breathing.

The pads of her fingers graze my forehead, riding my face of any loose strands of hair. I hear her swallow and then we are suspended in silence.

My eyes fall shut, and I grip her bedding tight in my fist.

I feel it before I'm ready—the soft, cautious flutters of her eyelashes against the top of my cheekbone. I vibrate with each pass of her lashes, my chest swelling. Somewhere in my Alma-induced stupor, the truth registers with me. Her butterfly kisses and my tiny violins are one and the same.

My eyes fly open.

Her movements are languid and carefully calculated as she pulls herself away from me. Rather than sitting back on her heels, she stretches her body out beside me, hands below her cheek, our heads sharing a pillow.

Her breath moves across my lips as she speaks. "I hope one day you'll feel thousands at once." Her hand settles on my chest, my heartbeat knocking into her palm.

"My mom used to do that when we were kids." Her eyes fall shut. "Even back then I knew it was something special."

The pulse in the tip of my finger pounds when it makes contact with her forehead, brushing bangs from her face. Maybe it's because she has her eyes closed, or maybe it's the silence begging to be filled but I find myself confessing, "I wish I knew my mom."

Her eyes stay closed but the hand on my chest grows heavier. I find it in me to keep talking.

"I never cared before. I had a great childhood, a mom around wouldn't have made a difference. My dad worked his ass off to make sure I didn't want for anything. Even at a young age, I respected that." I place my hand over hers. "I didn't ever ask. I had sort of an attitude toward her. Like 'I don't want to know you if you don't want to know me' sort of thing."

She links our pinky fingers.

"The first and only time I got curious was when I needed my birth certificate to get my license. He was super strange about it. When I confronted him, he told me her first name and that she grew up in Flat Rock, Michigan. I didn't ask any more questions after that."

"Why not?"

"It seemed to upset him." My eyes drift. "He meant more to me than a woman I'd never met, anyway."

"Rumor." She was holding my hand now, squeezing with all she had. "Wondering about your mother doesn't make you a bad son to your father."

"I know, but I never really wondered. Not until he died and made me an orphan."

Her eyes peel open, a curtain of moisture against emerald irises. "I'm sorry. I can't even begin to imagine what it is you went through."

"When I was a kid, I used to wish for a hand so other kids would leave me alone. Now, I'd give up my other hand just to bring him back."

Her hand leaves mine and falls against my face, palming my cheek. With a swipe of her thumb, she rids me of a tear I didn't know escaped. The pain that comes with losing my dad is a silent one. One that comes from cuts and bruises that can't be seen but are more painful than anything a weapon could do.

"If I dwell on him for even a fragment of time, I lose it. So I just don't dwell. Even though I think that's what you're supposed to do."

"You lost one of your parents and then jumped on a bus all alone to find the other one. There is no rulebook that says you have to feel a certain thing or react a certain way."

"Do you think I'm completely mad for jumping off a cliff without knowing what's at the bottom?"

Her smile is soft. "I think you're filled with buoyancy and courage. You may be a little mad, Rumor Rawlings, but don't you know your fairytales? All the best people are."

I snort. "That's her name."

"Whose?"

"My mother. Her name is Alice."

"Well, maybe she went back to Wonderland and that's why she's not here."

"That's wishful thinking." I rest my hand on her waist, my fingers tangling with the fabric of her shirt. "You think she's out there?"

"I do, yeah. I think she's somewhere out there, and you'll find her."

"I don't even know how she met my father or how long they were together. He never opened his book to that chapter."

"What was his name?"

"Simon."

"Tell me about him." She brushes my hair back, knotting her fingers in the strands at the nape of my neck. "What was he like?"

"He was smart. *Really smart.* He was a software developer and all around amazing with computers. He could fix or re-wire just about any machine. He had a special calculator inside his brain." My lips twitch, remembering. "I had no idea how he did it. I used to offer him foot rubs to do my math homework. It never worked."

"That was a good try." Her grin grows. "My dad would've taken the foot rub and still not helped with the homework."

"Oh, he did that." I laugh. "Plenty of times. He used to have to threaten to leave me at home while he went out and did fun things without me. That got me moving pretty quickly."

"Did you spend a lot of time together?"

"Oh, yeah. Dad and I did just about everything together. He taught me everything I know. Man was fifty-years-old on a skateboard, right beside Josh and I." My everything aches. "I miss him, Ace."

Instead of telling me it will get better or changing the subject, she wipes my cheek again and puts her forehead against mine. "There's no rulebook, Rumor."

My hand against her twitches.

"Alma!"

Her bedroom door swings open abruptly.

The silence convulses around us, the intrusion of another voice shattering the stillness into a thousand pieces that suspend over our heads. The sudden noise makes her jerk, her head connecting with the low ceiling above her.

"Shit!" I sit up swiftly, reaching for her. "Ace, you okay?"

Rubbing the back of her head, she mumbles. "This is not going to be good."

I look over my shoulder. Two dark eyeballs are glaring at the placement of my hand on Alma's head. "Who the hell are you?"

Ah, shit.

"Shepherd," Alma groans, wincing as she lifts her head. "What's up?"

Shepherd takes a heavy step forward, still staring at me with hooded eyes, probably wishing the gaze would be enough to set me on fire. "What's up with me?" He smacks his chest and thrusts his hand towards us. "What's up with you?"

"Oh, you know." Alma smiles weakly. "Just the usual."

"Alma." He takes another step. "There's a man in your bed."

"*On.*" She corrects, coughing nervously. "He's *on* my bed. I was just drawing on his nub."

His nostrils flare. "You were *what*?"

"Christ." I hold my nub, displaying her artwork. "Nub."

He studies me with cold, unblinking eyes.

Alma sighs and maneuvers around me, slipping off the bed and onto her feet. "Shep, take a breath, you look like you belong caged in a zoo."

He crosses his arms over his heaving chest. "Why is there a dude in your bed?"

"*On* my bed!" she huffs. "And we were just hanging out. I met him when I was at the school getting my schedule. He just moved to town."

He narrows his eyes at me. "You got a name?"

"Rumor."

"Is that your real name?"

I lift my chin. "Is Shepherd yours?"

"Oh, for Pete's sake," Alma grumbles.

"Where you from?" Shepherd addresses me.

"Chicago." I stand from the bed. I kind of want to punch him but I offer him my hand instead. "Alma's been really cool to me since I moved here."

"Yeah, I'll bet she has."

"Shepherd!" She pinches the bridge of her nose. "What are you doing here?"

"I live here."

"You *live* in Ann Arbor."

He takes my hand in his and gives it a hard shake before confronting his sister. "Class got canceled, figured I'd come home for a long weekend."

She nods, still rubbing at her head. I turn my back on Shepherd and move toward her with rapid strides. I wrap my fingers around her slim wrist and tug. "Ace, let me see." Her hand falls away. With gentle movements, I peel back her short strands of hair and inspect the area.

"No blood, but it looks like there's a small bump forming. Say something if you feel dizzy, yeah? That was a hard hit."

"I'm fine." She turns around, my hand slipping from her skin. She grasps it before it can get too far away and gives it a squeeze. "Promise."

Shepherd makes a noise. Alma and I both jerk, casting

him our gazes. His shoulders seem to have lost some of their tension, and he's attempting to smile.

"It's nice to meet you, Rumor," he says, and I think he felt true pain with those words.

"Nice to meet you, too. I've heard a lot about you."

He runs his hands through the tousled locks on his head, the same color as Alma's. "Yeah?"

"Oh, yeah. Alma told me all about her family. Congrats on not being named Colon."

"Thank you. It's my greatest relief in life."

"See?" Alma beams. "This is great. You guys could be friends."

"Sure." I'll be friends with the Gingerbread Man if it gets her to smile like that.

Shepherd gestures toward the door. "I was gonna get the crew together and watch some movies. Kitchen sink night."

Alma looks at me. "Want to come?"

I have no idea what the hell a kitchen sink night is but I nod anyway.

"Cool. I'll get the rest of them." Shepherd rotates, heading for the bedroom door when he stills. "What's with the pool float on your floor?"

I track his gaze to my duffel unzipped beside the giant pizza, my clothes spilling out next to a pile of my toiletries. The vein in his neck pulses when he notices the pool float has a sheet draped over it and a pillow resting in the corner.

"Alma—" His fingers curl into his palms. The storm inside his eyes has just reached its peak.

"I can explain." Her laugh is flat. "It's kind of funny, really."

Shepherd pops his neck. "Family meeting," he growls. "Downstairs. Now."

We both jump when he slams the door. The ceiling rattles like it's about to cave in. The sounds of his footsteps on the stairs puncture the air. The two of us stay motionless, listening to bedroom doors fly open and Shepherd's shouts about a family meeting.

After the creaking ceases and we're back to the silence, she grips my hand and sighs. "This ought to be good."

And then we're moving.

11

FAMILY MEETING

RUMOR

Alma maintains a vise-like grip on my wrist as she ushers me down the stairs. I feel a little bit like I'm being led to my execution. Judging by the look in Shepherd's eyes, he's either going to kill me or send me back to Mo.

"Alma, wait." I dig my heels into the ground. Her small body jolts and she pivots. I drop my eyes before she can capture my gaze. "Before we go in there, I just want to—" My throat grows thick. "I just, uhm, I want to say thank you."

"For what?"

"For—" My stomach knots. "For, ya know—"

"Not really."

Bouncing on my toes, I take a few shaky breaths and look her in the eye. Her big, toothy grin makes my kneecaps wobble. "I'm going to miss you, Ace," I blurt. "I'm just, uh, really going to miss you."

Her eyebrows dip. "Are you going somewhere?"

"Ah, well, Shepherd." I scratch my neck. "He looked real pissed."

She scoffs. "That grizzly bear brother is not about to kick out my best friend."

Did she just... "Your best friend?"

"Let's not make a thing of it, yeah?" She starts to fidget. "Echo, Arthur, and Lenox all think they have the title."

"But it's me?"

A flush sweeps her cheeks. "Yes."

My grin is massive.

"Alright, well, now that we know who the real Slim Shady is." She swipes her palms down the front of her denim shorts. "Let's go face the firing squad."

With her nose high and shoulders pulled back, she strides through her house, determination and purpose in each of her steps. When we emerge into the living room, the hushed conversation ceases, and four sets of eyes fall on me.

"Okey dokey." Alma claps her hands and moves to the center of the room. "Let's get this meeting started."

"Hold up." Shepherd advances on her, abandoning his post by the coffee table. "Why do you get to lead this meeting?"

"Because Rumor is my friend."

"I'm the oldest. I always lead the meetings."

I roll my eyes.

"This is a special circumstance, Shep." She pats him on the arm. "Now step aside."

Smoothing out her shirt, she takes up stance in front of a mantle, a small television perched above it, flanked by two family photos of her entire family in denim I'll never be able to not see.

"Let's begin this meeting with some introductions. I'm sure Shepherd has already blabbed, but seeing as how Rumor is *my* friend, I think it's only fair I properly introduce him." Alma gestures toward my position, half in the room, half out. "This is Rumor Rawlings. He's here from Chicago. His favorite color is forest green. He enjoys skateboarding and clean clothes. His dog of choice is the mac daddy."

I fight back a laugh.

"Rumor, this is the Underwood clan." She narrows her eyes at the eldest. "You know Shepherd, and his actions do not need any further introductions."

He starts pacing.

She disregards him and points toward a figure sitting cross-legged on an old wooden rocking chair, draped in an oversized fur coat the color of a ripe plum. "This is Lenox. My sort of twin."

Alma warned me she and her family are like something out of a bad budget horror film but I suppose it's one of those things you can't fully believe until you witness it with your own eyes.

They're identical. All of them. Like a matching set you'd pick out at the store.

Lenox lifts her hand in a cautious wave. She flashes Alma a look and they seem to have a quick conversation with their eyes before Lenox's lips curl into a smile. "Hi."

I nod in response.

That interaction seems to satisfy Alma and she directs my attention to the people sitting side by side on a big blue couch.

The girl is upside down, feet pointing toward the ceiling while the tips of her dark hair sweep the floor. Beside her is a dude sitting ramrod straight, stroking the strangest looking dog I've ever seen.

It has hair, but also it doesn't, and I'm not sure what to make of it.

"Rumor, this is Jackson and Holland. The real twins.

They enjoy all things sciencey. Later, I'll receive an essay under my door, schooling me on why sciencey is not a proper word and should be expunged from my vocabulary."

I flash them both a polite smile.

"Okay." Alma takes a step forward. "Now that we have the introductions out of the way, who has questions?"

Jackson's hand shoots up into the air. He rotates his upper body, moving the dog to his shoulder. "Are you a born amputee or did you suffer some sort of tragedy?"

"Jackson!" Lenox shakes her head, fingers to her temples. "You can't just ask people where their hand is."

"Nah, it's fine." I move deeper into the room, my face neutral. "I fell into the lion's den at the zoo when I was five. No, I didn't feel any pain and I don't remember a thing."

Alma slaps her hand over her mouth.

"Well, shit." Jackson muses. "I am never going to the zoo again."

Swift tension is severed by Alma's exultant giggle. It goes on for a full minute, hand still pressed against her lips, shoulders quaking. When our eyes finally meet, hers are smoldering behind tears of laughter.

"I don't get the joke." Holland frowns, eyes moving quickly, Alma and I their targets. "What's funny?"

Alma beams. The light in her is infectious.

"He's kidding." She dabs at her eye with a knuckle.

"I was born like this." I hold up my nub. "It's called con—"

"Congenital Amputation. I've heard of it," Jackson finishes, disappointment lacing his face. "Dude, you should've stuck with the zoo story."

"Can we get down to what's important here?" Shepherd marches to the center of the room. "I'm about ninety percent sure Rumor is living inside Alma's room."

"Huh." Holland cocks her head. "How does another person fit inside that room?"

"He sleeps on a pool float." Alma's answer is quick. "It's a bit tight but we make it work."

"Which one?" Lenox inquires, sliding to the edge of her rocking chair. "The pizza one, right? It has to be. It's the only one big enough."

"Well, there's the taco," Holland throws out. "But it's shape wouldn't allow for a good night's rest unless he sleeps curled up in a ball." She looks at me. "Do you sleep curled up in a ball?"

"Uhm..."

"Have you all lost your minds?" Shepherd squalls. "There is a stranger sleeping in our sister's room and you're all wondering what his preferred sleeping position is?"

"Shep, keep up." Lenox sits back, arms crossing over her chest. "He's been here for weeks."

My jaw unhinges.

Lenox snorts. "A, you are terrible at keeping secrets and even worse at being sneaky. You've been taking random plates of food up to your bedroom for weeks. There's suddenly an extra bath towel in the laundry load, and a random toothbrush forgotten about on the bathroom sink. Not to mention the backdoor is kitty-corner to Holland and I's bedroom. The two of you creep in every night, arguing over whether or not someone can hear you."

"You might as well be speaking into a megaphone," Holland agrees.

Alma sways. I take two giant steps, positioning myself behind her.

"I can't believe you two knew!" she shrieks. "Jackson? Did you know?"

He shrugs, still caressing his dog. "My sisters keep me informed."

"But nobody thought to call *me*?" Shepherd's back to pacing, hands linked behind his neck. "What the hell? Nobody in this house can make a courtesy call?"

"Eh." Lenox picks at her fingernails. "It slipped our minds after a while."

Shepherd explodes. "*Slipped* your minds? Are you kidding me right now?"

"Shep, he's been here for weeks," Jackson says. "If he was going to kill us or eat Charlevoix he would've done it by now."

"Eat your dog?" I deadpan. "Really?"

He shrugs. "I don't know you."

"You're all insane." Shepherd's laughter has an edge to it, his face burning so hot, we could roast marshmallows over his cheeks. "Each and every one of you is completely insane."

"Excuse you!"

Alma's bark makes us all flinch. She whips around, finger inches from Shepherd's face. Her dark eyes are feral, calculating Shepherd's movement with an icy intensity I had no idea she was capable of. All two hundred and six bones in her body are quivering with each word she snarls. "Before you start calling our entire family insane, stop and consider where Rumor was before I met him." A muscle in her neck twitches. "Rumor is here because he has nowhere else to go. He is going to stay here until that changes. If you fight me on it, I will fight back."

"Alma." The irritability in Shepherd's gaze eases. "I'm not about to call the cops or drag your friend out by his collar. I just want to know who he is and why he's living in your room."

She rises to her tippy toes. There's a slight shake in her voice when she says, "then ask him."

"Ace." I turn away from the attention, pressing my fingers to my lips. My nose burns, and I bite the inside of my cheek as if that is going to keep me from deteriorating. Alma makes eye contact with me, and she's the only person in this room I allow to see. Giving her a wonky smile, I mouth *thank you*.

Wrinkles form around her mouth while her lips purse in uncertainty, unable to interpret my gratitude.

She doesn't know.

Her kindness and willingness to go up to bat for me since the second she met me is like a break in the storm clouds. She is a *someone* when I thought I had no one. If I tell her thank you every day for the rest of my life, it won't be enough.

Her hand on my arm pulls me out of a trance. "You okay?"

"I'm fine." I bow my head. "Alma, I don't want my presence here to make anyone uncomfortable."

"Shepherd just has some questions." The pressure of her grip increases. "But you don't have to answer anything you don't want to. Okay?"

Okay.

I shake out the tension in my muscles and plant myself in front of the infamous Underwoods. Shepherd has taken up residence on the edge of the couch, arms crossed and back rigid. I look toward Alma. She makes no moves to leave my side. I let her stay.

I want her to stay.

"So, I'm Rumor." I lift my chin in greeting. "Yes, that is actually my real name. Who has a question?"

Shepherd leans forward. "How did you meet my sister? Where are your parents? Are you really from Chicago?"

"That was three questions, Shep." Holland frowns. "Don't be rude. Leave some for the rest of us."

"Yes, I'm really from Chicago." I kick off Shepherd's three-parter with the easiest answer. "Alma found me living in a train car. She kidnapped me. As for my parents, my dad is dead and that's why I'm not in Chicago anymore." Shepherd's mouth pops open. I hold up my hand. "My dad was my only family. I got shoved in a group home after he died. It sucked there so I ran. I'm here now."

"My turn to ask a question!" Lenox looks to me. "Was the train car Alma found you in named Mo? If so, did she threaten to juice you?"

"Juice me?" *What the hell does that mean?* "No. She ordered me to go find a new one. I didn't want to because Mo was the warmest so I suggested we be neighbors. Somewhere between that conversation and her astute observation skills, she pegged me for being homeless and demanded I come live in her attic."

Alma makes a noise and steps closer to me. "You didn't tell me Mo was the warmest."

"It didn't matter." I widen my stance. "Next question?"

"Yeah." Instead of raising his hand, Jackson lifts the dog. "Why did you choose Flat Rock? There are cooler places."

"What do you mean?" Alma huffs. "Flat Rock is cool. We have Doggy Style and Krispy Kreme. What's not to love?"

She's doing it again.

Saving me.

She doesn't have to but she does anyway. Steps right up and goes toe to toe with her brothers and sisters, side-stepping their questions and babbling facts about why Flat Rock is a great place to visit. All so I don't have to provide an answer that makes me uncomfortable. I've gotten good at that in the last few weeks.

Avoiding.

It's exhausting.

Somewhere between my dad's death, the group home, and living in a train car, I transformed into a person I don't always recognize. I'm a liar. A master of evasion.

I don't exactly relish in the idea of playing dirty. Actually, it kind of makes me want to vomit, and I'm tired of walking around with a stomach full of bile. My hands were tied in regards to her parents. But her siblings deserve some semblance of the truth for staying mute when they discovered where I was living.

They're good people.

I almost forgot how to be one myself.

"My mother lives in Flat Rock," I speak over Alma's chatter, letting out my truth in a whoosh before I lose my nerve. "I chose to come to Flat Rock because this is where my mom is."

"Awesome," Shepherd drawls. "Go live with her."

"I would love to." I claw at the back of my neck. "I just, uhm, I have to find her first."

Holland lifts a finger. Her mouth opens and then shuts again.

"The last time my mom saw me I was a newborn. It's a long shot she's even here anymore, but my dad told me once that she grew up in Flat Rock. That's all I know about her."

The room is cast in silence. All four of them deflate, donning sloped eyebrows and downturned lips. Even Shepherd has a hand over his heart like he's just now remembering it's there. Lenox and Alma are doing that thing again—talking with their eyes. The rest of them are looking at anything but me.

"Do mom and dad know?" Lenox murmurs, still looking toward Alma.

My roomie shakes her head. "They met him a few days ago. He's going to do some work at the motel but they don't know he lives here. Can we please keep it that way?"

They all nod. Even Shepherd, though it was slight.

The room is soundless, and I feel like I just sucked the life out of each of them.

"I'll find her," I say with a firmness I don't feel. "It may take me a while, but I'll find her."

"Of course, you will," Alma says with a fresh smile. "I'll help you."

"We all will." Lenox stands from her seat. "This town isn't that big. More than half of the elderly population has lived here their whole lives. It'll just take some quality snooping."

"We'll have to be smart about it." Jackson taps his chin. "But it's definitely a do-able mission."

"Are there stipulations?" Holland asks me.

"What?"

Her hands move as she talks. "You know, certain stipulations you'd like this mission to follow. A timeline? People or areas to avoid?"

"Uhm." I consider it. "Well, I guess the only thing is that I'd like to lay low until I turn eighteen. If someone finds me it's possible they'll—"

"Send you back to that shithole?" Shepherd questions, standing to his feet.

"Uh... yeah."

"How do we know they aren't looking for you?"

"Runaway teens are a dime a dozen in Chicago. Even in

the suburbs where I lived. I doubt they're looking for me if there isn't a parent in the station demanding a search party on my behalf. I can't be sure but I'm counting on the system ignoring my absence unless it's dangled in their face."

He gives me a curt nod. "Then we'll make damn sure that doesn't happen."

"Thanks." I shove my hand in my pocket and let my hair fall into my face some. All of this sympathy toward my unpredictable future makes me uneasy. I've never enjoyed being the center of attention and the last thing I thought I'd do was involve other people in what has become my wreckage.

But I won't pretend the dryness in my throat or my newly rapid heartbeat isn't there.

You don't always value what you have until it's all ripped from you in the amount of time it takes you to skateboard from one side of town to the other. Standing in this brightly colored room, with five people who just pledged help to a stranger, I feel like I got some of it back.

"Thank you." I look them all in the eye. "I'm not sure how long this will take but I don't want this to hold precedence over your own lives. You're all going back to school soon. That should come first."

"Noted." Holland bobs her head. "Does anyone else know you're here?"

"Alma told her friends."

There is a consecutive groan.

"Well, there goes that." Shepherd snorts.

"The whole school will know soon enough." Jackson props his feet on the coffee table. "Arthur's a walking time bomb. Secrets make him jittery."

"He isn't going to say anything." Alma rolls her eyes.

"This isn't somebody's second-grade crush, its Rumor's life. He respects it."

Jackson isn't convinced. "Yeah, we'll see."

Alma rolls her eyes. "Are we good now? Should we adjourn this family meeting?"

"We could start looking for Rumor's mom."

I wince at Lenox's suggestion. "Uhm, we don't have to do that... right now, I mean. We can wait." My palms get sweaty.

"Geez, Len," Alma blurts. "Give the guy a break. He's had a day."

Thank you, Ace.

"Well, I vote we pull out some movies and have a kitchen sink night before I have to go back to campus," Shepherd suggests.

"I second that." Jackson raises the dog again.

"Alright." Alma smiles and claps her hands. "Meeting adjourned. Any final questions?"

I raise my hand. "What's a kitchen sink night?"

12

HELLO?

RUMOR

If I had an egg, I could crack it on the cement and fry it right here and now. I don't have an egg, so I'll probably just eat myself after the sun scorches me.

I sit back on my heels and wipe the sweat off my forehead, looking to the sky. The cloud directly above me looks like it's flipping me off. *Fitting.* I raise my hand and give it the bird right back.

"That mad at the big man, huh?"

Reggie hobbles toward me, his cane tapping against the sidewalk. I stop myself from jumping up to help him. If I learned anything from working here, it's that Reggie will beat me with his cane if I try to treat him like an old man. Even though I'm pretty sure he has arthritis in every bone of his body.

"Take this before you dehydrate yourself, son." He extends a bottle of water with his free hand and gives it a shake.

I jump to my feet and snatch it from him, unscrewing the cap and guzzling the whole bottle in one go. The cool water puts out the fire inside my gut and I feel less like I'm going to turn into dirt. "Thanks."

"Come sit in the shade for a minute, kid. You look like a lobster."

I stare longingly at the Adirondack chairs perched below the motel's awning. Reggie lowers himself into one and lets out a sigh, looking pointedly at the vacant one beside him. I move to join him before retreating at the last second.

I'm here to work.

"That wasn't just a suggestion." Reggie hollers when I turn my back on him. "Get over here and take a break. Lord Almighty, don't be a stubborn mule. You're going to faint and then what good will you be?"

"I'm almost done," I call over my shoulder, dropping back down to my knees.

I wrap my fingers around a weed peeping through the crack in the cement and pull. A gardening glove slips and slides on my sweaty hand, and I'm not prepared for what it'll smell like when I return it to Clare.

I toss the weed in a five-gallon bucket and inch forward. I'm more than halfway done, and there's hardly any of the smaller weeds left to fight with.

"Are you wearing sunscreen?" Reggie shouts at me.

"Nope! I didn't know I'd need it."

"Do you know how to check the weather? It's ninety degrees out and you're wearing jeans. Put on a pair of shorts before you have a heatstroke!"

"I'll do that."

Right after I buy a pair of shorts.

I didn't bother grabbing any when I took off. I figured if I was going to be sleeping in shady places, I wanted to protect myself as much as possible. Exposed legs made me feel too naked.

I pull a dozen more weeds, sweat dripping off the tips of my hair and running down my shirt. I roll my shoulders and pop my neck, my muscles screaming from the strain. Little pockets of fatigue are packed beneath my eyes. Weariness is tugging at me as I try to move on. I tug back.

It's my first day on the job, and I can't leave until I've mastered perfection. It isn't that hard to yank some asshole weeds from a few gaps in the concrete, and I'm not about to wimp out on two people who took a chance on me as a favor to their daughter.

I owe them more than a bucket of weeds.

By the time I'm done, I feel like I submerged myself in a pool of sweat. There's an ache between my shoulder blades and I'm so tired my nerves are throbbing.

I press my fist against my thigh, popping all my knuckles. My legs feel like two overcooked spaghetti noodles when I move to stand up. I stare at the overflowing bucket of weeds, waiting for the sun to set them on fire.

My muscles do some sort of dance as I wobble toward the shade, collapsing in my new favorite chair.

"Take this." Reggie's holding another bottle of water, eyes dropped low in annoyance. "Moron."

I snuff a laugh and grab the extra water, partially wondering when he got up to get it but also not caring. I chug half of it and dump the other half on my head.

I crunch the empty bottle in my fist.

"It's missing the hand." He nudges his chin at the prosthesis covering my nub. "What good is a prosthetic hand that doesn't come with a darn hand?"

I laugh out loud. "You're a blunt guy, Reggie."

"I'm too old to beat around the bush, kid."

"The hand isn't functional, and it's creepy looking. The socket gets the job done just fine."

His eyebrows pinch. "Socket?"

I lift my nub, knocking on the blue carbon fiber base that covers it. "Socket." I twist the small knob on the side, loosening it. Sliding it down my nub, I hand it to him. He inspects it with fraught eyes, running his crooked finger along the edges.

"This looks painful."

"Nah." I wave my nub. "I have a sleeve to put on first. I'd take this off too but it's neoprene and drenched in sweat. I'm sure it smells like a hamper."

"What good does it do if you don't have the hand?"

"See that?" I point towards a silver plate at the bottom of the socket. "If you pop that off, it'll reveal a hole for me to screw my hook into. The silver plate is just an attachment to keep dirt or something else from getting inside. I use it for when I want to put pressure on my socket. Like push-ups or crawling on concrete to pull weeds."

He pops the plate off and looks down the hole like it's a microscope.

"The myoelectric hook is actually ten times more practical when it comes to holding things for cooking or building purposes."

Reggie's gaze is anchored to the device in his hand, shaky fingers fiddling with the knob, expanding and contracting the sides of the socket. "How does that work?"

"The hook? Simple." I lean over the arm of my chair and point to the power button right above the knob. "I'd have to screw it in first, but then once I turn it on, I flex my forearm muscles and that's what open and closes the hook."

"Well, I'll be jiggered. This is fancier than the car I drive."

I chuckle. "It took six months to make. The goal is to have this one for the rest of my life since I should be done growing. It's why it's so high tech."

And the reason I never let my dad buy me a car.

"It must be hard for you, having to do everything with one hand."

I catch the socket when he tosses it to me, sliding it back into place. The knob clicks each time I turn it, compacting the sides so it's snug against my skin again. "Not really. I mean, it's all I've ever known. Some people are born with two hands and then lose one and have to adapt. I've been adapting since the day I was born."

My dad always told me I lived a normal life in a remarkable way.

I'm not sure if I'll ever believe my nub and socket make me remarkable. Living life with one hand is basically the same as living life with two. The only difference is that I had to learn my limitations and blessings in life at a much earlier age than most.

"The worst part is when people look at me like I'm contagious. Like if they are around me for too long their hand will fall off."

He grunts. "People are dipshits."

"My dad told me God left me one hand to flip off the assholes with."

"Your dad sounds like a great man."

Pressing my lips together to keep them from trembling, I right my posture so I don't collapse. Too much mention of him sparks suffering in parts of my body I didn't know existed. Like a scar on my soul that keeps reopening. A wound that won't heal.

I'm not sure I want it to.

"He was the best." I manage to say.

If Reggie picks up on my use of past tense, he doesn't mention it. He clamps his boney hand on my forearm and gives it a squeeze like he's passing along strength he shouldn't know I need.

"I bet Alma loved that contraption," he says after a beat. "With her obsession for random objects."

"Treasures," I correct him, appreciating his attempt to change the subject. "Alma would not tolerate you calling her treasures objects."

"That's precisely why I do it, son. Riling that girl up is the extent of my old age entertainment. A man can only watch so much *Wheel of Fortune*."

My small laugh is somewhat therapeutic. "She did go nuts over it. She tried to ball her hand into a fist and try it on."

Her little nose crinkled with displeasure when she couldn't get it over her wrist. Slim shoulders shook while she puckered her lips in a pout. I think she was trying to look like the Incredible Hulk but she really just looked like a more adorable version of Grumpy Cat.

"That girl is a weirdo."

"No, she's not." My jaw goes rigid. "She's fine the way she is."

More than fine.

"Relax your face, son. You'll have double the wrinkles I do." His grin grows when he scans me, ocean eyes lingering on the fist I've got clenched so tight, my veins are bulging prominently from my skin. "The whole family is a rowdy bunch and I wouldn't change any of them. Though I could do without Jackson carrying that dog everywhere."

I try to stifle my laugh. "I feel like it's always watching me."

"Jackson or the dog?"

"Both." I recline back and prop my foot on my knee.

"So, you've met the rest of the clan?"

"Yeah, a few nights ago. I'm not sure Shepherd likes me very much."

"Of course not. You're a male hanging around his younger sister. It's in his nature to worry."

"I can respect that."

After learning that kitchen sink night is the actual cause of diabetes, I decided to partake in it anyway. I ran around the Underwood kitchen, helping Alma and her siblings collect every dessert item in the house and toss it into a Rubbermaid tub that looked like it could hold about ten gallons. When we successfully emptied the cabinets of anything that might contain sugar, Shepherd dragged it into the living room and we all sat around it, eating the strange mixture with serving spoons. There were several times throughout the night when I wasn't sure if I was loving the taste or completely repulsed by it.

Jackson asked me hundreds of questions about my nub that night, ranging from how I hold a pencil to why I chose the color blue instead of a color that matched my skin.

Answer: because blending in was never going to work for me.

Shepherd didn't bother to join in on the conversation, or even glance in my direction for too long. I tried to put myself in his shoes, consider how I'd feel if I came home to find a teenage guy living in my little sister's room.

It only made me angry he thought I'd somehow hurt Ace. As if hurting her wouldn't completely wound me.

"Shepherd has been the alpha of that crowd since they were kids. He used to tuck them all in at night, lay with them if one had a nightmare. He was the parent when Harrison and Clare were here working. He wouldn't ever admit it, but it was a struggle for him to move to Ann Arbor. Less than an hour away and to him it probably feels like he's across the ocean." Reggie turns to look at me. "You have someone like that?"

"I don't have any siblings."

He bats his hand. "Not a sibling. Just somebody who'd knock down a brick wall with a hammer if you asked them to."

I immediately think of Josh.

My insides burn like somebody just poured a pitcher of acid down my throat. My stomach squeezes, unable to handle the torture.

"No," I lie, closing my eyes and forcing my chosen brother from my brain. "I don't."

Reggie drums his wrinkly fingers against the arm of his chair. "Because you moved?"

"No."

"Ya know, kid, the strange thing about abandonment is that we spend so much time fearing the response of the one we left behind, we forget to consider what we're doing to ourselves."

I crack my eye open.

"By walking away from a person like that, we walk away from a part of ourselves we found peace in. Sometimes we're okay and sometimes we're not."

I am not okay.

"The interesting thing about walking away is that there's always a path to take you back."

Who the hell gave this old man a crystal ball?

I watch his movements from the corner of my eye. "Sometimes it's just too late."

"With the right friendship, it's never too late."

His words drape me in a sense of longing so substantial,

my throat starts to shrink. I breathe through my nose violently, my heart knocking around in my chest. The absence of my brother is an ache that comes and goes. I forget... but only long enough to remember again.

There's a man on my shoulder, scolding me and telling me what I already know.

I lost two best friends when my dad died.

One is gone forever. One I can get back.

I want my brother back.

"Do you ha–" I clear my throat and start again. "Do you have a phone I can borrow?"

His smile is slight. "Sure thing, kid. There's one on my desk. Just press star and dial any number."

Pushing myself out of my chair takes five big breaths and a pep talk from Alma I make up in my head.

I feel heavier with each step I take. The air conditioner makes me shiver when it blasts me, turning the droplets of sweat across my body to ice. My hand shakes as I reach for the phone. I pick it up and put it back on the receiver seven times. It slips off my shoulder and dangles over the edge of the counter. I almost give up right then and decide strangling myself with the old phone cord would be easier than pressing the damn star button.

Beep. Beep. Beep.

My eyes watch the phone swing back and forth, the dial tone haunting me— moving through me like the after effects of a bad dream. It's my new least favorite sound and I rush forward and hit the star button just to make it stop.

I'm on autopilot as I type in the nine digits, fingers numb and tongue thick.

My lungs stop working when it starts to ring.

"Hello?"

The sound of his voice is like a rock in my ribcage.

"Hello?"

I pound my chest, a sound eerily close to a bark escaping my chest.

"Who is this?"

Say something!

"Josh?" I sound like somebody sanded down my vocal cords. "It's me."

There is a hitch in his breath and a noise that sounds a lot like a sob. "Rumor?"

13

TAMPONS, TRASH & TIME

ALMA

"I cannot believe I just climbed through trash for you."

Lenox grins, clearly pleased with herself. "Dad is going to be so proud."

"Uh..." My lips smack together. "*Why?*"

"This was his idea."

"A giant trash pile on his back porch was his idea?"

"It was his idea for me to join the art club." She drops cross-legged on the porch and starts poking at the mound of trash we spent two hours dumpster diving for. I smell like a skunk, and Lenox has a jelly-like substance in her hair. Not my first choice of a nightly activity but when my sister says she needs me for something important, I steal some surgical gloves from Jackson's room, shove a tampon up each of my nostrils, and dive in.

"All this for the art club?" I squat down and use two fingers to lift some packaging for Fruit of the Loom underwear. "I'm not sure how this translates."

She swats the package out of my hand. "Our first task was to create art out of something unusual, and what's more unusual than trash?"

Girl has a point.

"Are you going to help me sort this or what?"

I arrange myself so I'm sitting on my knees. "How does one sort trash?"

"I'm not sure yet. We can definitely ditch all the food items. Those won't work. Maybe by plastics and paper?"

I recoil at the way she rubs her glove covered hand over her chin in thought.

Trash germs. Ick.

"Ya know." She tosses an apple core into a trash bag. "I figured you of all people would be excited about this."

I jerk. "Why me?"

"Because you collect treasures and this is practically the same thing."

I throw my hand over my heart, germ-filled glove be damned. "How could you even begin to compare my treasures to this heap of garbage?"

This girl has the nerve to roll her eyes at me. "It's all stuff nobody wanted."

"Because who wants this?" I lift an empty carton of fat-free vanilla yogurt. "There's mold in the inside."

"We just have to find the right thing," she says, sifting. "You know the saying 'one man's trash is another man's treasure.' Huh." Her lips purse. "Maybe that's what I should call my project."

"Lenox, none of this is treasure. It's all trash."

"What about this?" She flings something at me.

I dodge it quickly, pressing my lips together to keep any trash molecules from soaring into my mouth. An object thumps against the side of the house and rolls across the wood pallets of the porch, spinning and spinning in circles until I reach out and snatch it.

My fingers tighten around the object once I get a good look at what's in my grip.

Treasure.

"I stand corrected."

Lenox chuckles. "You can keep it."

"Her," I correct, suddenly wide awake and feeling much more exhilarated than I was two minutes ago.

My new treasure is a doll head. She has porcelain skin and long blonde hair I run my hand down. The little plastic crown on her head deems her a princess. She winks at me every time I tilt her, only one eye opening and closing the way it should. Flipping her over, I give her a good swat on the back of the head. Sand falls from her eyelids and sprinkles the wood below us. The wires coming from her neck tell me she used to have a voice box before someone or something decapitated her.

She's perfect.

I set my princess aside carefully, my brain already running through the endless possibilities of her past. Her story will have to be a tragedy. Something morbid and filled with misfortune. I'm thinking toy maker gone rogue after facing an event that could only be described as an utter calamity.

"Alma!"

I jerk, blinking to bring Lenox back into focus. "Huh?"

Her smile is smug. "Still think everything in here is trash?"

I flick an old bottle cap at her. "Keep digging. Maybe we can find her body."

What a story that would be.

"I think I want to keep all the shoes and ditch everything else." She yanks a red suede stiletto from the heart of the pile. It's missing its heel and covered in a dark liquid. "There's a story about the woman who wore this shoe."

"That's an idea." Plucking a banana peel from the edge of the pile, I toss it back into the trash bag it came from. "Maybe you could make some kind of sculpture with all the shoes, representing different walks of life and what not."

She beams, hugging her shoe to her chest. "I'm an artistic genius."

"Dad will be so proud." I free a blue tennis shoe with missing laces from the pile and hand it to her. "Why'd he encourage you to join the art club, anyway?"

"It wasn't art club specifically. I told him I was struggling to decide what I wanted to study in college. He suggested I find a creative outlet."

My knees aching against the unforgiving wood, I shift to sit on my butt. "You think art club is going to give you some insight into your future?"

"Maybe. Maybe not." She shrugs. "If anything, it'll be something fun to keep me busy."

"Why's everybody so stressed about the future?"

Her nose twitches. "Why are you not?"

"I guess I am on some level, but I also don't want stress to be the only thing I feel for the next year." I flick something brown off my arm. "Look at Arthur. We are less than two weeks into school and he's already losing it because his parents won't stop badgering him. He came to school this morning and announced he was an octopus."

"An octopus?"

"Because apparently, octopi eat themselves when they get stressed. Poor guy is one family dinner away from putting himself in the oven." I pull my knees to my chest. "I don't want to eat myself, Lenox."

"Well I'm not about to start blending my limbs or anything, A. I think of it more like an adventure."

I crack a smile. "An adventure?"

"Yeah. High school is sort of like the map for the rest of our lives. I'm just having trouble choosing which road to take." Her fingers find a bald cap and she pulls it free, dangling it between us. Eyes matching mine gleam with laughter. "Which road do you think this bald cap is telling me to take?"

"I think you should ignore any whispers that come from that thing. It's going to lead you toward rice pudding and gingivitis."

She tosses it over her shoulder. "See? This trash is helping already. I just crossed one road off my map." She adjusts the tampons sticking out of her nose. "Maybe if we lay in it, it'll tell us exactly what to do."

"I would not recommend that."

"You basically already laid in it. Don't be a ninny."

There's no time for a protest to leave my lips before she's falling backward into a trashy bundle of God knows what. She shimmies her upper body, slender shoulders relaxing against an old coffee can. Her lashes dance against her cheekbones, eyelids settling shut and her hands falling into place against her chest.

"You look like a homicide victim," I tell her.

She shushes me.

I pinch my inner thigh.

Yes. The sight in front of me is live and in color. My sister, *Lenox Underwood*, who wears bologna masks and sleeps with mayo in her hair is completely at peace surrounded by the remnants of a dumpster.

I fear that I've lost her to the desperation and desolation

high school bestows upon eager young adults with minds that can't be made up.

"Get your ass in this trash with me, Alma." Her demand forces my attention. "Hurry up."

"No."

"I will drag you in here."

She's not joking, and my choices dwindle down to two.

1. I run

2. I snuggle with my sister in a pile of trash.

My mind is already made up.

I pop my neck, bouncing on my knees and rolling my shoulders. My warrior cry makes her flinch, and I go for it. I dive into the garbage and wiggle around until I'm comfortable. She seeks my hand and squeezes, something sticky coating our gloves.

I pretend it's not there and close my eyes, concentrating on the garbage whispers. I breathe slowly as I wait for the coffee cans and bald caps to tell me which road to drive down. The longer I wait, the heavier my skin becomes as it fills with apprehension.

I feel compacted by time. Restricted by deadlines.

The faster we move in life, the less we feel. And I want to feel *everything*.

"Is it working?" Lenox asks me. "Do you see visions of the future?"

"Nope. I'm not sure I want to look just yet."

"Why?" Her head turns, something crunching beneath her cheek. "Are you afraid of what you'll find?"

"No." I stare up at the sky, observing the way a cloud morphs into an apple. "I'm afraid of what I'll miss."

"I don't understand."

"I don't want to choose a road with a high-speed limit and

miss out on all the sights to be seen. Eventually, we are going to forget the quadratic formula and what the powerhouse of a cell is called. All that's going to be left are the pivotal moments in our lives and what we felt during them." I squeeze her hand. "If we increase our speed, we become numb. We lose the difference between having a life and actually living."

"You are wise beyond your years, Alma Underwood." She whistles. "I think that bald cap is speaking to you."

"Reggie gets credit for my wisdom."

"Girl, do not tell him you said that."

I chuckle, watching the sky shift. "He told me we spend most of our lives treating time like it's disposable, and then we run out, and we realize what a luxury it is."

"You ever wonder if that old fart is like the second coming of Jesus?"

My body quakes with my laugh. I roll to face her, ignoring the thick matter on my chin. Our noses are almost touching, tampons strings tangling together. "If Jesus is next door, what the hell are we doing laying in a pile of trash?"

She sighs, pulling a pop bottle from beneath her hip and chucking it. "I don't like not knowing."

"Me neither."

Actually, the unknown and lack of answers sort of make me feel like I have ants in my pants. Every once in a while, I have to dance around to shake them out before I'm okay again.

"I don't want to graduate high school with no sense of direction," I say. "But I'm okay with my turtle pace if it means I'll remember what matters."

"You're sacrificing answers for experiences."

"Sure, I suppose. I just know I'm not going to pick a road for the sake of choosing. I want to uncover all the feelings and possibilities before I commit. If it takes me a while, so be it."

"I don't think you'll have trouble finding the right one."

"No?"

"I think you'll end up saving people."

"Saving people?" A deep V forms between my brows. "Like a doctor?"

"Maybe. Not necessarily." She licks her lips. *Brave girl.* "Just saving people... or *helping* people might be a better way to put it. Like you did with Rumor."

"You think I saved Rumor?"

"I think *he* thinks you saved him. You sort of— " She smiles. "— gave him a road when he didn't have a map."

"He would've paved his own road after a while. That's just who he is."

Rumor Rawlings possesses a hidden resilience people twice our age just don't. Every day, his dark eyes open to find a world that hasn't been so great to him but he laces his shoes anyway and steps into unknown territory with one foot in front of the other.

"I believe that." She scratches at something that dried on her forehead. "But I think he's better off now that he's met you. I think a lot of people would be better if they met you, A." The corners of my eyes start to tingle. "I'm just saying if this trash pile doesn't work for you, then maybe you should look down those roads."

"Roads that lead to helping people?"

"You said you want to feel things." Her grin goes wonky. "And Rumor obviously made you feel something."

Did he ever.

Rumor stirs something inside me. The feeling is different now than when I first met him. Sometimes it's confusing. Like I can't decide if I want to talk to him or just stare silently at him and memorize every second of the moment. Sometimes I want to hold his hand and other times I'm scared to.

Our roads are aligned but he's searching for a new one, and my feelings toward that confuse me too. My butterfly kisses are fleeting. They are rare. Something peculiar I've never felt until Rumor Rawlings tried to steal my train car.

"I think I'd love to figure out a way to help people," I tell Lenox.

But it's here, in this pile of trash with a tampon up my nose, that I discover the absolute truth. As much as I refuse to live my life in increments of time, there are no roads or future careers, no experiences or feelings that will match the butterfly kisses.

My hand squeezes hers again.

"I'm better off now that I've met him too."

14

ARE YOU MY MOTHER?

RUMOR

Alma and I have been assigned to the Slytherin group. It makes zero sense. She's clearly a Hufflepuff. I typically identify as Ravenclaw, though I'd stretch and settle for saying I'm a Ravenpuff. But a *Slytherin?* No. Just no.

"I'm gonna rage." Alma's upper lip is curled into a snarl. "Who the hell chose these teams?"

My eyes find Jackson. With fingers loosely curled around a Harry Potter wand, he saunters around the room in a perfect circle, sporting an onyx cloak and hooded eyes. He's arranged Charlevoix on top of the coffee table and strapped a pair of wings to her back.

"Alma, please stop pouting." He props his foot next to the dog. "What did you want me to do? Half of this house is a Hufflepuff."

"Does half of this house own the amount of Hufflepuff merch that I do?" Her small body starts to shake. "*No!* Besides, I'm the one who called this meeting to order. Why did you get to choose the teams?"

"Because you don't have a wand and I do."

She mumbles something under her breath, eyes at half-mast and filled with utter annoyance. I can't help but laugh when she pulls her Hufflepuff pen from the back pocket of her shorts and displays it proudly behind her ear.

Jackson looks disgusted. "You may only exhibit colors from your assigned house."

"Bite me."

He pinches the bridge of his nose. "Rumor, please control your teammate."

She rises to her knees and pounds her chest. "I will not be silenced!"

I raise my hand. "Is all this really necessary?"

"Rumor." The tips of his fingers come to together in front of his face. His eyes roll and he takes a dramatic breath. "If you want to find your runaway mother, this is the only way to do it."

I blink. "Alrighty then."

"Well, you can all thank me for coming up with this idea." Alma throws her foot into the side of the couch. "You're welcome."

"Thank you." Jackson bows. "But you're still a Slytherin. The teams have been set. Once our final teammate arrives, we can begin the search."

When Alma first revealed the plan she constructed for tonight, I had some reservations. Looking around the room, I have those same reservations and maybe a few more.

Jackson has divided us into four teams of two, each team claiming a corner of the living room. He assigned us Harry Potter houses he deemed fit. That's probably why he and Holland are Hufflepuff and Alma's sitting next to me with steam coming out her ears.

Lenox and Shepherd are Ravenclaw because Shepherd's home. *Yay me.*

The Gryffindor team consists of Echo and—

"I'm here! I grabbed some of my dad's old booze and I have on my best pair of underwear."

Arthur.

He cocks his hip in the open doorway, running his palms down the front of his silk shirt. His eyes find mine almost instantly. "Nice to meet you, Rumor. Do you think I look like Lenny Kravitz?"

"The dude from the Hunger Games?" I scratch the top of my head. "Uhm, sure."

He grins. "And if you were named Spencer would you date me?"

"Oh, here we go." Echo mumbles. "Just get in here. We're team Gryffindor, and you're late."

"I brought you decade old booze to make up for it." Kicking the door shut behind him, he struts inside and falls gracefully to a cross-legged position, next to Echo.

"So, Rumor." His eyes are luminous as he unscrews the cap to what looks like a bottle of Captain Morgan. "Alma told me she's helping you study for the GED."

I nod, running my hand through my hair.

"What exactly is that code for?"

"I'm sorry?"

His eyebrows dance. "Is it like a Netflix and chill sort of thing?"

"Order!" We all jump when Jackson slams his foot against the coffee table. He picks up the dog and starts walking again. "Now that we've all arrived, it's time to go over the rules."

Lenox crawls across the carpet and jacks the bottle of booze.

Jackson ignores her. "As you can see, each team has a dozen yearbooks and a few Post-It notes in front of them.

The object is to find and tag as many women named Alice as possible."

Echo clears her throat, tightening the thick ponytail on the top of her head. "Do we know the last name?"

"That's a negative." He lifts his wand. "However, tonight is not about hitting the bullseye but rather finding the correct target. Any other questions?"

"Yeah." Shepherd grunts. "What if she's not in any of these?"

"I believe you were instructed to leave your pessimism at the door." Jackson looks less than amused. "We have accumulated enough yearbooks to span across ten years."

"That's if she is even within ten years of our parent's age."

Jackson's eye twitches. "Are you a team player?"

Lenox burps and passes the bottle to Shepherd. "Take a swig, Shep. You look like you need it."

He takes one hell of a sip.

"Damn it." Arthur throws himself in a heap on the faded carpet. "I should've brought more booze."

"Can we just get started?" Alma grabs a yearbook from our stack and flips it open. "Tonight is about Rumor."

That sentence makes me feel itchy.

"That's the Slytherin spirit!" Jackson claps his hands. "Everybody begin."

Alma snorts. "I am so not a Slytherin."

I chuckle and look down at the yearbook in front of me. My fingers fumble when I move to open it, and I'm stuck there, looking at the once glossy cover, dull due to time and improper care. I get caught up in the swirls of yellow and green, my eyes content with what's on the book rather than what's inside of it. I add a sheen of moisture to the front by running my thumb across the lettering, sweat transferring from my skin to the hardcover.

"Rumor?"

I jerk.

Alma frowns, glancing at my thumb tapping the edge of the book. "You good?"

"Gre–" I drop my head, attempting to swallow the baseball that was hit into my throat. "Great."

Her gaze feels heavy against my chest, and I wheeze just a little, trying to cover it up with a cough.

"Rumor."

"I'm fine." I sweep my head up. "This is great, right? There's probably like fifty yearbooks here." My laugh is shrill. "I mean, fifty is a lot. That's like half of one hundred."

She blinks slowly.

I look around the room for the nearest hole to crawl into.

She leans close to me, talking out of the side of her mouth. "Should I fake a heart attack?"

"That's a bit extreme, don't you think? Food poising might be a bit more believable."

"Yes, but it's not nearly as dramatic."

My lips tug.

"Just say the word." She clicks her tongue. "I got an A in theatre class."

Her eyes light up with an inner glow of mischief, and it's impossible not to grin.

"We can postpone this, Rumor," she says, placing her hand over mine. "Did I jump the gun planning this? You told me you were ready."

I did.

I took the stairs to her attic two at a time and tossed her

bedroom door open, Josh's name and my phone call confession on the tip of my tongue. *'I'm ready to find my mother'* came out instead.

And now I'm here, a rubber band fastened around my lungs and my fingers numb, unable to turn a book page.

"It may have been a hasty confession."

Alma tosses her pack of sticky notes over her shoulder. "Then we won't do it. You aren't ready."

"Yeah, but that's the thing, Ace." I bounce the yearbook off my knee. "I don't think it's smart to wait until I'm ready. I have this awful, barf in my mouth sort of feeling that I'll never be ready. I mean, this is why I'm here. I didn't run away from something. I ran towards it."

"You're the most courageous person I've ever met."

I snort. "The sweat running down my back right now would disagree with you."

"Isn't that sort of the definition of courage, though? Being scared shitless but doing it anyway?"

I cock my head.

"You're sweaty and a little green, but so what? It's a lot braver to voice our doubts than to gloss over them and make things look prettier."

Her fingertips move in slow motion over my knee. I feel a few pounds lighter just with the touch.

"You have this way of disregarding your strength because you get a little nervous. Whatever feeling it was that had you announcing you were ready, latch onto that."

"It was Josh."

"What?" She adjusts her body to face me, her hand slipping off my knee. I grab it and put it back.

"I called Josh."

Her eyebrows fly up to her hairline.

"Reggie let me use the phone in the motel. I'm really

not sure how it happened. The old goose started spouting stuff about friendships, and I got all dizzy. My shirt felt too tight, I couldn't move my tongue. Next thing ya know, I have a phone to my ear and a sense of regret so heavy, I worried about upchucking all over his desk."

She opens her mouth and slams it shut. Her eyes shrink two sizes, lips flattening.

I have no idea what to make of the look. I don't like it.

"Do you regret coming here?"

"No. Not at all. I regret not telling Josh."

"Well, how'd it go?" She starts picking at her bottom lip. "What'd you say?"

"Uhm, he was as pissed as I imagined he'd be."

He screamed at me, and I let him. I deserved all the f-bombs and the *'what were you thinkings?'*

The guilt trip he doused me in was *thick.*

When he brought up the day he called a bunch of hospitals to make sure I wasn't hurt or dead, I had to press my face in the crook of my elbow to stop the burn behind my eyes.

"Well, was he happy to hear that you're safe? Is he coming to visit?"

"About that." My grin is sheepish. "I didn't tell him where I was."

She lifts a finger, halting the conversation as if she needs time to replay my words and make sure she registered them correctly.

Her fingers curl into a fist. I brace myself.

"Are you kidding me?" She cuffs me in the head. "You called the guy you consider a brother to tell him you ran away but refused to tell him where you are?"

"Ah, yes. Basically."

"He probably wanted to crawl through the phone and kick your ass."

I laugh out loud. "I told him I was in Michigan. I just didn't get more specific than that."

"Why?"

Because he'd beg me to come back when I just found a home again.

"I just wasn't ready to explain everything yet." I look down to where we're connected. "And I think part of him knows. He was the only other person I told about my mom and Flat Rock. I'm sure he's put the pieces together by now."

"So how do you know he won't show up asking around?"

"Josh isn't pushy." I lift my head. "I also promised to call him twice a week."

Her fingers slip between mine. "I'm proud of you, Rumor. That must've felt great, hearing from him."

"It was awesome, Ace." His voice was like the raft that kept me from sinking. "After he bitched at me the first time— and then bitched at me again— we just talked. Like we used to. He told me his class schedule, and I told him about the GED. We were just shooting the shit back and forth about skateboarding and the sludge his sister keeps making him taste test for her culinary class. The whole conversation just slowed me down, ya know? Made me feel—"

"Like you could do anything?"

"Yeah. I guess after hearing he wasn't absolving me from his life, I was so compelled to find my mom, telling you about my phone call with Josh just didn't matter anymore. I was on top of the world." I run my thumb across her knuckles. "And then I woke up the next morning and it sort of felt like the world was on top of me."

She palms my face, and I lean into the touch. The tips of her fingers trail down my neck, whispering across my skin — a barely there touch I'm afraid will disappear if I breathe too hard. The touch continues up and over my shoulder, sweeping down my back. I close my eyes and imagine the butterfly kisses she's drawing with the tip of her finger.

And then she's pulling me close. Our chests meet, her cheek falling against my shoulder. I let go of her hand to fist the back of her shirt, forcing her closer. Putting my nose to her neck, I breathe.

She smells like home.

"You don't have to do this. Not tonight."

I shiver at her breath moving down my neck. "Yes, I do."

"Hey!"

We jerk apart with the yell. Peering over Alma's shoulder, I welcome Shepherd's glare.

Worth it.

"What are you guys doing?" Shepherd grinds.

Arthur makes a tsking noise. "Looks to me like they're studying for the GED."

Alma curses under her breath and then whips a pack of sticky notes at him.

"Team Slytherin is losing by a lot," Jackson announces, scanning the pile of yearbooks we haven't even opened.

My ears perk up. "This is a competition?"

"Winner gets a gift card to Doggy Style sponsored by Doggy Style."

Alma's brows dip. "You bought a gift card for this?"

"No. They donated it." He shrugs, uncapping a pen. "I told them it was for my handless friend searching for his mother."

I bark a laugh.

Alma throws her hand over her mouth as if it will tame her giggle. She holds up a yearbook. "Are you ready to win this thing?"

Translation: are you ready to find your mom?

"Ready."

I shake out my limbs and flip open a yearbook. She flashes me a million-dollar smile, and I almost keel over.

Every time she smiles at me, I can't decide if I'm dying or getting more life pushed into me.

Alma Underwood doesn't give out counterfeit smiles. There is nothing more real than the curve of her lips and the radiance in her eyes as she stares at me.

"Rumor?" She waves her hand in front of my eyes. "What are you looking at?"

"Nothing." I lie, flipping a page. "Let's find my mother."

15

IF YOU WERE A STAR

ALMA

When I was a kid I asked my parents to get me wings because there was nothing I wanted more than to fly.

Then I met Rumor, and I discovered what it's like to *soar*.

It's euphoric, really. To feel so weightless in the presence of another. Rumor draws the breath right out of my lungs and then gives it back with his laugh and the way he says my name.

"Alma."

Yes. Just like that.

I turn, resting my head in the crook of my elbow. "Hm?"

"Are we supposed to be up here?"

"On top of Mo? Absolutely not."

He smiles, and I'm floating— right next to the butterflies that appeared when he did.

"What if someone catches us?"

"We run."

He laughs with no limitations or reservations. It's full throated and choppy, the type of laugh that makes his sides crumple up and forehead pinch. It's his happy sound, and there is nothing better.

For the moment, his shoulders are free of weight and the burden of the future. His mind is vacant and at peace. I revel in seeing him this way because I know it won't last long.

His brain will catch up to the night's events, and it won't be nice to him. The heart resting inside his chest will suffer, and he'll fight the tremble of his chin.

I'm defenseless in the face of his past and the pain that still lingers there. I attempt to shield him anyway, walking side by side down the road he chose, putting my own on hold because there's nowhere else I'd choose to be.

"If you were a star, you'd be the brightest one." He tells me, hand behind his head as he gazes into a phenomena of dark and light. "You wouldn't need the other stars to light the way but you'd make them feel like you did anyway."

I look up at the stars above us, dotting the dark sky for miles. "If you were a star, you'd be the rare one everyone looks for, only appearing for something special."

"I'll always appear for you."

"What if we were both stars?"

"I'd wish for the sun to never rise again."

I don't remember climbing upward, but I fall anyway.

The rush from the descent begins in my stomach and extends to the very top of my head.

The inevitable drop that comes with falling is nowhere in sight. It's just me—drifting.

"If my mother were a star she'd be the impossible one to find. One that only emerges sometimes, and never in the same place twice."

"I think those are the types of stars that shine the brightest. So you can find them when you're ready to look."

"They all look so similar." He turns his head, eyes wild and vulnerable. "What if I choose the wrong one?"

"You try again."

His hand falls off his chest, resting palm up in the sliver of space between us. I set mine over top. This time, there are no hesitant fingers or twitching wrists. We link together and I squeeze.

"Sixteen, Ace." He blows out a breath. "Sixteen women named Alice and one might be my mother." He's completely on his side now, cheek against the blanket spread out beneath us. "What do I do now? Google them, get their address, knock on their door, and ask if they gave birth to a one-handed baby seventeen years ago?"

I inch closer.

"We are working off the assumption she is similar in age to your parents. What if she isn't any of the Alices we found?"

"What if she is?"

"That's a good thing then, right? *Gah.*" He brings our joined hands to his forehead. "I should just do it, right? I mean what's the worst that can happen?"

I push one of my legs between both of his. "You tell me, Rumor. What's the worst thing that can happen?"

His eyes become misty, and I watch him struggle to blink it back. His lip suffers beneath the assault of his front teeth. "She won't want to know me," he rasps. "That's the worst that can happen."

My heart weeps.

"Then what, Ace? I am constantly teetering between desperation and distress. I want to find her so badly, look into her eyes and see if they are the same as mine. Ask her if she loved my dad and why she ran away. I never cared about answers before but now they are all I think about. Except

I'm not sure I can step on a porch and make myself knock. Because what happens when the door opens only to be slammed shut again?"

I sweep the pad of my thumb across his lower lip, seizing some of its trembling.

"What if I stand there, in front of that door, and I break?"

"I'll put you back together."

A tremor moves through him. His forehead comes to rest against mine and he whispers a tortured, "Thank you."

There are a lot of ways to say 'you're welcome' and not one of them feels right.

"I asked my dad if it was my nub."

I pull away from him. "What?"

"The reason she didn't stay. I asked if it was because of my nub. He swears it wasn't but I'm not so sure. Having a kid is scary enough, let alone one so abnormal."

Babe.

"There's something peculiar hidden in each one of us. If we were all the same, we'd live life in black and white. There'd be no color." I bop his nose with the back of his own hand. "That would be a shame, don't you think?"

His nose twitches. "That's true. You are pretty strange."

"*So* strange." I laugh. "The only difference is that your rarity is constantly on display. Me? It takes some digging to see what makes me special."

"Not that much digging, Ace. I knew you were special the second you sat down in that Big Joe."

I think I swoon.

"You know, you're the first person who has looked at this thing and said it was cool over asking a ton of questions."

"For real?" I knock on the side of his socket with my free

hand. "I think this is badass. Especially the hook. You look like you could be in a Marvel movie, except better because you aren't in costume. You're just you."

His lips curve into a massive smile, and Lord help me, I get dizzy.

He holds it up, admiring it with a smug smile I'll miss when it disappears. "I am pretty good with this hook."

"Rumor." I school my expression. "You do everything with that. You can sign your name faster than I can."

"Am I detecting a hint of jealousy in your voice?"

I make a face. "It's not my fault the stupid socket wouldn't fit over my fist."

"Ah, come on, Ace. Don't pout." He bops my nose, mimicking what I did to him. "We all can't be Marvel heroes."

"Well, I—"

Clink!

Rumor jerks and propels himself forward with impressive momentum. Jumping to his feet, he holds himself in a squat, shoulders tense and eyes vigilant. "Ace, did you hear that?"

Clink!

He throws his arm outward, creating a barrier between me and the noise. "There's somebody out there."

I scramble to my knees.

He spins and puts his hand on my shoulder, halting any further movements. "Ace, I'm not playing."

Clink!

"Clearly." I try to shrug his hand off. "I want to see who it is."

"Yeah, nope." His fingertips dig into my shoulder. "Stay behind me."

It takes me a second to understand his urgency, but

when I do, my heart all but melts. "Rumor Rawlings, are you protecting me?"

"Trying to," he grunts, dropping his hand. "Just stay behind me, yeah?"

The butterflies rise to the surface of my skin and bat their wings like never before.

"I think it's a guy."

I inch closer to Rumor, putting my chest against his back so I can peer over his shoulder and make out the intruder. "Oh geez." I snort when I spot the familiar beard. It's braided tonight, and it's kind of cool. In a homeless, Dumbledore sort of way. "That's just Ralph."

"Who the hell is Ralph?"

"He works here." I watch Ralph move, scratching at his beard while he hobbles down the line of boxcars, tapping his fist against the steel siding every few steps.

"People actually work here?"

"Well, yeah. Not a lot of guys hang around the back of the lot with the reject train cars. I'm not exactly sure what Ralph's job title is but I think he's like the keeper of them."

He peers over his shoulder, eyebrows raised. "The keeper of the rejects?"

"Sure. Why not?"

Ralph is singing now, and Rumor is lit up with silent laughter.

"What is he doing working in the dark?"

"Like I said, I have no clue. Let's just let him do his thing."

"If he finds us, will he try to make us leave?"

"Oh, definitely."

At a leisurely pace, Rumor lies down beside me, pressing his finger to his lips. I follow suit, stretching out on our blanket bed.

"Do you do this often?" he whispers.

"Stargaze on top of Mo? Sometimes." I run the tops of my fingers over the moonlit shadows cast on his face. "It's better with you."

"I like it up here. We aren't too elevated but I feel like I can see things differently." He takes my hand again and tugs it close to his chest as if he's decided it no longer belongs to me. "We can't always grasp how big the world is when we're only looking at it from one point of view. Being up here really puts into perspective everything I would've missed out on if I hadn't found it in me to run."

Except he's not looking at the sky. He's looking at me.

He presses his nose to our hands. "This is kind of like camping."

"I'm glad you're enjoying it. We might be stuck sleeping out here. Ten to one says Arthur's asleep in my bed in his underwear and Echo stole the pizza."

"Sleeping outside with you? There are worse things." He flops to his back and drums his fingers across his chest. "Get comfy."

My limbs feel heavy, my movements sloppy as I slide my body across the blanket and lay my head over his beating heart. My hand falls lightly against his chest, and my leg is tingling when it throws itself over both of his.

His arm moves around me, holding me flush against his body. He drops his cheek to the top of my head. "You comfy, Ace?"

I hum. "Never better."

16

I DON'T EVEN GO HERE

RUMOR

"Does he even go here?"

I shove my thumb and forefinger into my eye sockets.

No. I don't even go here.

"You are popular today, my man." Arthur slings his arm over my shoulders, towing me into his side. I can see myself in the reflection of his oversized sunglasses.

I look like a crotchety jackass.

Around me the air is thin and stale, shared by hundreds of mouths talking all at once. I lurch forward when somebody jogs past me, waving a pamphlet in the air like they're about to go cash in a lotto ticket.

With each body that wedges itself through the front door of the school, the impatient faction of teens gagging to have answers inflates and presses against the sturdy walls. The foundation beneath my feet threatens to crack.

It's suffocating. The lobby is so full I feel like I have to step outside just to have space to think.

"Want to escape out the side door and go munch on some weenies at Doggy Style?"

Tempting. But no.

Lingering eyes give me an itch I can't make go away no matter how many times I scratch it. But I can't leave. Not when one pair of eyes belongs to her.

Not when she looks at me like that.

Mesmerized.

Like she's woken up from a dream only to realize it wasn't a dream at all.

Cue the tiny violins.

Arthur fans himself. "Hot damn. She's all the way across the room and I can still feel you two studying for the GED."

"Am I supposed to know what that means?"

He dips his chin, sunglasses coasting down the bridge of his nose, allowing him to gaze dubiously at me over the slim frames. "Oh, you know what it means."

I really don't.

Using his pinky finger, he pushes his glasses, letting them settle in the space between his eyes. He takes back the hand that's resting on my shoulder and starts to pick at his pink nails.

"What's with the sunglasses?" The fluorescent light strips hanging above us are bright but not *that bright.*

"If recruiters can't look you in the eye, it's less likely they will try to talk to you."

Any other day I would've found his logic amusing. Now I find nothing but a blanket of jealousy as it drapes over me.

"My outfit was also designed to repel people."

My eyes roam his all black ensemble. "I was wondering who died."

"My soul as soon as I stepped through the door."

I bite my lip to cover my smile.

Arthur is nothing if not dedicated to his mission to revolt against all things regarding his future. He isn't just wearing black. *No.* In a full suit the color of ink, accessorized with a matching scarf wrapped around his neck, he doesn't seem concerned he'll drop dead of a heatstroke. The get up is a stark contrast to the neon colors he normally slathers himself in, typically dressing like this decade's Fresh Prince.

I rapt my knuckles on the wall behind us. "So, what's your plan?"

"Stand here until I spot the guidance counselor, and then move in the opposite direction of her. I'm not above collapsing if that's what it comes to."

"Could you take me down in the process? I wouldn't say no to a mild concussion."

He holds out his fist. "I got you."

One shouldn't attribute misery with a career fair, but for a couple of dudes like us, you might as well throw our tortured bodies down a well.

The only reason I'm spending Saturday afternoon inside this stuffy, teenage trap is because Alma begged me. And trying to say no to that girl was like ripping off my own skin.

"This is like one of those nightmares that robs me of a wet dream." Arthur's lips curl in disgust. "There are forty-seven colleges being represented in this lobby today. That's basically half of the higher education in this state."

"I know." I drag my hand down my face. "That's what Ace said. She kept going on about how the trash whispers didn't work and it was time to find the right road."

"The trash *what*?"

"I have no freaking idea."

"I don't know who that girl is trying to kid." He folds his arms over his chest. "We all know she and Lenox are going to pack their bags and zip off to the University of Michigan.

Same as Shepherd did. Same as their parents did before that."

No truer words have been spoken.

Just a fraction of her body was through the door before Lenox grabbed Alma by the wrist and they practically sprinted to the gold and blue booth. They've been there ever since.

I'm happy against this wall.

"I mean, damn," Arthur spits. "I can't even leave the classroom to take a piss without needing a hall pass first, and these slave drivers want me to choose a career I'm supposed to do for the next fifty years. How about no thank you?"

I lift my palm to the sky. "Preach, man."

"I mean, do I want to live with my parents for the rest of my life? Hell no. I'd throw myself off the second-floor balcony, but give a brother some time to figure out his thing."

"I feel you." I drum my fingers against the side of my leg. "I tossed a few ideas around last year. My dad was a software developer and taught me a shit ton about computers. I'm not sure I want to go as far as he did education wise, but basic computer science didn't sound so bad. With everything he taught me I could probably do it in my sleep."

He sneers at me, his jaw a sharp, distinctive line. "Excuse me, but what are you doing over here becoming one with the reject wall? Get your ass in the heart of that monstrosity and find a college."

"No thanks." My stomach drops to my shoes with just the idea. "I don't even know if I'm sure."

He scoffs, jerking against the wall. "You sounded pretty sure to me."

I was.

I was sure up until the minute my dad dropped dead

and now I'm not sure of anything. His death was the cata-lyst to everything else in my life erupting into unrecogniz-able fragments.

Nothing makes sense anymore.

"Hey, you okay? You look ready to projectile vomit all over this place." He lifts a finger. "On second thought—"

"I'm fine." I rub at the scab inside my chest.

Arthur's everything droops. "Oh, Rumor, I'm sorry. I didn't mean to press you into talking about your dad."

"Don't worry about it. It's just, uh, not something I do with anybody but Alma."

"There's no one better to talk to."

"She carries some of the grief for me. I don't know, but around her, I don't feel so heavy."

"That girl may be small, but she is stronger than the both of us. Must have something to do with growing up in a house with four siblings. Girl would forget to feed herself making sure everyone else is fed, ya know?"

Oh, I know.

Alma was made with the perfect blend of selflessness and kindness. From just observing her, I'd learned most of her beauty is crafted from the moments she goes out of her way to make other's lives fulfilling. It took only a short time for me to realize the questions she was so eager to ask me weren't so she could have answers.

They were so I could.

Somewhere between answering and being in awe that she cared enough to ask, I didn't think to ask anything in return. I didn't have to. Everything I know about her is all by happenstance—how she got her name, her treasures, her favorite hot dog, her best friend—all facts she volunteered to make talking about myself easier.

When I discovered Alma, I discovered pieces of myself.

My heart searches for her as much as my eyes do. She hasn't moved at all, still smushed in the maze of college booths and future students, standing side by side with—

That is not Lenox...

Every muscle inside my body snaps.

Worse than if I was kicked in the chest, the breath inside my lungs is knocked out while the rest of my insides twist around themselves, from my gut and up to my chest, snaking its way to my heart. *Squeezing.*

"Who the hell is that?"

Arthur's head snaps up. A facetious grin creeps up his cheeks, reaching the edge of his sunglasses. "Oh, that's Lenny. He's harmless."

"He's touching her."

"Dude." Arthur snickers, clapping me on the shoulder. "Are you jealous?"

"Is that what this is?" My breaths become coarser, faster. "I feel like I'm on fire."

I watch with pinched eyes as *his* forearm muscles flex where they're resting on top of her shoulders.

"You're looking a little hostile, my friend."

"I kinda want to break his arm."

The belligerent remark catches even me off guard.

What is this girl doing to me?

But then his boney hand starts to rub her shoulder, up and down, up and down, up and down, and I couldn't care less about what happens to his arm.

I move one step forward. I don't make it to two before I'm yanked back by Arthur, the pulse in my wrist going wild beneath the grip he has on me.

"Man, do not go up in there and throw a hook. Lenny has been in love with her since ninth grade. She didn't give a damn then and she doesn't give a damn now. That arm around her shoulders thing is just as platonic as when I do it to you."

"I don't like it."

His laugh his quick. "Obviously."

"I'm not going to do anything stupid, man." I pop my neck and work my jaw, ridding myself of the tension there. "I'm just going to ask him to remove it."

"I can't let you do that."

"If you don't let me go right now, I'll start shouting that Arthur is in the building dressed like an intern for the secret service."

I feel the breath from his gasp on my cheek. "You wouldn't."

"Try me."

"What kind of friend would I be if I let you go over there and make a fool of yourself?"

My patience thins. "*I told you.* I'm not going to make a scene, I'm just going to intercept whatever he thinks he's doing."

"Looks like he's flirting with her."

"Yeah, that doesn't work for me."

"Fine." He drops my wrist. "Let's go."

"Wait. You're deserting your wall?"

"For this?" He claps his hands. "Hell yes. You're about to turn this career fair into a theatrical production."

I mutter a disagreement and start walking, shoulder checking my way through the crowd. Arthur is hot on my heels with giddy giggles escaping his mouth. Despite the newfound flames beneath my skin, my goal isn't to be violent. That's not the kind of guy I am, or even the kind of guy I want to be.

Especially around her.

I just want Lenny The Loser to take his paws off my girl.

The walk lasts less than a minute but it feels like I've been walking a mile before I finally reach her.

"Rumor!" The look she greets me with is as radiant as ever. She spins on her toes to face me, the action forcing his hand from her skin.

Mission accomplished.

"Look." With the trust of her pamphlet in my face, the nostalgic smell of ink and paper slithers up my nose. "I think I found something perfect for me."

"Yeah?"

"Yes. Once I pictured myself in the role it was like *bam!*"

I chuckle at her enthusiasm and pry the paper from her anxious fingers. Two words are protruding from the glossy paper. "Social working."

"Yeah. I'd spend every day relieving people of suffering and improving their lives." She bites at her bottom lip. "What do you think?"

"There's nothing more perfect for you, Ace."

She beams, and *God.* That smile.

The rumble of a throat clearing interrupts our moment. Over Alma's head, I spot Lenny looking me up and down with pinched lips.

He flicks his chin at me. "Who are you?"

A muscle in my cheek flexes.

"Oh!" Alma palms her forehead and whips around. "Lenny, this is Rumor. Rumor, this is Lenny."

"Hello, Rumor." He extends his hand. "Nice to meet you. I'm one of Alma's good friends."

And I sleep next to her bed.

"Cool." I return his handshake with a little more force than necessary.

Lenny's eyes resemble two raisins as he memorizes every inch of me from my head to my toes, stopping to linger on my prosthesis. "Do you even go here?"

"The career fair is open to the public, Lenny," Alma says, the tips of her fingers whispering across my wrist subconsciously.

"Doesn't your school have its own career fair?"

With a flick of my wrist, I capture my hand in hers. "I'm homeschooled."

He jerks his chin in an attempt to toss dirty blond bangs from his eyes. "You must not get out much. How do you know Alma?"

I run my tongue along my teeth. "I work for her parents."

"Cool." He bobs his head and shoves his hands deep in his pockets, going for a nonchalant look though I'm pretty sure he's planning my murder.

"Oh, shit." Arthur starts pulling his scarf over his face. His words are muffled when he says, "Counselor alert. Got to split. Tell Alma about the computer thingy, Rumor." There's a spring in his step as he weaves through the crowd.

Alma tugs on my hand. "What computer thingy?"

"Eh." I shrug half-heartedly. "Just something he thinks I should look into."

"Well, then let's go." She smiles politely at Lenny. "I'll see you at school on Monday."

And then we're moving. We take maybe two dozen steps, her resolve prominent before it registers she doesn't actually know what booth she's leading me toward.

"Rumor." She pivots. "Where are we going?"

"Home?"

"Oh, come on." She drops my hand to place both of hers at the top of her waist, cocking her hips. "You didn't come here with even one program or college in mind?"

"Nope. I came because my girl asked me to."

Her jaw unhinges, and then slowly closes again, her bottom lip clamped fully between her teeth. With her head now tilted, bangs sweeping her eyebrows, she flashes me a wonky smile with question and elation lingering in her eyes.

Smoothing out the sunflowers on the little yellow skirt she's wearing, she starts to stammer. "What, ah, what was that computer thingy ma bob Arthur mentioned?"

My eyebrow lifts. "Computer thingy ma bob?"

Damn. She's cute.

She rocks on her feet, toying with the ends of her T-shirt. I almost ask her if she's okay.

And then I remember.

I called her my girl, and no sentence has ever felt so effortless.

I match her smile and watch hers double in size, the space just below her eyelashes flushing. I don't have to wonder if she likes the idea of being my girl. Whatever that would mean for us.

"So, uhm, the computer thingy?"

"It's nothing, Ace."

"It doesn't sound like nothing."

I gnaw at the back of my neck, the tile floor streaked with dirt is suddenly a really interesting focal point. "It's just... something my dad taught me. Computer science. Last year, I thought maybe that's what I wanted to study. But now I don't know." I dig my toe in the ground. "Anything too far past today is hard to picture."

"Hey." The tips of her mismatched flip flops touch my

worn-out tennis shoes. She rests her head on my bicep. "You want to go home?"

No.

Yes.

No.

Yes.

"No." An ounce of hot air leaves my chest and I seize her hand. "Walk with me?"

"Of course."

17

A CRACKED COASTER

RUMOR

This place doesn't smell anything like mothballs or urine.

My experience with homes owned by senior citizens is limited and unpleasant. For a brief period, my dad and I lived next door to an eighty-five-year-old woman who liked for us to call her Tabby. Because he felt guilty her owns kids didn't visit her, Dad hauled me to a dinner she hosted once a week.

Between the faint smell of pee I wasn't sure was from her or her cat, and the burnt smell of coffee because she left the pot on all day long, I walked out of that place feeling like I needed an extra layer of deodorant.

Reggie's house is the polar opposite of Tabby's. The walls aren't stained yellow from excessive smoking, the couch is sans plastic, and the TV isn't lit up with a soap opera.

With warm beige walls dotted in clocks, a few framed photos, and dozens of paintings, Reggie's house feels lived in and cozy. Plushy carpet oozes between my toes and the fireplace below the television makes the house feel friendly, despite the cranky old dude who owns it.

Dropping to my knees in the center of the room, I take a test whiff, detecting only the smell of rain drifting through the open window and the fresh wood laid out in front of me.

I lift my chin to the sky and whisper a thank you.

"You have everything you need, kid?"

"Oh, yeah." I flip open the instruction manual and position it beside the unboxed furniture pieces settled against his carpeting. "It looks pretty straight forward. I shouldn't need anything more than an allen wrench."

With a tight grip on his cane, he lowers himself into a cushy recliner. "Thank you again for helping me out."

"No problem, Reg. I don't mind."

"I tried to buy the display that was already put together but the damn thing wouldn't fit in my car."

"That's because you drive a Cadillac from 1962 and this coffee table is almost as long as me."

Waving an airy hand, he rests his cane between his legs and tugs a worn-out paperback from inside one of the pea-green cushions.

I take that as my cue to start working.

The project is as simple as screwing four legs into the glossy wooden slab that will act as the top of the coffee table. Acutely familiar with how pigheaded Reggie is, it astounds me he didn't insist on doing this himself.

When he approached me to inquire if I had any interest in making some extra cash, the only acceptable answer was yes.

The thump of his air conditioner and rustle of book pages accompany me as I work. I'm no stranger to this type of task. Josh and I used to build shelves and different variations of tables for his mom all the time.

He claimed she had an obsession with Target.

Relatable.

Hovering over the top of the table, the veins in my forearm extract while I work to make sure the fourth and final leg is secure. I'm not about to be the reason Reggie breaks a bone because the coffee table collapses on him.

With the help of my foot, I get the table standing upright and give it a shake to ensure its sturdiness. "There ya go, Reggie. Is this spot okay?"

Studious eyes peel from the pages of his book. "Can you drag it toward me more? So it's centered with the couch?"

"Sure thing." I drag it slowly, an inch at a time until he tells me to stop.

"Looks good, kid. Thanks."

"Not a problem." Jumping to feet, I scoop up the plastic wrap and foam pieces, dumping them in the now empty cardboard box. "Anything else I can help with?"

He scratches at his silvery mustache. "You could fix my TV."

"What's wrong with it?"

"I can't find the damn remote."

My laugh comes out of my nose. Dropping to my knees, I start shoving my hand inside the couch cushions. The sagging state of them tells me this khaki colored couch is well loved. I figure it's safe to assume the same for the end tables on either side of it, sporting mismatched lamps and a mountain of coasters.

I'm shoulder deep in my journey when my hand closes around something slim and foreign. I pull it free, my brows drooping. "Uh, Reggie." I hold up my discovery, wiping dust from its small screen. "Are you missing your home phone?"

"My... what?" He leans closer to me, eyes squinting. "Oh. Well, I'll be damned. Looks like I'm gonna have to start answering when people call me."

"I could put it back," I joke.

He flashes me a gummy smile. "Do that, would ya?"

With his book now covering his face, just the top of his head is visible. The old toot has a full head of thick hair that's apparently unfamiliar with the idea of balding. The short locks are milky white, cropped just over his ears. I feel for all the young dudes putting garlic juice in their hair every night to avoid resembling a naked mole rat.

Cough, Josh, cough.

Placing the phone back under the center cushion, I drop to my stomach. Beneath the couch is a dead zone and I army crawl across the muted red carpeting, scanning the dark crevices that are below the end tables.

"Are you enjoying Flat Rock?" he asks, shutting his novel. "Have you had a chance to visit town?"

"Oh, yeah." I lift myself to my knees. "Alma has shown me just about everything over the past couple of months. We always end our day at Doggy Style though. That girl has a thing for wieners."

The wrinkles in his face pull tight. "Maybe don't mention that to Shepherd."

I press my palm to my forehead and count backward from ten. "Please excuse my word vermin."

"Is that teenage talk for putting your foot in your mouth?"

"Uh, yes."

His foot stomps in tune with the hoarse laugh scrapping against the walls of his throat. The sound completely betrays the no-nonsense attitude he typically conveys.

"Son, you just turned white as the snow on my back porch in December."

Because I don't want Shepherd to get the wrong idea and castrate me.

I make a noise and return to my mission, effectively ending that monstrosity of a conversation.

Pulling open a drawer on the end table closest to me, I shuffle through a few wrinkled Sudoku books, a handful of pens, and a pocket-sized Bible. "Are you a hoarder?"

Thwack!

"Ow!" My hand flies to the crown of my head, rubbing away the sudden jolt of pain. I gape at Reggie. "Did you just thump me with your cane?"

"I didn't like your question."

"Clearly." I wince when my fingers meet tender flesh. "Damn."

Thwack!

"Dude!"

"Don't use that language in my house, and I am not your dude."

I scoot away from the crazy old man in the recliner and his weapon, massaging my abused noggin. "Sorry," I mutter, yanking open the other drawer, finding similar items plus a membership card to Sams Club that expired four years ago.

I'm tempted to pocket the item and take it to Alma.

"Are you liking school?"

"Hm?" The drawer shuts with a click. "Yeah. I guess. I don't mind it, but it's not my favorite thing."

"Any plans for the future?"

Find my mother, stop sleeping on a pizza slice, ask Alma Underwood out on a date...

"I'm helping Alma study for her Spanish quiz this weekend."

He regards me with a straight-laced expression I'm all too familiar with. "That is not what I meant and you know it."

"Ungh." I throw my head back and flap my arms

dramatically. "I don't know. Alma dragged me to a career fair a few days ago."

"And?"

I look up. "I don't know."

Hand in hand with Alma, I walked out of the career fair, my back pocket stuffed with eight pamphlets. I haven't looked at them since.

Signing off on a decision so paramount, without my dad, is not only exhausting but agonizing in a way that tugs on all my joints. Pulling myself off my pizza bed the next morning was damn near impossible.

Some days, I just need to catch my breath.

"Well, if all else fails, you have a career putting together furniture for old men with arthritis."

I snort. "How reassuring."

He winks.

I shuffle across the carpet on my knees. "Could you lift your feet, Reg?" I poke the top of the slipper he's wearing. "I need to check under this chair."

He looks severely unhappy about it but lifts his feet with an annoyed huff anyway. I make quick work of wedging my upper body beneath the chair and feeling around blindly for the long lost remote. Wrapping my fingers around something solid, I start to wiggle my way free, hoping it's not another phone.

"Bingo." I blow off the dust. "Found the remote, Reggie."

"Good. Now get out of there so I can put my feet back down."

I scramble free and try to hand the remote to him.

He shakes his head. "Just put it on one of the tables."

Extending my arm, I place the remote among the coaster collection. My nosy eyes skim the coasters, and I'm caught off guard when I spot Reggie's face on one, attached to a much younger looking body. Curious fingers hold the ceramic disc up to the light.

Reggie has kids?

"Is this a photo of you and your kids?"

"Yep. That's them."

I squint, trying to make out the figures in the faded photo. Reggie's clearly in the middle, a broad smile on his face with an arm around both his son and daughter. He's wrinkle free. *Weird.*

"When was this taken?"

"Oh, about twenty years ago." The recliner creaks when he starts to rock. "The coasters were a gift to my wife before she left me."

"Oh." My throat threatens to close. "I'm sorry for your loss."

"What?" The blue in his eyes twinkles. "Oh, kid, she isn't dead. She's living in a swanky retirement home with her boyfriend."

I bite my cheek to cover my smile.

"We divorced about a decade ago. She was a great woman and a wonderful mother, but we weren't a perfect pair."

I wave the coaster. "Who needs a fancy retirement home when you got to keep these bad boys in the divorce?"

"Exactly." He snaps his fingers. "It was the only thing I wanted. I said, 'take the house, but by God don't take the coasters.'"

My laughter is sudden, and I can't control the way it lurches out of me. Reggie's smirking, his own chuckle rich and booming. When a snort escapes his nose, he throws his hand over his mouth in shock.

I double over.

"It wasn't that funny."

"It was," I argue. "The first time I met you, you were like a brick wall with eyes. And now you're snorting and telling me you own coasters with your kids on them."

What a trip.

"Where are they now?" Laying on my back, I lift the coaster still in my hand and run my finger along a crack on the edge. "Your kids, I mean."

"Davis lives across the bridge with his wife." The air moving around us comes to a standstill. The hair across my arms rise, and the action is a mystery until he says, "Allison passed about a few years after that picture was taken."

The bones beneath my skin feel ten tons heavier. "I'm sorry, Reggie."

I want to ask him if it ever gets better. If there will ever come a day I won't wake to a rock in my throat and its twin inside my chest.

I can't manage the words.

"Allison's biggest fight was the one she fought against herself." The traces of cheer in his dialect are long gone, replaced with something more pained not everybody would notice. "Her smile was her greatest feature. She gave it freely to everyone but herself."

She's wearing a smile in this photo, an arm around her father, her head on his shoulder. Long, chestnut waves cascade down her shoulders, sweeping the top of her waist.

I brush my thumb over the smile she's giving me. I give one back.

"There's a larger picture over on the mantel."

I scramble to my feet, taking the two hefty steps required to put me in front of the fireplace, the concrete shelf on top home to a golden-edged frame with only one face inside.

Her cheeks are tinted the same color as the rose tucked behind her ear. With a smile baring all her teeth, she has a hand over her heart playfully, staring into the camera with—

"Hey." I blink slowly, carefully. "She has eyes like mine."

"She sure does. Noticed that about you right away."

"When I was a kid, my dad used to tell me the little flakes of gold floating around my pupils made me magic."

"Allison was a magical girl."

My fingertips trail over her cheek. "I'm sorry she can't create magic anymore."

"She can. She just does it in a different way."

I turn around. "Do you really believe that?"

"I do." He sits up, the groan of the recliner obtruding on the moment and its delicacy.

"Do you still miss her?"

"Every second."

I press my eyes closed.

It never gets better.

"You know, Rumor, grief is really just stored love."

"Love?" I open my eyes and damn them for the sheen of moisture they wear. "How so?"

"Losing Allison didn't make me love her any less. When she was gone, I had nowhere for her love to go. So it found other places to gather—my throat, my chest, my eyes. At the time, it felt a lot like an ache, but now I recognize it for what it really is."

"Love."

His nod is slight. "That's what got me out of bed every day."

I look down at the coaster still clutched in my hand. It's hard to imagine her not smiling. "I'm sorry your love had to be stored up."

"One day, I will see her again. Until then, I'll have you to change the lightbulb in the bathroom upstairs."

My smile is only a little bit watery. "Is that my cue?"

"Lightbulbs are under the sink."

That's my cue.

Walking across the carpeting, I gently place the coaster back where it belongs. The staircase is just behind the couch, leading up to what looks like a hallway. "How many bedrooms do you have, Reg?"

For the first time since stepping inside, I really comprehend the idea that Reggie is living all alone in a big house with a staircase.

I don't like how toxic my insides feel.

"Three bedrooms. One for me and two are for strays."

"Strays?" I recoil. "Like cats?"

"No like people. Davis used to tell me I should take in a few roommates since I refuse to live in a suburb of old people."

"I have a hard time picturing you with a roommate."

"As long as he or she cleans up after themselves and finds my television remote from time to time, I wouldn't mind some company."

With those words, I uncover the notion that Reggie and I share the same truth. In a world full of people, we're both all alone.

18

KEEPING UP WITH THE COPELANDS

ALMA

If this social worker thing doesn't work out, I could be a ninja. Or an FBI agent. Or wear a suit and protect the president.

I'm *that* good.

A sharp chin rests on my shoulder. "Your tongue is hanging out."

"It's the face of concentration."

"Looks like the face of someone trying to slurp their boogers."

"Hush." I bat my hand in Echo's face. "I'm on a stealth mission."

The spring on the rolling chair beside me squeaks when Echo drops into it. "You're on Google."

"Google is an avid companion in this mission." Ignoring my burning retinas, I lean closer to the library's oversized computer screen.

From the corner of my eye, I spot her pull a pencil from the bun on top of her head. She starts gnawing on it. "How long have you been in here? The bell *just* rang."

Busted.

"I may have skipped music appreciation and came straight here after lunch instead." My fingers click against the keyboard, moving in rapid succession as I type in a few identifiers and press the search button with fervor.

"What are you searching? I thought we already established typing Alice's name and the town Flat Rock into Google wasn't getting us anywhere because Rumor's a chickenshit."

I pound the desk hard enough to rattle the keyboard. "Don't call him that!"

She flinches, biting down on her eraser. "I just don't understand what his hold up is. I mean, we found the address."

"We didn't find *the* address, Echo. We found nine addresses."

Sixteen yearbook Alices became nine Alices that still live in Flat Rock. Nine addresses written in Jackson's scrawl on the back of french fry printed wrapping paper. Rumor took those fries, folded them up, and tucked them in his wallet. They haven't seen the light of day since.

I don't blame him for not being keen on the idea of perching himself on the stoop of a stranger's house, clutching desperately to the dream of meeting his mother.

That sort of plan would set him up for nine disappointments. *Nine* potential letdowns that would weigh on his soul. Each time a door closed in his face, a teeny fissure would develop on his heart until a crack so big formed, the piece of his heart he saved for his mom drifted away from the rest of him.

I refuse to let his heart get away from him.

"I'm sorry." Echo pulls the pencil from her mouth, eyes cast low. "I didn't mean to be insensitive. I sort of get the gamble he'd be taking by just showing up and asking. Not to mention the idea that his mom could straight up lie and he'd never know."

"Exactly. He wants more proof."

Some protection before he leaps off a cliff.

"I just don't know what else we can do. Google only gets us so far." Slim fingers start to fiddle with her pencil. "Maybe we should hire a hacker or something to stalk all nine of them."

"I didn't realize going to prison sounded fun to you."

"Oh, hell no. It sounds horrifying. The orange jumpsuit would totally clash with my hair." She runs her tongue along her bottom lip. "We just have to find a way not to leave a paper trail."

"Hackers don't use paper, Echo. That's sort of the point. Besides, I don't know any hackers and I'm not about to post an ISO on my Facebook."

Her mouth forms a perfect oval. "Touché."

She goes back to shaving down the pencil's eraser with her teeth and watching me as I scroll through my searches. "How do we get more proof?"

Clunk!

"We don't."

I lurch in my chair, my hand leaving the mouse and flying to my chest. A pair of feet decorated with tie dye converse find a home beside my keyboard.

"Unless she runs a mommy blog and made a four-page post about giving up her one-handed kid seventeen years ago."

My gaze travels up his denim overalls and lands on his lips wrapped around a jumbo pickle. "Are you trying to give me a heart attack?"

Arthur makes a slurping noise in response.

"What are you even doing? You can't eat in the library."

"I missed lunch. Did you not notice?"

"I noticed," Echo says. "It was the most peaceful meal I've had since meeting you."

He flips her off. "I missed lunch because I was making out with Spencer in the supply closet."

I choke on my own spit.

Echo flies from her seat, the wheels and the force of her action catapulting it half way across the room. "Shut the hell up. Are you for real?"

"Hell no, girl." The pickle makes a crunching noise between his teeth. "That man still doesn't know I exist. I did spend lunch in the supply closet, though it wasn't because I was locking lips with the reason for my constant erection. I was hiding from Ms. Bailor."

I press my palms against my eyes. "Arthur..."

"What? I heard she was looking for me."

"This is getting out of hand," Echo chides, before stomping off to retrieve her chair.

"I agree, Art. Just tell Ms. Bailor you don't know what you want to do yet. I'm sure she can help you figure it out."

"Or try to glamorize the dry, mundane world of finance and politics like my parents." He shoves the rest of his pickle in his mouth, catching the juice that runs down his chin with the tip of his finger.

I interpret his gesture for what it is. The end of that conversation.

Swiveling on my chair, my butt cushioned comfortably against the cotton, I place my hand back on the mouse. "I doubt Rumor's mom has a mommy blog."

"What's a mommy blog?" Echo saddles her chair up next to mine, repositioning herself so she can peer at my screen.

"It's a blog where mommies post about meal prep, craft

time, and the horrors of non-organic Ketchup." With his pickle gone, Arthur reaches into the breast pocket of his overalls, retrieving a mini bag of pork rinds. "My aunt has one. Her last post was condemning Harry Potter. Like, excuse you bitch."

I snuff a laugh. "Well, thankfully, I've developed a new plan that doesn't include mommy blogs."

Echo snatches my mouse and scrolls to the top of my webpage, inspecting my search with a bemused wrinkle above her eyes. "Who is Simon Rawlings?"

"Rumor's dad."

"Uh, A." Arthur pops a pork rind in his mouth. "He's dead."

"Thank you, wise one." I roll my eyes and apprehend my mouse from Echo's grip. "I thought that if I searched Rumor's dad, it may lead me to his mom."

"Rumor's dad is from Chicago, A." Echo points at the screen. "Why'd you search Flat Rock?"

"Because he had to have lived in Flat Rock at one point, right? Long enough to meet Alice and—"

"Do the bow chicka wow wow?"

"—have Rumor." I push the bangs off my face. "I'm sure there were a lot of men named Simon in Flat Rock at one point. But how many were named Simon Rawlings?"

Echo clicks her tongue, seemingly impressed.

"Have you tried going through the library's database and searching his name there?"

"We aren't looking for an academic article, Art."

"Well, duh." He sits forward, his feet smacking the thin carpeting. "I meant newspaper articles. You can go to the library's database and search his name in the archives. Even the small-town newspapers that no longer exist will show up."

Laying my head against his shoulder, I wrap one arm around his middle. "You're a genius, Arthur."

"Well, they don't call me the futureless Valedictorian for nothing."

"You aren't futureless." I kiss his cheek and straighten my spine, rocking excitedly in my chair. "And also, you smell like the pork rinds you're inhaling."

"It's not the chips, girl. It's my new cologne."

"No wonder Spencer hasn't come near you," Echo drones.

With a shake of my head and a smile peeping out from the corner of my mouth, I close Google and log into the library's database. Typing in Simon's name with rushed, anxious fingers, I'm forced to hit the backspace button four times before I'm successful.

Echo's impatient groan is loud in my ear. "Finally."

With my pointer finger on the scroll of the mouse, the three of us put our heads together and lean forward simultaneously. My restless eyeballs track the results, ignoring all the articles penning news of a Rawling's Grocery Store that must have existed and died before I was born.

"There! Go back." Arthur smacks my shoulder and presses the tip of his finger against the screen so hard, the skin beneath his fingernail lightens. "Click that!"

I click the article he's referring to, skimming the headline about Flat Rock's community fair.

"Scroll down," he instructs. "I just saw Simon's name in the fine print."

"I didn't see anything." Echo leans closer.

Feeling like a marshmallow in a straw between these two, I hunch my shoulders forward and keep my eyes peeled, bypassing the long list of marathon participants and photos of the event.

"Art, are you sure you saw—oh." My hand flutters against my throat, my fingers spreading out across my collar bone as I stare, stunned. "Holy shit."

Leaning across my body, Arthur hits the keyboard and increases the photo size. "We found her!" He flails in glee, clapping his hands and littering the desk with pork rinds.

SIMON RAWLINGS (38) and Alise Copeland (29) enjoy large buckets of cotton candy as they wait in line for their turn at the dunk tank.

UNBLINKING, I read the description over and over, logging every detail of the old photo that captured the couple. With their hands linked, Simon and Alise are smiling proudly at the camera, each holding a plastic bucket of cotton candy by their sides.

My mind dances, inserting a modern day Rumor into the picture. He's standing between them, devilishly hand-some with a bucket of sugary goodness in his own hand. The smile he's giving the camera is more bashful than the toothy one his father is sporting, but the merciless curves in their cheeks are exactly the same. With hair the same shade as Simon's, and a nose as slight as Alise's, he is the perfect blend of them both.

"A, that's her," Echo says, giving my shoulder a shake of excitement.

I barely register the movement.

Rubbing my arms absently, I sit back in my seat, eyes on the photo, convinced it will disappear if I look away. If it weren't for sweat on my temples and the hair on the back of my neck standing straight up, I'd think this whole moment is the climax of a very vivid dream.

My brain sort of feels like a pan of scrambled eggs. After weeks of searching and staring up at the stars, Rumor's mother is right in front of me.

A stuttered, watery breath escapes my lips.

He gets to keep his heart.

"That's an odd way to spell Alise," Arthur mumbles. "With an S instead of a C."

"Typo, maybe?" Echo suggests.

"Could be." Arthur hums. "Alise Copeland. Is anyone in school named Copeland? Maybe Rumor has a sibling."

I almost fall out of my chair.

"One thing at a time, Art. Yeah?" Echo giggles and steadies her hand on my shoulder. "I don't know anybody with the last name Copeland."

"Me eith— wait." I hold up my hand, silently asking the world to slow down. "Reginald's last name is Copeland."

"Girl, what?" Arthur coughs. "Old man intern Reggie?"

"Yes."

Is my tongue dry? My tongue is dry.

"His last name is Copeland. I'm positive of it."

"So?" Echo's eyeballs do a dance in her head, the same dance my brain is now doing. "It's possible Reggie knows Alise?"

"I could ask him." I shake out my arms. "He mentioned a few nieces and nephews once. He isn't big on talking about himself."

"What about kids?" Arthur props his elbows on the table. "Did he mention those?"

"Yeah. He has a son named Davis and a daughter named—" My hand moves to cover my mouth, the blood beneath my skin vibrating. "Allison."

"Holy shit, it's not a typo." Echo's eye size doubles. "That's why her name is spelt with an S. It's not Alise, it's—"

"Allison." I tap the side of my head to make sure it's getting enough blood. "Allison Copeland."

Arthur chokes on a pork rind. "But if Allison is Reggie's daughter that would make—"

I hold my breath and squeeze my eyes shut, not ready to turn down the abrupt bend in Rumor's road, but unable to stop myself from candidly gasping the words anyway.

"Rumor is Reggie's grandson."

19

PLOT TWIST

ALMA

There are so many ideas in life I can't wrap my head around; fire breathing squirrels, the practicality of a coconut bra, the function of a spleen, Justin Bieber, mushroom pie, zebras...

So. Many. Things.

But even the idea of flying fish doesn't make my brain whirl the same way seeing that photo did.

Rumor is Reggie's grandson.

Like... what?!

It's the biggest plot twist since Darth Vader revealed he was Luke Skywalker's father. Except, instead of the entire country being left in dismay with thousands of questions and jaws sweeping the floor, it was just the three of us.

Echo, Arthur, and I sat there like three wind-up dolls whose voice boxes were never installed. I'm not sure if I took a breath until the bell rang and forced us out of our chairs in a haze. I don't remember the rough feel of the dial beneath my fingers as I entered in my locker combination. Slinging my backpack over my shoulder and walking to the parking lot is all a blur, and I can only just recall getting into the car with Lenox, lying to her about what was wrong with my face and the color that had left it.

I lied.

Lied to my sister for the first time in forever.

The whole way home I stayed mute, my gaze fixed on a crack in the dashboard while my mind sorted through a reel of what ifs.

What if we have it all wrong?

What if Alise isn't actually Allison?

What if there's no relation and it's just a mere coincidence?

What if I get Rumor's hopes up and totally crush him?

What ifs are my new least favorite things in life.

The print out of the article has been burning a hole in the pocket of every outfit I've worn over the last two days. Twice I almost cracked and told Rumor before envisioning myself in an ice bath, cooling my excitement for something I wasn't sure warranted it.

I refused to pump him with flawed optimism before I was absolutely sure.

"Rooms two and four aren't going to clean themselves. You've been staring off into space for long enough. Up and at 'em."

I palm my back pocket at his gravely demand, the article wrinkling in the tight denim. The last forty-eight hours passed by in a cloud of questions while I struggled to keep my mouth shut, strategically planning my words and how I would confront Reggie.

This entire situation and the possibility of who Reggie is has my brain throbbing and the area around my eyes fogging. I could've walked right into the motel after school that afternoon but I wanted to tread carefully.

"Young lady, are you listening to me?" I make out the

click of his cane against the floor. "Teenagers and their daydreaming. Back in my day, we didn't have time to daydream. If we weren't working, we got thumped."

Running my hands along the handle of my maid cart, I peer over the piles of linens, studying Reggie and the way he hobbles across the lobby, toward my position in the doorway of the laundry room. If there is a resemblance between him and Rumor, I don't see it.

Maybe it's all the wrinkles, the salty hair, or the scowl he's got creeping up his lips. When I picture Rumor seventy years from now, I don't see him with subtle cheekbones, long earlobes, and thin lips.

"You aren't going to find any treasures standing there with your thumb up your butt."

"I'm sorry... what?"

"It's a figure of speech. It means you're being pokey." Crooked fingers scratch the top of his head, fluffing the smokey locks.

And that's it.

The similarity between Reggie and Rumor.

Despite the century age difference and the age spots above his temples, Reggie's hair is still full. His gray is a stark constant to Rumor's rich brown, but the volume and slight wave are alike.

I shuffle through the dates in my brain, looking for a moment I might have seen a picture of a teenage Reginald. I'd be interested to know if the locks he exhibited back then are the same as Rumor's right now.

Unless...

"Is your hair real?"

He flounders in his trek to me. "Excuse me?"

"Your hair. Is it real or is it a toupee?"

"Is this another old man joke?" He stabs his cane at the

floor. "Young lady, this hair is all real. My grandfather was the same way. Died with a full head of hair."

"So, it's genetic then? Your son must be happy about that."

"Davis?" He bats his hand. "That boy started balding in college. They say young men take after their mama's fathers."

That bodes well for Rumor.

"Do you believe that?"

"I sure do. Eleanor's father was balder than a baby's bottom."

"Eleanor is Davis's mother?"

Rumor's grandmother.

The corners of his eyes pinch. "Why are you asking me so many questions? You have a job to do. Those clean sheets aren't going to put themselves on mattresses."

I run my hand along the seam of the pale blue sheets. Not the standard white for a motel but my parents have this thing about wanting our guests to be one with the Great Lakes. "I suppose I'm just curious."

"Well don't be," he gripes, knocking his cane off the top of my cart. "I'm not paying you to be curious."

"You aren't paying me at all." Giving the cart a small push, it slides past the doorway into the lobby. I pull the laundry room door shut behind me. Much to Reggie's displeasure, I give the wheel its usual rapid kick and position the hunk of plastic against the wall adjacent to his desk.

"This is not the front door, young lady."

I lean back against the wall beside my cart, folding my arms across my chest in a gesture that's supposed to be nonchalant. "I bet your grandsons love the whole hair thing."

"Why are you still talking about my hair?"

"I'm doing a genetics project for one of my classes," I lie.

He lifts his cane off the floor and points it at my chest. "I am not your project. Do it on your own family."

"That's totally lame."

His blank face and even features tell me he couldn't care less. Pivoting cautiously on his loafers, he turns his back on me and begins the trip back to his desk. Fingering the article in my pocket, I open my mouth and verbal diarrhea pours out, drowning my carefully rehearsed words.

"I bet Rumor will love the idea of never losing his hair."

Reggie pauses, his cane slipping from his hand in surprise. The clank it makes is indistinct against my words and their meaning.

He looks over his shoulder at me, eyes hooded, masking the disbelief I know is there. "What did you just say?"

"Rumor."

"What about him?" With a hand on his lower back, he bends at the waist, stretching for his cane.

Shoving off the wall, I race across the lobby and sweep his cane off the floor. He takes it from me tentatively, grasping the dome handle with both hands. I'm a foot away from him yet he doesn't look at me. My throat is dry as dust when I say, "he takes after you in the hair department, doesn't he?"

"Young lady, I'm not sure why you would think that."

"Because it's true." With hesitant movements, I pull the article free of its confines. Reggie's leer is heavy as he observes me from the corner of his wary eyes, tracking each motion my quivering fingers make as they unfold the article.

I smooth it out against my chest and hold it out to him.

His knuckles whiten where they are, making no moves to grasp the paper.

I lift it in front of his face.

"He takes after you," I whisper. "His mother's father?"

My accusation thickens the air and the pressure is almost too much. Reggie assesses the article briskly, and then his eyelids slam shut like old shutters. His bunched up cheeks and the wrinkles around his lips are his tell.

He still sees it.

Because that's the thing about the truth. It's most prominent in the dark.

"Alma." Running his hands along the handle of his cane, I see the sweat there. "Where did you get that?"

"I printed it off a computer at the school's library."

"Why?"

"To bring to you. For, uhm, confirmation."

"Confirmation?" His eyes finally open. "Confirmation of what?"

"Is it her?" I point at the grainy photo. "Is Allison Rumor's mother?"

Everything stops.

The intensity in his eyes, the anxious flex of his hands, the purse of his lips, the bob of his Adam's apple. *Time.*

It all ceases and hovers in the air with my question, thick enough to rob us of air as we stand there—– not speaking, not blinking, not breathing. Time moves slow enough, I see more than I ever have. Colors are brighter, sounds are sharper, and the molecules in the air are visible as they float between our noses.

Time is at a standstill and doesn't resume until he blows out a tortured, "yes."

His verification is a ray of sun between two dark clouds. My jaw loosens and my shoulders sag, the article falling to the floor while my hands occupy themselves by resting over my warming heart. "Oh my God."

Rumor has a mother.

Reggie's foot covers the article. "Does he know?"

"Rumor?" I shake my head. "Not yet."

"Does he know you're looking?"

"Yes." I bob my head, some of my happiness dimming with the look in his eyes.

I can't read it, and that frustrates me. Is he angry? Bewildered? Overcome with joy? He looks the same portraying every emotion.

"Reggie, Rumor asked us for help."

He cocks his head. "Why would he need your help internet searching his father? That makes no sense."

"Not his father." I look down, making contact with the half of Allison's face that isn't covered by Reggie's foot. "His mother. He's, uhm, he's looking for his mother."

Reggie vibrates. "What?"

"Rumor is looking for his mother." I meet his eyes. "That's why I made the search, that's why I printed the article, and that's why I'm here. Because I—"

"Because you didn't want to tell Rumor until you were positive."

I rest my fists under my chin and nod. "Did you know who he was the first time you met him?"

"I had quite an inkling. There aren't a lot of one-handed teens with a name like Rumor Rawlings and eyes like his. It wasn't until he told me he came from Chicago with a father named Simon that I was absolutely certain."

"Why wouldn't you say anything?" It makes no sense. "Don't you want to know him? He's your grandson, and he's wonderful!"

His eyes are untamed, jerky movements as he looks

around the motel, confirming what we already know. We're alone. "Alma, that isn't how Rumor knows me. He's never known me that way. I can't just explain something like that to him while he's cleaning my ceiling fans."

"And why the hell not?"

He steps closer to me, proof of the truth tearing beneath his rubber shoe. "Simon would have my head on a stake if I went spouting off things about Alise." He taps my ankle with his cane. "Don't be sticking your nose in this, young lady. It's more delicate than you realize. If Rumor has questions, tell him to ask Simon."

Oh God.

"Reggie." I pinch the bridge of my nose, heeding the burn in my eyes.

He doesn't know.

Of course he doesn't know.

"When Rumor said he moved because his dad got a new job, I wondered if it was coincidence or if he finally planned to tell that boy who his mother is. I've thought about reaching out to Simon. Actually, I'm surprised I haven't heard from him. Unless Rumor doesn't tell his dad about the old man he does chores for."

"He's dead, Reggie."

"Who?"

"Simon died months ago." My lip quivers. "He lost his only parent and came all this way to find another one. He doesn't want to be alone."

There's a tremor in his hand when he presses it against his pale face. "No."

"He said his dad told him his mother's first name and where she was from. He came here to find her, Reggie. We've been searching for the right Alise for more than a month."

A puff of air rocks his chest. "Who on earth is he living with? I didn't know Simon had family here."

"He doesn't."

Reggie's thick, silver eyebrows dip in confusion. "Family friend?"

"You could, ah, say that." Wringing my hands together, I feel dizzy.

"Alma."

I meet his steely gaze. "He lives with me," I squeak. "Rumor lives with me."

I don't consider the consequence of my words. I bask in the veracity, desperate to show Reginald that while Rumor searches for his blood family, he has a chosen one keeping him safe.

"Nice try, girl. Tell me the truth. Your parents would never take in a teenager without— *Christ.*" He rubs at his forehead. "They don't know."

"I had no choice, Reggie."

His eyes narrow in a way that says *explain.*

So I do. I pace back and forth, my overwrought movements twisting up the floor, while I babble Rumor's truth. The words spew out of me, tasting pungent. The guilt that follows is heavy and thick, the way it wraps around my body and constricts, leaving me breathless and weak.

Each moment I reveal— from Mo, the pizza bed, Josh, and his lack of family— there's a voice echoing in my mind chastising me because these aren't my moments to disclose.

"You're telling me my grandson is sleeping on a heap of plastic with only a bag full of clothes and a dead cell phone to his name?"

With a weary sigh, I rub at my arms, feeling drained and hollow. My eyes are wet yet burn like they're dry. "He thought when he found his mom he'd live with her."

"And you and the rest of your siblings thought it best to help him on this journey?"

"I promised him I'd find her. Where is she, Reggie?"

His eyes blur, finding a focal point above my head. "She's gone."

"Gone? From Michigan? Can you call her or something?" Determination to give Rumor what he came for has been burning inside me since I met him. The flames grow higher now as I stare at Reggie, resisting the urge to shake him. "We have to tell him who you are, Reggie. And you need to call Alise. He has all these questions for her about why she left and why she didn't want him."

"It wasn't like that, Alma. Allison loved Rumor." His eyes, always filled with snark and a mischievous glint, fill with water and he places a hand over his chest. "She loved him so much."

"Loved?" I ache with that word. "She doesn't love him anymore?"

With a gentleness I didn't know Reggie was capable of, he places a hand on my shoulder. "She will always love him right from where she's at."

"From where's she at? I don't—"

She's gone.

All the air in the room seems to move right through the walls and as far away from me as possible. Slapping both hands over my mouth, tears spill over my eyelids.

He gnaws at the inside of his cheek, and it takes him a while to speak. "She passed five weeks after his birth."

"B–b–but...." The tears come faster, gushing out of me while my chest takes the brunt of the news. "He came all this way."

I'm in Reggie's arms, my head on his shoulder and tears on his collar before my next breath leaves my lips.

I cry for Simon.

I cry for Allison.

And I cry for Rumor, who lost his mother before he ever had her.

"What happened?" I speak into the cotton on his chest. "Was it an accident?"

He pulls away from me, cupping my damp cheeks and ignoring his own. "No, kiddo. I don't think it was."

20

A CREASE & A KISS

RUMOR

There is a crease on her forehead.

I want to lean forward and brush my lips against it.

It made its appearance five days ago when she came home from work, sans a lost treasure. I thought maybe her disappointment was cause of the crease. But as time ticked by, the crease deepened. And with it came friends— pale lips, dull eyes, fake smiles, and forced laughs.

I hate that stupid crease.

"Are you having any luck?" I ask her, and I know it's a stupid question. She's having zero luck writing her paper because in order to be successful she'd actually have to write the damn thing.

Her pencil hasn't moved once from where it's positioned loosely in her hand. She hasn't even summoned the energy to scrawl her name in the top right corner.

"Hm?" She tilts her head slightly, offering me her ear. I don't get her eyes though. No. Those stay cemented on Mo's steel door and the patch of rust that lingers there, adjacent to her Big Joe.

"Your paper, Ace." I try again, tapping my finger on the

edge of her notebook. Any hope it would jostle her out of her stupor fizzles when she doesn't even twitch.

I'm ready to rip my hair out.

Since the moment I met her in this exact spot, Alma has lived every day with abundant vigor. So much so, it would spill out of her and transfer to me. I took it willingly, submerging myself in her smiles and laughs until I heard nothing but tiny violins. Her energy was contagious.

The thing about energy is that it's not deceptive, and the energy I'm getting from my girl right now is flat.

And now I'm worried I selfishly took too much from her.

"Alma?" Fighting against the sudden mass in my windpipe, I hijack her hand and slip my fingers through hers. "Are we cool?"

Translation: Have I overstayed my welcome?

"Wait. What?" Looking down at our hands, she gives mine a squeeze. Her muscles tremor and the reaction must bring her back to the here and now because she finally —*finally*— lifts her head. The earthy forest that's routinely in her eyes is subdued and murky, the after effects of a storm I didn't realize she'd withstood.

"Why wouldn't we be cool?" she asks, her features twisted and laced in confusion. As if it doesn't register with her that she spent the last thirty minutes giving all her attention to a rust patch no bigger than my fist.

"You seem a little withdrawn."

"Withdrawn?" She tests the word, and the curl of her lip tells me she doesn't like it. "How so?"

"Well, Ace, you've been pretty quiet the last week or so."

Her chin dips, and I come face to face with that damn

crease. When it deepens, I battle against the urge to use my lips to smooth it out.

"Have I upset you somehow? Do you, uhm, need me to leave? Give you some space?"

I hold my breath. The wait for her answer feels like an eternity when in reality, it's less than a second.

"No!" Her head snaps up, eyes wide with ardor. "Rumor, of course not."

Her free hand comes to rest on my neck, and I'm positive she can feel my overactive pulse. Soft fingers pepper the hair above my ears before she flattens her hand against the side of my head. I lean into her touch.

I breathe again.

"Have I done something to make you feel that way? I love having you here."

Did she say love?

"Alma." I find my words. "You've just sort of been out of it the last few days. Like you're here but not really. If Charlevoix were to start reciting Shakespearean quotes, I'm not sure you'd even notice."

The smile she gives me is the polite, stoic one she gives customers at the motel. Her hand falls from my face. "I suppose that wouldn't be too farfetched. I wouldn't put it past Jackson to put headphones with audiobooks over her ears."

She tries to drop her head again but I catch it lightly with the side of my hook, searching her eyes. "Are you okay?"

"I guess I just have a lot on my mind."

"Anything you want to talk about?"

Talk to me, baby.

"The future, mostly. I don't know."

"The future?" I drop my arm from her chin, using it to

wrap around her waist, tugging her forward. Her Big Joe slides across the steel ground, wrinkling the blanket I'm sitting on. "Are you having second thoughts about social working? You can change your mind, ya know?"

"I know. It's not that." The hair tickling her cheek is blown away from her skin with the pucker of her lips. It's much longer now than it was two months ago. The peak of her bangs is past her eye now, and she picks a few stray pieces from her eyelashes. "It's just the future in general." She tells me with a huff. "There are so many unknown variables. It's starting to petrify me, Rumor. I can't sleep." There's a void in her eyes. Darkness taking over. And *that* petrifies me. "I don't like not knowing everything is going to be okay."

"Baby, what wouldn't be okay?"

A beat goes by. One. Two. Three.

Her bottom lip starts to shake, and I feel like I've been shot in the chest at the sight of it.

"When I was a kid, my parents used to ask Lenox and me what we wanted to be when we grew up. Lenox always said she wanted to be a cowgirl. Me? I wanted to be happy."

"Happy?"

"Happy. It's an odd answer for a kid but it was the only one that made sense to me. A spectacular life for me would be one where I laughed every day. Where a smile was more frequent than a frown and there were lots of lost treasures to save. Beyond happiness, I wasn't sure what I wanted."

"Are you saying you don't want to be happy anymore?"

"No, I do. I just..." She bites at her lips, eyes cast downward. "I'm saying that I want other people to be happy more, and it sort of kills me I'm not in control of it."

This. Girl.

The multitude of her authenticity astounds me. She is genuine. She is kind. She is considerate.

She is everything a person should be, and how lucky am I to have been saved by her?

"You're kind of magnificent, Ace." I pull our joined hands to my chest, closer to the pounding heart. "You're going to be one hell of a social worker."

Her lips curve. It's slight. Not a full smile, but progress. "You think so?"

"Ace, I've never been more positive about anything in my life. Your consideration for others isn't artificial. It's real. You were made for this job."

"Thank you." Her words hold nothing but sincerity. When she rests her hand on my thigh, her thumb moving slowly across the denim there, my breaths become stilted. "You'll be amazing at computer science or whatever you choose to do."

"I sure hope so." I didn't believe that yesterday, but now, with her hand in mine and her eyes coming back to life, I believe.

"I'm sorry if I've been ignoring you these past few days. My brain sort of feels like that one time I forgot to take the plastic wrap off a microwavable brownie."

I raise an eyebrow.

"Gooey and slightly flaming."

My laughter is sudden and low. The sound seems to medicate her. I watch with warmth in my chest as her cheeks pink with a giggle.

"You're crazy, Ace."

"But the good kind though, right?"

Leaning forward, we're an inch apart. So close I can feel her breath on the tip of my nose. "You're the best kind of goddamn crazy there is. There's nobody like you."

"You say that like you've met everybody there is. Like you're certain."

"I am. Don't need to meet billions of people to know you're one of a kind. You, Alma Underwood, broke down my walls with your smile faster than anybody with a hammer could've. First night I met you I was showing you my nub, giving you hints about my mom and letting you slather green paint between my toes."

The pressure on my thigh increases. "I'm happy you chose green. That it's your favorite color. Nobody ever chooses it, and I like that you stand out. It's the first pair my eyes go to. It seems fitting."

"Confession? Green isn't my favorite color. Or, it didn't use to be. It is now."

Her nose wrinkles. "You didn't choose forest green because it's been your favorite color for all of eternity?"

"Nah, Ace." Slowly pulling my hand from hers, I run my thumb just below her eyelid. "I chose it because it matched your eyes. Eyes I wasn't afraid to let see me."

Her breath catches.

"I didn't understand what they were doing to me then. I do now."

"What were they doing?"

"Healing."

The silence that follows my admission isn't awkward at all but rather the most soothing moment of my life. It's a comfort I found only with myself, but I know now it's better to share it with her.

The look in her eyes is almost my undoing. It isn't just stars I see. It's the rebirth of a galaxy, lit up and glowing right in front of my eyes. *Just for me.*

The effect it has on me is sweeping. I almost can't breathe. The tiny violins are deafening, and I swear I feel pieces of my soul leave my body and find more peace with her.

I don't know what this feeling is. It's terrifying and thrilling all at once. My stomach has bottomed out and my hands are clammy, but I can't stop smiling.

And I think, maybe, I'm in love with her.

"Rumor? Can I ask you something?"

"Ace, you can ask me anything."

She smiles and *holy shit* it's a real one.

"Why do you call me Ace? Is it because my name starts with A?"

As much as the truth is going to reveal, I don't even think about lying to her.

"A few months ago, life dealt me a really shitty hand. I shuffled that damn deck for weeks. I came up empty." I palm her cheek gently, caressing the soft skin with my callused fingertips. "One day, in this very spot, I looked at my hand and right there on the very top was an ace."

Her hand falls over mine, eyes wondrous and wandering through the meaning of my words. The light in her returns, luminescent and dazzling. "I'm your ace."

"You're my ace." Stretching upward, I breathe in her scent and press my lips to her forehead. *Finally.* "I've been winning ever since."

21

CURVEBALL

ALMA

When I was in the fifth grade, I tried my hand at softball. I enjoyed it up until the last game of the season. I was standing at home base, nervous hands wrapped tightly around my bat, eyes on the pitcher.

I remember watching her chest expand when she took a labored breath, expelling her nerves. I remember the slap her glove made when it smacked her thigh and she wound up her pitch. I remember the bright yellow ball as it sailed toward me and the bob of my bat as I got ready to swing.

That's when everything went wrong.

Instead of flying across the plate, the ball curved and smacked me right in the mouth.

I screamed.

Dropping my bat, I bent at the waist, holding my hands to my mouth. Blood seeped between the cracks of my little fingers and hit the dirt below me in steady drips.

Leaping over the fence, my dad sprinted across the field, arms stretched and eyes ready to inspect the damage.

The tears on my face were monstrous, soaking the collar

of my shirt while I wailed and begged my dad to count and make sure all my teeth were still in my head.

They were. But I never played a game of softball again.

You could say I was scared. Or maybe I was just pissed that softball wasn't actually played with a *soft* ball.

Nevertheless, I've been free of curveballs since. I stopped looking for them to hit me because where would they come from?

Life.

That's where.

Standing in that lobby, poised in front of an old man, I got hit with my second curveball. And it was so much worse than the first time.

"Hey, do you want to stop for dinner?"

"Hm?" My eyes are weighted when I pull them from the windshield. Turning my head, I look at Lenox perched behind the steering wheel. The movement feels colossal. "What did you say?"

"I asked if you wanted to stop for dinner."

A yawn tears out of me. "Sure."

Lenox slows at a stop sign. Peering into her rearview mirror, she seems satisfied finding the absence of any headlights creeping up behind us. She throws the car in park. "Alright, what gives?"

"What?"

Her upper body spins, giving me as much attention as the restrictive seatbelt will allow. "You've been a zombie for almost a week. I haven't heard you talk about one lost treasure, haven't seen you with your notebook, Rumor said he finds you staring at the ceiling instead of sleeping in the middle of the night. Are you sick?"

My chest hurts this time, and if I could open myself up, I bet I'd find it bleeding the same way my mouth was.

The pain is significantly higher and even after eight days, it hasn't lightened. I know it's because it wasn't a ten-year-old girl with muscles the size of green beans behind the plate. It was life that hit me.

And there's nothing more forceful.

Reaching across the console, Lenox presses her balmy hand to my cheek. "Your skin looks like old dishwater."

"Rumor said the same thing."

"In those words? I highly doubt that. That guy is obsessed with you."

The butterflies I would typically feel with her words are drowned out by the recurring ache. "He said I looked like I was sleeping through life."

"Well, I don't disagree. You're starting to sweat. What the hell is wrong with you, A? And don't you dare say nothing."

"Curveball."

"Curveball? What is that supposed to mean?"

Headlights light up the old Toyota we're in. I look over my shoulder, spotting a truck rolling to a stop behind us. "You should drive."

"They can wait."

Beep!

"Actually, it doesn't sound like they can, Len."

"Oh for the love of—" Her seatbelt disengages with an aggressive punch of her thumb. The bottom of her shoe makes contact with the door and it flings open. "Go around!"

"Lenox." I slide down into my seat. "Oh my God."

Half her body exits the car, one hand braced on the door handle and the other on the headrest of her seat, she shouts into the afternoon air. "My sister is having a teenage crisis! She may be pregnant with a homeless man's child. Show some respect!"

I throw my hands over my face, the skin beneath my fingers heating. A noncommittal laugh escapes my lips.

Tires squeal and the truck weaves, leaving Lenox satisfied as she slams the door shut and pushes the lock down with her finger. "So, do we have ourselves a Lenox Jr. on the way or what?"

I find her in my peripheral vision. "Lenox Jr? What if it's a boy?"

"Lenox is a unisex name."

I snicker, a rare smile creeping up my face. "I'm not pregnant."

"Duh." Her seatbelt is refastened with a click. "Can you imagine what Shepherd would do to Rumor?"

A shiver runs through me.

"Dad would totally get over it and try to build that kid a crib from scratch. But Shep?"

"Oh, he'd kill him," I say, propping my foot on the dash. "And why was teenage pregnancy the first thing that came to mind? Rumor isn't even my boyfriend."

The skepticism on her face is vivid. "Are you sure about that?"

No.

Checking her mirrors, she starts driving again. "My twintuition is giving me major lovey-dovey vibes. You like him, don't you?"

I'd give up all my treasures just to keep one. Him.

"He kissed me."

"Hold up!" The car groans when she hits the breaks suddenly. The force of the jerk has my forehead making contact with my kneecap.

"Shit! Lenox, what the crap? I think you just gave me a concussion."

"Screw the concussion. Did you just say he kissed you? Was tongue involved? Did he get handsy? Did you do the Princess Diaries leg pop?"

"It was on the forehead."

"The forehead?"

It doesn't sound like much, but *wow* it was everything. The second his tender lips floated across my skin tentatively, I stopped thinking about how I was supposed to break his heart and let him capture mine instead. If I would've been standing, my leg would've been popping, right before my knees gave out at his words that followed.

I've been winning ever since.

"You're telling me Rumor kissed you, basically claiming you as his girl, and you're still walking around like you did when George was killed off Grey's Anatomy?"

The car starts rolling again and I drop my knee, keeping both feet planted firmly on the floor for what I have to tell her next. "I found Rumor's mom."

"That's it. I'm pulling over." Foregoing her blinker, she yanks the steering wheel and whips into a Dollar General parking lot. Her haphazard job of parking between the lines doesn't faze her in the least as she flips off the ignition and turns completely in her seat. "Say that again?"

"Her full name is Allison Copeland." I press my tongue to my cheek, looking up at the cloth ceiling, shadows cast on my face from the sunlight streaming through the window. "And she's Reggie's daughter."

All hell breaks loose. A slew of curse words and questions leave her lips, and I answer what I can, explaining that moment in the library and confessing my confrontation with Reggie.

"So what is going to happen? Is Reggie going to call her? Did you get her address? *Oh my God!* Did you meet her? Is she pretty? What did Rumor say?" She backhands my chest. "Why did you wait eight days to tell me?"

My face scrunches, my only defense against the burn that hasn't truly gone away since I found out the truth. It vanishes for a moment, long enough to keep me functional for a conversation, but then returns with a vengeance at the mere thought of Allison's son. "Google her name."

She teeters on her seat, fighting with the vinyl still across her body. She frees herself. "Huh?"

"Type her name into Google." I wrap my hand around my scratchy throat. "Type her name next to Flat Rock. Tell me what comes up."

Clearly perplexed, she fumbles to pull her phone from her purse in the console. The tap tap of her fingers against the digital keyboard haunt me, and I hold my breath while the search engine loads.

I know the moment she understands. The air in the car becomes too hot to handle, and I open my mouth, unable to catch my breath. What she's looking at is tattooed in my memory. I can't seem to unsee the words. Every time I close my eyes, they are right behind my eyelids.

ALLISON (ALISE) COPELAND (30) *is survived by her mother, father, and older brother...*

HER JAW HITS HER LAP. "This an obituary."

"Yes."

"No." Holding her phone closer to her face, her pointer fingers sails across the screen, scrolling through the paragraph like she's hoping the word '*Gotcha!*' will start flashing across the screen. "But——"

The effervescent light that was in her eyes when she woke up this morning dims considerably. She places a hand on her chest, and I know just what she's feeling.

Curveball.

"That's just——" Her lips can't form the words.

"Devastating," I say. "It's devastating, Len."

Her eyes are captivated with the words in front of them. They reveal so little, yet so much at the same time. "This says it was an accident. What kind of an accident?"

"She drowned in the lake at Huroc Park."

As I repeat Reggie's words, and Allison's fate, I'm struck with disbelief that manifests as a numbness. I feel nothing and everything at the same time. Things have just stopped making sense.

"A park ranger found her a few weeks after Rumor was born."

The color drains from Lenox's body, leaving her gray and dreary looking. "That's tragic. I don't... I can't comprehend how that happens."

"She was drunk." Reggie's admission about his daughter exits my throat. I'm a robot, reciting the truth, devoid of emotion—basking in the insensibility I never wanted to feel but am grateful for in this moment. "She was drinking and alone and Reggie doesn't believe it was an accident."

"He thinks someone did this to her?" The wetness in her eyes is enough to lure me back into all she's feeling. I struggle against the curveball and weaken with the blow to my chest.

"No, Len." I catch her gaze. "He thinks she did it to herself."

Silence.

The occasional beep of a horn, faint conversation of those walking past us, the clank of shoppers returning their carts— it all fades away as Lenox takes in my words and their underlying meaning.

My tears fall now, trailing slowly down my cheeks, splashing the cotton dress covering my thighs. And like everything else lately, they make little sense.

Allison was not my daughter.

She wasn't my mother.

I'd never even met her.

But the idea of her was meaningful to me. I basked in the hope she represented for the person I've come to care most about. She was Rumor's comfort when he needed it most, his luminescence in the shadow of his grief. It was her, and the thought of seeing her again, that taught him how to smile again after losing his father.

"I wanted to give him this treasure so bad, Len." I catch a tear on the tip of my finger. "I don't think I'm capable of taking it away. Every time I try to say something, the words get stuck in my throat."

I tried for four days straight. I'd call his name, he'd look at me, tears would claw their way to the surface and I'd fall mute. When he asked what was wrong, I'd lie. Because how do I take away something he never even had in the first place?

"Rumor knows something is up," I say. "It's starting to scare me how easy lying is becoming."

"Of course he knows something is wrong, A. You have a severe degree of compassion for other people. So much so that it can't be hidden. You're upset because you know what this news is going to do to him but—"

"Exactly!" I sniff. "How do I tell him something I know will completely destroy him? There is no instruction manual for breaking someone's heart. No damn guidebook that lays out the perfect way to tell your best friend that his mother submerged herself in a lake with no intention of ever coming back up!"

I can't breathe.

I scramble for my seatbelt, tugging at the belt desperately and taking oxygen in big gulps. Lenox's fingers replace mine and the belt comes loose, freeing my chest of the weight.

The rumble of the engine can barely be heard over the ringing in my ears. The blast of the air conditioner cools the tears on my face, and I lean toward it. "I can't keep this secret and I can't tell him."

Her hand hits my lower back, rubbing the way our mom used to when we were kids. "This is an impossible situation."

I angle my face, seeking her. Unshed tears are balancing cautiously on her eyelashes. "I don't want to tell him, Len."

She nibbles on her quivering lips. "I'm trying to comprehend the best way to do this and I'm coming up short."

"Because there is no good way to do this."

"But that doesn't mean you keep this from him. He is bound to figure it out eventually. What if he googles his dad the same way you, Arthur, and Echo did? What happens when he finds out you already knew? He's going to think you—"

"Betrayed him."

"Exactly." The pressure on my back increases. "What about Reggie? Is he going to say anything?"

"I begged him not to say anything yet. He told me he'd be there when I was ready to tell Rumor."

I am not ready.

"Did Reggie say anything else about Allison and—"

"The way she might have died? No. Mom came into the lobby to talk to Reggie about a schedule change, and I escaped to Room Two and cried into a towel."

"Have you talked to him since then?"

"Reggie? No. I can't bring myself to ask any more questions. Rumor is the one who deserves these answers, not me. The more I know, the harder it will be for him.

"But you can't tell him?"

"Not yet."

"You have to."

I sigh. "I know."

We fall silent. I sit there, an ache in my head that could be due to it ricocheting off my kneecap, or it could be just my brain on overload, begging for a break.

I'm speechless for so long, Lenox puts the car in reverse and pulls from the parking lot. When she turns left, heading in the direction of our house, I know she's abandoning the Target run we were supposed to go on.

The brakes squeal when she comes to a stop in our driveway and pulls the key from the ignition.

"You can come hang in my room for a while."

I know what she's offering. It isn't necessary but I appreciate it nonetheless. "Rumor's at the motel painting trim."

Stumbling from the car, I walk through the house, succumbing to dread and worry. Lenox's footsteps are behind me, her words patronizing me with each step I climb.

You have to tell him.

I make it to my bedroom, Lenox by my side, unwilling to leave me by myself. Pushing open my door, my heart sinks. My mom is sitting on the edge of my bed, staring down at the pool float like she isn't quite sure what to make of it. Clutched in my dad's fist is Rumor's duffle bag.

"Oh shit." Lenox's outburst announces our presence

I slam my eyes shut, count to ten, and reopen them. My parents are still here.

I brace myself for the blow.

"Alma." My mom rises from my bed, her expression unreadable. "We need to talk."

The curveball hits.

22

CRISIS OF LOVE

RUMOR

Staring down at the sticky note positioned beneath my pen, I recoil at the strokes I left behind.

A heart.

I doodled a damn heart complete with the letter A inside.

I've got it *so* bad.

With the old phone wedged between my ear and my shoulder, I pull the sticky note off the pad in front of me and wad it up. As quickly as I crumple it, I smooth it back out nicely. Not a cell in my body can handle squashing Alma, or a mere representation of her.

Christ.

"Hey, brother."

"Dude. What the hell?" I drop the pen. It rolls across Reggie's desk and falls over the edge with a faint *clink.* "That was like nine rings. What took you so long to pick up?"

"I was taking a piss. Damn. Let a man put his dick back in his pants."

"I couldn't care less about your dick right now, Josh. I have a crisis."

"A crisis?" The sound of a sink running greets me through the speaker. "Rumor, the last time you called and told me you had a crisis, I got so worked up thinking you were back living in Dumpster Alley and what did you tell me?"

"That was a crisis, man. Jackson made me a *Slytherin.*"

"Jackson's inability to correctly assign a Hogwarts House is not a catastrophe, and I'm willing to bet whatever you're calling about right now isn't either."

I pinch my drawing between my thumb and my forefinger, lifting it so it's the only object in my line of vision. Staring at my light sketch, my first thought is that I should put it in my wallet and keep it forever, maybe display it at our wedding or something.

And yeeeaaahh. Crisis.

Slipping the doodle into my back pocket, my eyes find Reggie in my peripheral. At first glance, he appears like any other old man sitting on a couch in the motel's lobby, reading today's paper. But I've memorized his mannerisms and the subtle tilt of his head by now.

The old bastard is trying to eavesdrop.

"Does this crisis have to do with Alma and those... what did you call them? Tiny—"

"Violins."

I professed the rest of my truth to Josh weeks ago. The first time I spoke of Alma, he knew. He knew she wasn't just some girl offering me a place to stay as a way to clear her conscious or gain good karma.

He knew.

"Ah, yes. Tiny violins." His soft chuckle is a familiar, nostalgic sound. An image of him lingers on the edges of my mind. I can almost make out his exact features—the shaggy blonde hair he never combs, the crooked slope of his nose from that time I kicked him in the face with a soccer ball, and the crinkle around his dark eyes that typically goes hand in hand with a laugh so boisterous, he possesses the ability to shoot chocolate milk from his nostrils across his kitchen.

A wave of longing has me feeling unbalanced but the sensation isn't painful like it used to be. It's simply a drumming in my chest—a reminder that he isn't gone the same way my father is.

"Let me guess, you kissed her, sucked at it, and you're calling me for advice."

"Piss off."

He cackles, and the picture of him is vivid now. I can see him right in front of me, his hair flopping on the sides of his head when he directs his laugh to the ceiling. "I'm kidding. What happened?"

"I did kiss her but that's not wh—"

"Back the hell up. You kissed her?"

"Yeah, I kissed her on the forehead but that—"

"*The forehead?* Dude, that's how I kiss my gran. No wonder she has no idea you're head over ass for her."

"It was not a granny kiss, J. It was a million times more intimate than that, okay?"

"Did you just say intimate?"

Oh for the love of... "Are you going to shut up and let me talk?"

"Right. Sorry. Lips are sealed."

I doubt that. "Anyway, like I was saying, I kissed her forehead. Yes. But it was after I called her baby and basically admitted that I equate her as the illumination that scared away the shadows surrounding my life. And now I'm thinking about us in nursing homes, planning our wedding, and doodling hearts with her initial in them."

"Ah." Now he gets it. "Crisis, I see."

"Told you it was a real one."

"Rum, are you... in love with her?"

I close my eyes, and like always, she's right there waiting for me. Her hand is outstretched, fingers wiggling and urging me to grab hold. I do, and I pull her to me, tilting her chin. She reveals her smile.

It totally wrecks me.

"Yeah," I say into the phone, body going lax against the desk. "I'm totally gone for her."

"Tell me about her."

"What do you mean? I've told you all about her."

"Uhm, not really. You told me about her treasure obsession, the pizza slice bed, and her habit of eating hot dogs named after sex positions. You haven't told me how she makes you feel."

"Do you care about those details?"

"Rumor, come on." He clicks his tongue, and I know he's scratching the top of his head. "My brother is telling me he's in love with some girl I've never met. I mean, sure, she sounds great but I need some confirmation this isn't a heavy dose of infatuation or an odd case of Stockholm syndrome."

Stockholm syndrome?!

"What the hell, Josh?" Dropping to my elbows, the wood clunks beneath my movement. I catch the phone with my hook and hold it so it doesn't slide away. "Are you serious right now? Alma didn't actually kidnap me. She isn't holding me captive. I can leave as soon as I find my mom. Hell. I could leave right now."

"Okay, so maybe not Stockholm syndrome. But what about some sort of hero worship?"

"Hero worship?"

"Yeah, like, have you considered the only reason you think you love her is because she saved you?"

I frown.

"I'm just wondering if after you find your mom and get your feet back on the ground, will you still love her?"

Flipping my palm over, I spot the butterfly she drew there this morning, lines representing their kisses wrapped loosely around my fingers and wound around my wrist. "With everything I've got."

"That's a hefty admission."

"I didn't fall in love with her based on what she did, J. I fell in love with her because of who she is." Now that I'm able to recognize this weightless, breathless, all-consuming feeling for what it is, I'll say it over and over again. "Alma is remarkable, man. She excites me, inspires me, makes me want to improve in whatever way I can so I can be at least one percent of what she is. Everything I'm afraid of is minuscule in the face of the strength she shares with me. I'm just sort of awestruck when I look at her."

My best friend is mute. The quietness and lack of snark have me chewing on my tongue nervously and winding my whole hand in the phone cord.

"In this unstructured world of cruelty and unfairness, nothing ever makes sense. After dad died on me, I was convinced nothing would ever make sense again. But Alma? Alma makes sense, Josh. She. Makes. Sense."

"Wow." He lets out a low whistle, and that's how I know he gets it. "I'm happy for you, Rumor. Truly. I don't like that you're stuck in limbo with a list of sixteen women named Alice you don't know what to do with, but if you're happy, so am I."

I'm happy.

At times, I'm also unsure, pessimistic, irritated, resentful, overwhelmed, wary, withdrawn, and achy. But when all that passes, the guilt subsides and the tears dry up, I'm not left feeling bitter.

I'm content.

I let the phone cord drop to my side before I lose feeling in my only hand. "Jackson actually narrowed it down to nine Alices that still live in Flat Rock."

"How do you know your mother didn't move?"

"I don't. But it's a good starting point. Sixteen is less intimidating than nine. Alma's still trying to narrow it down from there. The idea of approaching one of them and laying all my cards out on the table has me in hives."

"I don't blame you."

A rush of water has my ears perking up. "Are you still in the bathroom? It sounded like you just turned on the shower."

"I did. My mom is walking up the stairs, and I'm trying to drone out our conversation so she doesn't knock on the door and ask me who I'm talking to. I wouldn't have to, but you're a shitface and won't let me tell her you're alive."

The guilt starts to nibble at me, inch by inch, taking over my body until I feel it snaking up my spine.

"Josh, come on. You know if you told them, they'd make me come back."

"Not if you told them that group home was the seventh layer of hell."

"Dude." A beat goes by. Then another. And one more before I slump over the desk, pressing my forehead to the wood, muffling my next words with the desk calendar. "You know as well as I do they wouldn't approve of my living arrangements. And what happens when the state shows up looking for me?"

"They did that once in all the months you've been gone, and honestly? They didn't even look around. We could've been hiding you in the next room and they wouldn't have given a shit. The dude in the suit was just collecting his payment."

"That's actually super depressing for the teens who are actually missing."

"The system is screwed, man."

"Yeah, and now you know why I'm laying low with a plastic bed and two pair of pants for a few more months."

"You need money?"

"No, I don't need money. I told you I've been working at the motel and doing some odd jobs for Reggie."

"Right. The intern who bosses everyone around. How's that going?"

"Not bad, actually."

Reggie's company has become a source of escapism. The stories he's willing to share about his life are endless. I've gotten lost in the tales of his past—his childhood, his work as a nurse, the first time he drove a car, the day he asked his wife to marry him and forgot the ring. His opinions and views are sort of their own treasure, but they come with their own story, and they're something I can keep with me without needing a big plastic bin.

I don't have to talk about myself, but I usually do. He's the only other person besides Alma I'm comfortable opening up to. There's a vibe Reggie has that's familiar to me. One lone wolf to another, maybe.

"The first time he paid me, he slapped some cash in my hand and demanded I get a haircut and a pair of shorts so I didn't die of heatstroke."

He barks a laugh. "Did you listen?"

"Hell yeah. It was hot as hell. I bought two pairs of shorts and an ice cream cone."

"And the haircut?"

"It was, ah—" I smirk to myself. "A hair *trim*. It just brushes my shoulders."

"Isn't that how you always have it?"

"Yup. Reggie wasn't impressed until I showed him how I tie it back in a knot with only one hand."

"That's how you should make some money." I can practically see the mischievous look in his eyes. "Charge people to witness your one-handed wonders."

"Pimp me out? That's your solution?"

"Well excuse me for trying to get you some fast cash. Maybe if you did that you could afford two ice cream cones and ask Alma to go steady."

"Piss off." My tone doesn't match my harsh words. There's laughter behind the insult as I push up to my elbows. The desk creaks under my weight. "I will ask Alma on a proper date. She deserves that."

Alma deserves everything under the sun. If it were possible, I'd spend forever traveling the world and collecting it all for her.

"But for real, my next shopping endeavor is going to be a coat. Apparently, it's supposed to be fifty degrees next week. I swear, man, Michigan's weather doesn't know how to act."

"Hey, why don't you give me the address to the motel? I can send you some of the stuff you stored here before they shipped you off to the hellhole. Mom won't notice."

Drumming my fingers against the desk, I find his idea doesn't totally suck. It sure as shit would save me some money. "Let me ask Alma for her house address. Her parents are at the motel more than the house."

He makes a tsking noise. "You don't even know the address of the place you're sleeping."

"Oh, bite me. It's not like I—Ace?"

I come off the desk with the sight of my girl. Cocking my head, I watch her pull open the glass door, the movement seeming to take a lot out of her. Small feet covered in shoes with cat ears are unhurried as they make their way across the room. The dress she's wearing is vibrant—fire engine red with matching socks that go up to her knees. The lively outfit is bursting with a charisma she normally wears like a second skin.

Today is different.

"Ace, you okay?"

She doesn't answer me, and it doesn't matter. The slight hunch of her shoulders, the refusal to meet my eyes, and constant wringing of her hands are enough to tell me something is wrong.

I move to walk around the desk, halted by the damn phone cord. I fight with it, untangling my arm. Alma raises her chin at the sound of my struggle. Our eyes meet, and I want to hit something.

Tears.

There are tears swimming just below her forest green irises.

"Baby, are you—"

My tongue dries up, and I lose all communication skills when I catch sight of the two figures stepping up beside my girl.

Harrison and Clare are staring at me, not with anger, but with an expression that says I'm not who they thought I was.

"Rumor, dear?" Clare steps forward, approaching me as if I'm a wild animal.

I don't understand until I see it. My bag hangs loosely from Harrison's fist. My knees buckle and I reach out to steady myself. The desk rocks with my movement.

"Dude, are you still there? I'm assuming you drowned me out because Alma showed up. I am definitely not your baby."

"Josh, I gotta go."

The line goes dead, and I'm afraid a piece of me dies with it.

23

JUST A NAME

RUMOR

This is not happening.

I'm sinking. From the inside out, I'm sinking. My organs are submerged, drowning alongside my heart. My lungs sputter, unable to pump under the weight of all the water.

It fills me, rising up my throat, seizing any chance I may have had at talking or gasping for air.

I look at Alma beside me, focusing on the rise and fall of her chest. I try to mimic it.

Up, down.

Up, down.

Up, down.

It's no use. With every pull of air, I choke, my throat burning as though it's been ripped open and exposed.

"Rumor?"

Both of her hands enclose around mine. My fingers twitch beneath her touch but it's all the movement I can manage.

"Rumor?"

Her eyes are wide now, and her hands drop mine to

palm my face. She turns my head from side to side. I'm not sure what she's looking for.

"Rumor, are you okay?"

With a shake of my head, I wrap my hand around my throat.

"I'm sinking." My eyes say.

"Swim." Hers scream back.

So I do.

With my eyes locked on hers, I swim just enough to breach the surface and allow my lungs some relief. I cough, my nostrils sizzling and chest like lava. Despite my ability to breathe, I'm not home free. With half of me still sinking, I'm trapped. Stuck in limbo. Breathing but still fighting.

"I don't want to go back," I say when I've found my words.

Her face is granite. "Over my dead body."

"Rumor? Honey?" I don't want to look at Clare and Harrison but I do it anyway.

Sitting on the couch opposite of Alma and me, they hold hands, regarding us with cagey expressions.

Reggie's off to the side, leaning against the nearest wall, tapping his cane in time with my breaths.

"Rumor." Clare moves forward so she's perched on the edge of the couch. With her hair held together by a pencil on the top of her head and the avocado people holding hands on her T-shirt, I shouldn't be afraid of her.

I am.

"Alma told us you've been living in her room. Is that correct?"

I clear my throat. "Yes, ma'am."

Harrison makes a noise. "I'm going to assume everything Alma told us was accurate."

One look at my girl's face is all the confirmation I need.

"Yes, sir." My knees bob as I look him in the eye. "I'm sorry for being so deceitful. My intention wasn't to work here under false pretenses or disrespect you by living under your roof without your knowledge. I just, uhm, I didn't know what else to do."

"Ah, son." Harrison rubs at the back of his neck. "I'm so sorry about your father."

My throat constricts. "Me too."

"Alma said you don't have any family back home but I need to hear it from you."

"I don't. I have a best friend. Josh. His family tried to get custody of me but there were a lot of hoops to jump through. I ended up in a group home. It was, uhm, a—"

"A shithole." Alma jumps to her feet. "It was a real shithole, Dad. He wasn't safe there. He wasn't safe anywhere until he got here. Okay? I know the set up wasn't much but he felt safe, and if you try to make him leave, I will riot."

She shocks the shit out of me by plopping right down in my lap and wrapping her arms around my neck.

"Call this a symbolic protest," she announces. "Like when people chain themselves to trees to protect them from being cut down. Rumor is my tree. You cut him down, you cut me down."

Harrison slaps a hand over his face.

Me? I wrap my arms around my girl's waist, burying my face in her neck. I press a kiss to the skin below my lips.

My love for her at this moment intensifies.

Just like she's been doing since day one, she stands up beside me, connecting her shiny shield to my dented one. Alone, I fight and I survive. With her, I conquer and I live.

"Rumor is my tree!" Alma shouts, and I hear Reggie's muffled laughter.

Harrison presses two fingers to his temples and looks to Clare. "She is so your daughter."

Clare smiles as though she's pleased. "Alma, sweetheart, we are not going to cut down Rumor. We want to help him."

"You are helping him," Alma says. "He has a job and a home."

"Honey, he is sleeping on a pool toy."

"In your room," Harrison adds. "Those living arrangements aren't acceptable. Not to mention, it is probably illegal for him to be here. He is a minor."

"It's not illegal." Alma crosses her arms over her chest.

"Actually, it might be, Ace."

Her jaw falls limp.

"Technically, if I were found, I'd be shipped back to the group home until I turn eighteen. But the thing, Mr. Underwood, is that almost two million teenagers run away from homes every year. Some are found by the police and are returned and some aren't. The ones that are returned usually run away again." I tuck my hair behind my ear, straightening my spine. "I felt safer sleeping in a laundromat and a train car than I did in that home. I'm laying low because I don't want to give them a reason to come after me. But the fact is, I'm just a name. I'm a name on a sheet alongside thousands of other teens who ran from a shitty situation before it became even worse."

My heart wilts thinking of the kids who are still running, searching for their ace card and a chance to catch their breath.

Alma's face is painted in shock. "I didn't realize there were so many."

"Neither did I." I capture her hand. "Not until I did some research."

"You are not just a name." She looks in the direction of her parents. "He isn't just a name."

"We agree," Clare says, and I try to keep the shock off my face.

What I can't stop myself from feeling is hope. My hope. Alma's hope. The intensity of our combined hope.

Don't make me go back.

"Rumor is not just a name, and I wouldn't dare send him back to a place he feels unsafe in. But your father is right. His living arrangements need to change."

"The living arrangements are fine."

Clare isn't buying it. "Alma, honey, he doesn't even have a bed. He needs more than that."

"I don't," I blurt. "Really. The pool toy is great, and it's only for a couple more months."

Thinking about leaving sheaths me in a blanket of desolation that wasn't in existence months ago.

"Alma mentioned you came here in hopes of finding your mother."

I simply nod at Harrison's remark, unsure if it was a question or a comment.

"I don't mean to be pessimistic, but what if you don't find her. Then what?"

"I'll be okay, sir. I have a plan for when I turn eighteen."

Bracing his elbows on his knees, I have his full attention. "Care to share this plan?"

"Alma's been helping me study for the GED. I'll pass that and apply for college. I should qualify for aid but if I don't, I'll receive social security money from my father's passing in about two months. I planned to buy a car and find a place to live with it but I could do without the car and put it toward college. I'm also not opposed to taking out loans."

Harrison looks like I just kicked his puppy. I'm not sure why. It's a good plan.

"I'm sorry, son. I'm sorry you have to deal with this when you should be out, enjoying your last year of high school and making memories."

I shrug. I haven't allowed myself to mull over all the extra things that disappeared from my life when my dad did. Why inflict that sort of pain on myself?

"Your job is yours for as long as you'd like it. When you turn eighteen, we will reassess. Do you have your documents?"

"You mean my social security card and all that mumbo jumbo? Yeah."

Clare rests her hand on Harrison's shoulder, rubbing. "We will do our best to help you out, Rumor. Your GED, applying for college, buying a car, finding your mom. Whatever you need."

"I—" can't speak. I'm capable only of steady eye contact I'm desperately hoping conveys the appreciation I feel. Even sitting down, the weakness in my knees is apparent. I drink in this moment at a leisurely pace, wishing to never forget its impact and vowing to pay back their kindness one way or another.

For all the days I have left, I'll take a second out of each of them just to say thank you.

"My children tell me you've been part of this family for some time now. Apparently, my husband and I were the only ones not in the loop. I'm so sorry about your father and all you had to endure before you came here. We're happy to help you get back on your feet. As for where you'll be living—"

Alma cuts her off with a wild groan. "Where is he supposed to go, Mom?"

"With me."

Reggie's been so soundless, standing motionless and becoming one with the wall, I forgot he was even present. His proposal leaves me flabbergasted.

I lick my lips absentmindedly, blinking ever so slowly. "Wait, what?"

He pushes off the wall, giving his weight to his cane. "Pack your stuff, kid. I'm taking in a stray."

24

STAY

ALMA

Stay.

I trace the word on his arm with the tip of my finger. Right below his elbow, I drag my skin across his, silently pleading.

Stay.

"Ace." His eyes are closed and he's lying on his back. He speaks from the corner of his smile. "I'm not going anywhere."

I stop.

He chuckles and rolls to his side, wrapping his free arm around my back. Before I can blink, I'm pulled across the mattress, his chest against mine, his lips on my forehead.

He does that a lot now. Kisses my forehead. The butterfly kisses are extra intense whenever he does, and I wonder what they'd do if he were to give me a real kiss. I want to find out, but also I don't because I'm not sure I'd deserve it.

"I miss you too, Ace. You know that, yeah?"

"Yeah." He tells me every day. "But this is a better place for you."

"I disagree."

"How could you possibly disagree? Look around."

The bedroom Reggie gave him is painted a light blue color. There's a window that opens to a balcony, and I know he stands out there at night, looking at the stars and wondering which is his mom.

The mirror on the back of the closet door and the drawers lined with floral paper are the only indicators this room used to belong to his mother. He thinks Reggie offered it to him because it was the largest of the three.

I know better.

Pushing my face into his chest, I rub my cheek against the cotton covering it. He hums and pulls me closer. With our movement, the mattress rocks. The bed we're laying on isn't just a slice but big enough to be the whole pizza. He has dresser drawers to put his things in and a bathroom across the hall he can use without tip toeing.

He's free here. Free to live and wander and wonder. And when it all comes crashing down, I hope this will be a place he finds peace.

His lips whisper across my exposed shoulder. "The best place for me, Ace, is wherever you are."

I shiver because *damn*.

He is my favorite.

My favorite friend. My favorite treasure. My favorite person to do everything with, to do *nothing* with.

Rumor is my favorite everything, and I love him the same way stars love the sky.

Palming the back of my head, he holds me tight to him, keeping me captive as if I might try to get away. With the tip of my nose in the base of his neck, I breathe in his scent. The aroma is familiar and comforting—a smell I'll always equate with love.

"We're supposed to be doing homework," I mumble but make no attempt at moving.

"What homework?"

I giggle against his collar bone, pulling my face free of its confines. The arms around me don't loosen but I do manage to wedge my arm between our bodies and brush the hair from his face.

"Those words don't sound like they're coming from a man who wants to pass the GED."

"What GED?"

"You're killing me."

His chuckle is rich, and he kisses my forehead one last time before reluctantly letting me go. With a quick roll of his body, he snags a textbook off a nightstand—because at Reggie's he gets a nightstand—and then he's beside me again, rearranging his body so he's sitting cross-legged.

I mimic his position, opening up my own textbook. Chemistry. *Gross.*

"Ace, you look like you just swallowed sour milk."

"I think I'd rather do that."

"Baby, that's college level Chemistry. Clearly, you know what you're doing."

I flip a page with a sad sigh. "Just because I'm good at it doesn't mean it's fun."

He lifts his own textbook. "Want to trade?"

"Kind of."

His smile is silly. He bops me on the nose with the book and lets it fall back on the mattress with a thud. "Learning is supposed to be stimulating but twiddling my thumbs is more fun at this point. I don't know how I'm supposed to pass this test because every time I try to study my brain starts to tell me that sleep sounds better."

I run my hands down my stone washed jeans, tracking

the movement with my eyes. "Have you, uh, ever thought about enrolling in school?"

"Nope."

I chance a glance at him. The twists in his features tell me all I need to know. "Okay then."

"Ace, what would be the point of me enrolling in school?"

"Because you hate studying for the GED?" I maneuver to my knees. "Rumor, you'll be eighteen in six weeks. You can enroll yourself in school and still have half a year to attend. You'll get the high school experience back, a diploma, and some counselors to help you navigate your future."

"I don't need anyone to help me navigate my future." His pencil spins in circles over his knuckles. "I'm doing perfectly fine on my own."

I can't argue with that. Rumor's more put together than most adults. While I'm proud of him, I'm also sad for him.

Death is a thief. It takes, and it takes, and it takes. Nobody is safe from being robbed. Not the deceased, not those who are still living. Everything Rumor knew about the world was stripped from him, and he was left on his own. Rumor isn't dead, but he was robbed of life all the same.

I just want to give it all back.

"Well, the option is there." I throw out, but his attention is already back on his book. "Calling your old school for transcripts would only take a few minutes."

"Ace. Drop it."

Message received.

The equations in my Chemistry book blur together, and I don't feel much like studying. I pretend to take notes so as not to distract Rumor who actually appears to be having a successful study session.

My thumbs punch buttons on my calculator aimlessly. Spelling out sentences with numbers and typing 1234567890 as much as the screen will allow. Every once in a while, I glance at Rumor to find him jotting things in his notebook or munching on the eraser of his pencil. His hair is a screen, and it makes it hard to see his face. Are his eyebrows scrunched in concentration? Are his eyes lit up with excitement or muted with boredom? Is he smiling? Frowning? Did my suggestion upset him? Why hasn't he looked at me?

"Ace, I can feel you thinking."

It's been quiet for so long, the sudden sound of his voice makes me flinch. I drop my calculator and it cracks against my kneecap. I hiss, throwing my palm over the spot and rubbing.

His pencil hits the bedding and he leans forward, nose-diving toward my lap. I'm unsure of his motive, so I just sit there like a statue, waiting for him to—*oh sweet Jesus.*

When his lips replace my palm, soothing the sore spot on my knee, I enter some sort of parallel universe where only Rumor and the butterfly kisses he makes exist. I'm no longer sitting on the bed, but floating, and it's not just my lips that are smiling. It's my soul too, and I bask in it before it's taken away.

He straightens. "You okay?"

Apparently, I forget what words are. I just nod, gnawing on my bottom lip. His laugh is breathy and it wafts across my face right before I get another kiss in the center of my forehead. It's the eighth one today, the third one since I've been here. And yes, I'm counting.

I count. I keep track. I replay every kiss on a reel inside my head because one day, he'll stop doing it and I'll miss them.

"Penny for your thoughts?"

I use my whole hand to remove the curtain of hair masking his face. It's soft between my fingers. "I just want to make sure you aren't upset with me."

His lips flatten. "Why would I be upset with you?"

"For pressuring you about school."

"You haven't pressured me, Alma." He plucks my hand from its position buried in his hair. Our fingers entwine like they have so many times before, but this time feels different. "I think it's nice you want to give me what you think I'm missing out on but I'm fine with the way things are, okay?"

I nod, using my free hand to play with his fingers absentmindedly.

"You don't look like you believe me." He squeezes my hand a second before he lets go. "Don't move."

I stay put, stalking his movements with a furrowed brow. He flops on the bed, inching toward the nightstand. The drawer opens with a groan and he shoves his hand inside, the rustling of papers heard beneath the rattle of the lamp sitting atop the nightstand.

With a triumphant noise, his hand emerges from the drawers, full of papers. He doesn't bother closing the drawer before he scooches his way back to me. Tucking his legs back under his butt, he pulls a piece of hair from his mouth and lifts his papers with a grin. "I've been thinking and screw computer science." He gives the papers a shake. "This is what I want to do with my life."

"You figured it out? That's great." I make a grabby motion with my fingers. "Gimme gimme gimme."

He laughs and sets the papers in my hands. "What do you think?"

"Uh." I flip through the pages. I'm not sure what I was expecting—college admission papers, a program pamphlet, information from a career website, maybe. None of those things are resting on my palms right now, but rather a list. A list of facts, states, addresses and— "Statistics of homeless youth?"

"Yeah. I did some research. Reggie has a computer and a printer in the room across the hall. It's dial-up and moves slower than hell, but it's not like I have anything better to do during the day than watch a loading bar."

He slides the pages from me carefully. "This is what I want to do, Ace. I want to help them. Millions of kids run away or are left behind every year. Whether their parents die, they're being abused, or just plain neglected—they have nowhere to go that feels safe. The type of physical and sexual abuse that can occur in group homes and homeless shelters makes me want to vomit." There's an intensity in his eyes that matches his movements— a fist pounding his chest, his nub punctuating the end of every sentence. "There are some safe houses, different charities around the country that are dedicated to giving these teens a place to live but not enough. The ratio of homeless youth to safe living spaces is heartbreaking, Ace. I just... I want to change that ratio." His inhale is heavy, and when he exhales, he doses me in his passion. "What do you think?"

I tell him the truth. "I think it's the most admirable thing I've ever heard."

His grin is blinding. "I haven't worked out all the kinks yet. I'm not sure what college I'll go to, what degree I'll get, or if one even exists but this is what I'm passionate about."

The pang of joy in my chest is all for him, because of him. Knowing Rumor, loving him, watching him transform from the cynical, dejected, mute man he was in Mo that day to a man who's animated and literally beaming with gusto about the possibility of a future that no longer frightens him into a corner.

It's quite possibly the greatest treasure the universe could create. Even better because it wasn't one I found but was gifted with.

And I hope, *pray*, that when the truth comes out, he'll keep his promise and stay.

"I've looked into programs for people who want to go into nonprofits." The look on his face is bashful. "I want to start my own, put a safe space for teens in every state. I'll call it Simon's Space."

With a hand on his neck, I kiss his reddening cheek. "Your dad would be really proud of you."

Those words give him more than I ever have.

"You think so?"

"I know so."

He flicks my earlobe. "Told you I had things figured out."

"You definitely do." I relax on the mattress, shoving my Chemistry book aside. "Though I did like the idea of you there every day, preferably in Chemistry class. You'd be a nice distraction from Mr. Stevenson's monotone lectures. It's merely selfish."

"You can be a little selfish every once in a while, Ace. It won't kill ya." He sets his self-made pamphlet aside carefully. "And I promise I'll come to any other career fairs or dorky dances or whatever."

"How chivalrous of you."

"Right?" He chuckles and sprawls out on his back. "In the meantime, I'll be here, living with the nosiest old man I've ever met and trying to find my Alice."

His words lodge a stone in my windpipe.

"I really want to find her, Ace. The idea isn't as horrifying as it used to be. And I don't know." His smile is all teeth. "I have a good feeling about it."

Oh, God.

My face must convey my panic because he pushes to his elbows and says, "you okay?"

I nod, clearing my throat aggressively and lying down beside him, in the crook of his arm with my face in his chest so he can't see my expression.

As we lay, the only sound our syncopated heartbeats, I open my mouth seven times only to fasten it tight again.

The words won't come, and they taste pungent in my mouth. As time ticks by, my panic grows and the dread I feel with the inevitable truth is too thick to breathe properly against. But like a coward, I stay mute.

I can't break him. Not yet.

And though I already love him at a record breaking capacity, I vow to love him harder. To give him my whole heart.

And when his heart breaks, he'll have mine.

25

YOUR SILENCE GAVE ME HOPE

ALMA

His head resting awkwardly against the cushion of his recliner and the flap of his lips with each pass of his snore is not enough to fool me. He's awake. Awake and watching my movements through his eyelids.

His pointer finger, crooked and boney, twitches against the opened Sudoku book resting in his lap.

It's a great ruse, really—pretending as though he's fallen asleep with the pen in his hand and his brain on overdrive.

Buried beneath silvery strands, his ears are wide open, and I know what he's listening for.

The truth.

"Reggie." The handle of my backpack slips from my fingers, thundering against the carpet running beside his front door. The action frees my hands so I can bend over and slide on my sneakers. "I know you're awake."

His eyes peel open and his head lolls, glaring at me over the faded cushions. "You didn't tell him."

"It wasn't the right time."

"Young lady, you were up there for four hours with him. You couldn't find the time to—"

"To what, Reggie?" My laces burn my palms when I pull too tight. "He just spent the better part of those four hours talking about this non-profit he wants to start and name after his father. What was I supposed to do? Shit all over that?" I move to the next shoe, lifting the limp laces with frustration and malice. "It wasn't the right time."

"Alma, it will never be the right time. There is no right time."

"Reggie!" With my shoes now tied uncomfortably tight, I have no choice but to straighten and lock eyes with him.

I falter at what I find below his lashes. The displeasure he normally looks at me with has been exchanged for something gentle. Setting his Sudoku aside, the recliner creaks as he leans forward. "Alma, I know this situation is unpleasant."

"Unpleasant?" *No.* "Reggie this situation is maddening."

I'm stuck in a place where life meets death, and it's messy.

Rumor's life is mixing with his parent's death and the chaos it's creating is almost impossible to navigate.

There's darkness in this spot, and turmoil is all I feel. I wonder if life and death conspired— came together to forge a path I'm forced to lead Rumor down.

My fury isn't directed at Rumor, or Reggie, or anything other than the force of nature that took away both his parents. Lingering just beneath that anger is fear. Fear of the untold and the voice in the back of my head that's taunting me, telling me I don't have the tools to put him back together after I break him.

"It has to be done, Alma."

"Obviously." My back hits the door and I run my hands

down my face, scrubbing and scrubbing, but the dread doesn't go away. "I need more details."

"What kind of details?"

I drop my hands. "Don't bullshit me, Reggie. When you told me about Allison's death, you hinted at something. My parents came into the room but they aren't here now. I need to know the rest of the story."

"There is no rest of the story." With the help of his armrest, he pushes to his feet. "Alma, it's a guess. I don't know what was going through her head."

Is this man for real?

"Reggie, you basically told me you think she drowned herself!" Pushing off the door, I stalk toward him. "Who makes that kind of assumption when they aren't sure about it?"

"The kind of man who knew his daughter. Allison had a beautiful soul but it was a complicated one." With a slow finger, he taps the side of his head. "Her mind wasn't nice to her, Alma. Allison lived every day in a pervasive state of suffering. Some days her only belief was that escape from it was hopeless."

His words aren't just words. They're hints. Bread crumbs leading to the past and the truth about the life Allison lived. "She battled depression?"

Reggie's nod is slight. "My guess, my hunch, is that she finally found a way to escape."

"*Your hunch?*" Chills racing up my spine hold me immobile "Reggie, how am I supposed to explain all this to Rumor based on a hunch?"

Uneasiness clouds his vision, and he makes a sound I know I will never forget. "You just have to say it. The same way I said it to Simon almost twenty years ago. If you can't say it, I will. You don't have to do this."

"I can do it." My voice wavers as I speak. "I just, I—" I need more time. More minutes to tack on to each day that can be spent drafting the words needed to recite this all back to Rumor.

"I need to wrap my words in the delicacy this situation requires. This isn't just me telling him the truth about his mother, Reggie, it's me taking away his purpose for this visit. The whole 'rip the band-aid off' mentality doesn't work for this scenario. I want to soften my words, make the curveball as painless as possible."

"The curveball?"

"Yes, Reggie, the curveball that this bastard called life just wailed at him. This isn't twenty years ago. Rumor's alone. Simon is gone, and Josh is five hundred miles away."

"But you're right here." With a slow step forward, he pokes me in the chest bone. "Why are you acting like he has nobody? You. Are. Right. Here."

I'm not enough.

"I'm not Allison, Reggie. Rumor came for her. My presence won't erase her death."

"Ace?"

No.

Please. No. Not like this.

"What did you just say? Alma?"

My chest tingles, and it's a warning. An awareness spreading throughout my veins, icy and frigid, cautioning me toward what's to come.

The spasms of alarm erupting beneath my skin are intense enough to bring me to my knees. But I stay upright and use every fiber in my body to turn and look at him.

Standing on the last step, an empty cup in his hand, he's staring at me with unfocused eyes.

"*Alma.*"

All the times he's said my name, he's never said it like that.

Like he's tethered to me, a string from his heart to mine.

And it's breaking.

And he's scared.

"Tell me what you said."

I am not ready.

I swallow hard, coaxing moisture into my mouth so my feeble answer can be hard. "She's gone, Rumor. Your mother."

The cup leaves his hand and rolls across the carpet, forgotten. "Gone?"

My blinks are rapid, and Rumor becomes a blur in front of me. Reaching outward, I wrap my quivering fingers around the base of Reggie's chair.

Say it, Alma.

"Dead." The word tastes venomous leaving my lips. "She's been gone for years."

He just blinks. "No, she hasn't."

"Yeah, she has, son." Without his cane, Reggie's walk is slow and deliberate. His slippers make the faintest of noise as he shuffles across the living room, toward the base of the staircase. "Come sit."

"No." Progressing backward, Rumor takes two more steps, and I know one wrong move will have him retreating up the staircase and shutting out what he just heard.

"Yes," I say, with a steadiness I do not feel. "Rumor, she died when you were five weeks old."

"Are... are you sure?" His hand carves into his hair, pulling back and releasing it. He does this, over and over and over. "There are nine of them. They are alive, all nine of them are alive. None of the Alices from that time are dead."

"That's because your mother's full name wasn't Alice." Keeping my tears in check, I reach for my backpack where his proof is concealed.

"Yes, it was. My dad told me her name was Alice. He wouldn't lie. Not about that."

"He didn't lie." The sound of the zipper makes my heart pound. Pulling back the canvas flap, my fingers connect with the torn print out of the article. "Alise was a nickname. Her full name was Allison." The article wrinkles under my touch as I press it to my chest and attempt to smooth it out.

I count five steps, and I'm right in front of him, at the bottom of the staircase and extending the picture. "Her name was Allison Copeland."

Moving back slightly, he increases his personal space. Unsteady fingers lengthen and snatch the article from my possession.

His agonized whisper and the way he hugs it to his chest is almost too much to handle. "*Dad.*"

Slow moving tears inch down his cheeks and stain the article below his chin.

"Where did you get this?" He's staring down at me now, blinking and trying to find my face behind the tears welled up in his eyes.

"I printed it at the school's library. I searched your father's name in an article database."

"But why?"

"I thought I could find her that way, and I did."

But I almost wish I hadn't.

"That's her, Rumor. In that photo with your dad. That's your mother."

His stance is restless as he stands there, head bowed and chest pumping. Twitching fingers toy with the top of the paper, pieces damp from his tears are sticking to the pad of his fingers. With a noise that's somewhere between a sob and a deep breath, he pulls the article back from his chest and comes eye to eye with his mother.

He frowns. "This isn't my mom. This is Allison." He looks past Reggie, into the living room. I track his gaze to a mantle, and there lies a photo of his mother, rose behind her ear and eyes a carbon copy of his. "This is Reggie's daughter."

Rumor descends one step. With refusal to set down the article, he gives Reggie his attention. "My father was friends with your daughter?"

The smile on Reggie's thin lips is fragile. "Ah, son, your daddy was much more than friends with Alise. The way he loved her was reckless. Sometimes it made me want to kick his ass. Mostly, I was just grateful she got to experience something so special."

"But—" He sways on his feet, rubbing at his chest with his nub and pressing down. "That would mean that—" He draws back, crashing into the banister. The article slips from his fingers and he points a finger at Reggie. "Holy shit."

Reggie nods, a fist to his mouth as he scans Rumor, allowing himself the opportunity to be vulnerable. "You look just like her, kid."

It's as though Rumor was just given a pair of brand new eyes. He gazes at Reggie like he's meeting him for the first time all over again.

And in some way, he is.

No longer just a co-worker, or an old man he does chores for.

Reggie is family.

His family.

And suddenly I'm intruding. Stumbling backward, I

trip over my backpack and tumble into the door. My elbow cracks against the wooden frame, and the sharp noise captures Rumor's attention.

His eyes, murky and spinning with questions, flick to me. My hand on the doorknob has him jumping off the step. "Are you leaving? Don't leave. I need you to stay."

I drop my hand.

He stares at it for another beat, ensuring I'll stay put, and then he starts to pace. One foot in front of the other, he makes a circle in the space between the kitchen and the living room, his brain whirling. "So, Reggie's my grandfather, and Allison's my mother."

"Yes," I say, though I'm not sure he was asking.

"But if Allison's my mother, then that means my mother is—" Smothering a sob, he looks at me with lost eyes and a quiver in his cheekbones. The shock slips away, and realization sets in. The black and white visions he had of Allison are replaced with color. "Dead. That means my mother is dead."

Boom.

The tears choke him but still, he doesn't weep. He just stands there, eyes moving from me to Reggie, to that picture of his mother with the rose in her hair, as he pieces together his puzzle.

He doesn't like his result, so he messes up the pieces and builds it again. He ends up with the same result every time and I know because the tears grow bigger as they fall down his face.

When he looks at me, broken and confused, a hot tear rolls down my cheek.

"I don't want her to be gone," he says, and the last traces of my control vanish.

I rush him, arms outstretched, but he halts my movements with the palm of his hand. He licks a tear off his top lip and asks what I was hoping he wouldn't. "Why didn't you tell me when we were upstairs?"

"I—"

"And how did you know she was related to Reggie?"

"They have the same last name. I didn't... I didn't tell you right away because I wasn't positive she was related. It could've been a coincidence." I wrap my arms around myself. "I had to be sure, Rumor. I didn't know she was gone until after I talked to him."

"Wait." His voice is sharp and it cuts right through me. "Is tonight not the first night you talked to Reggie?"

I shake my head and drop my chin, unable to meet his eyes.

"Alma, when exactly did you print out that photo?"

"Twenty-seven days ago."

"Twenty-sev—" A curse rips from his mouth. "Twenty-seven days ago?!"

I sweep my head up, and the fury in his eyes suffocates me and holds me prisoner in my spot, close enough to feel his wrath but too far away to hold him. "I should've told you, I know. But after I learned she was dead, I didn't know how to say the words."

A grunt comes out his nose. "How about how you just did? Give me the damn paper and tell me she's gone."

"It wasn't that easy, Rumor. You wanted to meet her so badly, and I didn't know how to take this from you. I was trying to—"

"So, you killed her then?"

I jerk. "What?"

"Did you kill her, Alma? Are you the reason my mom is dead?"

"No. Of course not, I—"

"So, you didn't take her from me." His interruption is steady but laced in his words is venom. "You aren't the reason she's dead, so what exactly was so hard about telling me?"

"Rumor." Reggie takes an unsteady step forward, and I didn't think it was possible, but the skin on his face seems to be sagging more than it was a few minutes ago. "She's been beating herself up for weeks, trying to come up with the best way to break it to you. She cares about you, son."

Rumor doesn't even look in Reggie's direction as he speaks. The words bounce and fall right off his back.

"That's why you've been acting so weird." He shoots me with a sour look, scoffing. "All that bullshit about being worried for the future had nothing to do with you. It was about me."

"Yes, but I—"

"You lied to me." His face pales with anger, and *that* I can handle. Barely. What wrecks me completely, tears my insides out and exposes them for all to see, are the tears of hurt. Of disappointment. Of betrayal.

Tears not for his mom. But for me. *Because* of me.

"You lied to me, Alma. Every night we lied awake together, I held your damn hand and talked about what I thought she'd be like! You looked me in the eye inside of Mo and told me nothing was wrong! Just today, upstairs in a goddamn room that belonged to her, you let me talk about her knowing she was dead."

The flash of loneliness in his eyes stabs me right in the gut. My own eyes become a faucet, and out of them comes tears, one after another soaking my cheeks, my neck, and the collar of my shirt.

"She's dead, Alma! She was dead then. She's dead now, and it sucks all the same."

"I didn't know how to hurt you."

"Hurt me?" His nostrils flare, and he lets out a nasty laugh. "Oh, that's nice, Alma. You didn't want to hurt me so you spent the last month treating me like a moron."

"I would never say—"

"You *listened* to me talk about her, excited and hopeful and scared! I rambled on and on and on about what it would be like to meet her." He bares his teeth at me, a vein in his neck pulsing with each word he spits. "You looked me in the eyes and lied straight to my face. Your silence gave me hope, Alma, and it was all bullshit."

His accusing voice punctures the air as though it's a balloon, and when it pops, the sound is deafening.

"How could you do that to me?" he asks, and his heartbreak quells some of the anger. He's staring at me, almost begging with his eyes, begging me to tell him none of this is true. "How could you let me believe in something that wasn't true? How could you be so cruel?"

I grasp at my chest, because *God*, the heart inside hurt. "I wasn't trying to be cruel to you, or inject you with false hope. I just... this isn't the ending I wanted for you. I was trying to come up with a way to make this better."

"You can't make this better!" His shout makes me flinch. With a fist to his chest, he steps forward, voice raised and hair wild. "I'm not one of your stupid treasures! You didn't find me, okay? I came to you, looking for something and you kept it from me. It was fun to pretend but this is real life, Alma! I'm not a freaking object. You don't get to set me aside until you're ready to draft a story for me!"

"That is not what I was doing."

"No? Because that's exactly what it sounds like to me. You placated me, fed me a bunch of shit to evade me from the truth because it wasn't what *you* wanted."

He tilts his chin up and wipes his cool eyes with the back of his hand. "You live in a fantasyland of clueless parents, treasures, and dumb twinkle lights over your bed. I live in the real world where there is pain and death and *liars*!"

I sniff, my arms heavy and limp at my sides. I pray for the strength to reach for him and for the strength to stay breathing when he pushes me away. "Rumor—"

"Get out."

You said you would stay.

"You... you said you needed me to stay."

"Yeah, well, that was before I knew that your kindness is a facade. Under all that crap about treasures and butterfly kisses and stupid ass violins, you're mean. You're mean, Alma Underwood, and I don't need you to stay. I need you to go away."

"Rumor, just calm down for a minute, yeah?" Reggie's hand is on his shoulder now, rubbing, trying to coax Rumor toward the living room. "You're just upset. You don't really want her to leave."

Rumor's eyes don't leave mine as he stumbles backward, away from me. "Yeah. I do. I want her to leave, this house and my life.

So I do.

With one last look at him, I leave. The emptiness in my chest is confirmation he has my heart, and I hope he keeps it.

I hope it's enough.

26

ALLISON

RUMOR

Up then down.

Up then down.

Up then down.

Up until the moment the door clicked shut behind her, I thought of a rollercoaster as a euphemism for my life.

I was wrong.

My life isn't a rollercoaster but rather one of those rides that spins really fast and pins you to the steel wall. It's uncomfortable, and you can't breathe, and your legs feel like jello when you try to step off the ride. It leaves you dizzy, with a throbbing in your temples and an ache in your gut that doesn't let you forget the ride's aggression.

I want to fall to my knees and beg whoever is up there to make it stop. I can't handle it anymore— the lies, the questions, the false hope. The pain is crushing. It hurts as though there's a war waging inside my body, and my only source of peace just walked out the door.

Peace is a traitor.

"Rumor."

It's the fifth time he calls my name, and it's the fifth time I ignore him.

My grandfather.

I'm astonished the world hasn't cracked beneath my feet with how quickly it's been changing. Everything looks the same, the stars haven't dropped from the sky, and the sun still rises each morning but it's different. I can no longer count on the world to comfort me when I open my eyes. My safety net of familiarity is gone.

From the time it took for the sun and the moon to trade places, my world as I knew it had vanished.

And so far, this new one sucks.

"Rumor. Royce. Rawlings."

His breath is hot on my neck, saturating the collar of my shirt, and did he just— "Did you just middle name me?"

Spinning on my heels, I come toe to toe with him, and it pisses me off he's so damn tall. Craning my neck causes the tears on my face to re-route, and I have to slap my hand over the droplets to stop them from running into my ears. My hair sticks to my skin when I try to brush it back, the adhesive a mixture of sweat and snot.

"I told you to get it cut," he says.

Unbelievable. "I like my hair like this."

"You're welcome then. You get your hair from me."

"Says who?"

"Science."

"You expect me to call you grandpa now or some shit?" I widen my stance, staring right into his old eyes. "Because I don't have a grandpa. He died when I was a kid. Where the hell were you?"

The tremble in my chin is fierce, and I gnaw on my lip to stop it. My head bobs on its own accord, and I think it's just an action—something to rid my body of energy.

Reggie's entire face frowns. One by one the wrinkles slope downward, and he starts rubbing at his chin, tugging on the loose skin. He nudges his head toward the sofa. "Let's sit."

"No."

When I'm asked to sit, people die.

"Rumor." My name is a sigh. "I have a bum knee and a cane that's all the way across the room. I will stand here all night with you if that's what you need but I'm warning you now that you better pick me up off this carpet in the morning."

Fuzzy eyebrows raise, disappearing behind his hairline and I interpret the action for what it is. A challenge.

With a slow roll of my head, I gesture toward the sofa with both arms. His hand pats my shoulder when he passes me, and I stay behind him, walking at turtle pace in case the old fart collapses. It isn't until he's settled in his recliner, rocking slowly, that I drop to the floor.

"The couch is comfier."

"I like the carpet." I press my hand into it, letting the soft microfiber ooze between my fingers.

The action grounds me. The strands may be small but I'm slipping and it gives me something to hold on to. Something to keep me present.

"You want a pillow or something, kid?"

"I'm fine."

"I learned from Alma that when teenagers say they're fine, it means they are minutes away from destruction."

"Can we not talk about Alma right now?"

Or ever again...

The recliner groans and he should probably think about getting a new one before he finds himself flipped over. "How close are you to destruction, Rumor?"

"Hell if I know." And it's the truth. The tears are a steady drip, running into my hairline. I've lost feeling in my palms, and I have this idea that if I lay here, staring at Reggie's popcorn ceiling for the rest of time, I'll be okay. "I think I stopped feeling."

"You're numb."

"I like numb. Numb is good."

Numb is not anger.

Numb is not sadness.

Numb is not pain.

"You won't be numb forever, Rumor. At some point, you'll have to feel, and I want you to know that I'll be here. When you start to feel, and you think you can't take anymore, I'll be here."

I sniff, and because I'm laying down, the snot slides down my throat. I gag at the taste.

My eyelashes are wet when they meet my cheeks. The darkness that's waiting for me isn't much different than what's in the light.

It's them.

First Dad.

And now my mother.

Dad's wearing trousers and one of the pressed shirts he wore to work. He skips the tie and leaves the top button undone because he's the boss and can do what he wants. I've got half a bagel in my mouth when he rushes into the kitchen, tucking his shirt into his pants. He's late. Which is normal. After he fills up a travel mug with coffee, he kisses the top of my head and tells me that drugs are for nerds. When the door shuts, I think I'm alone. But not a minute later he rushes back inside and sweeps his keys off the counter with a goofy grin on his face. The door shuts and I'm alone again. For real this time. Forever.

My mother is a blur. I see her face and the curve of her nose. Her smile is lopsided, and there's a damn rose behind her ear. I imagine she slides it free and bends at the waist, handing it to a little boy with only one hand. He looks over his shoulder to make sure his dad is watching but when he turns back, she's evaporated. And the boy is all alone.

"Why didn't she want me?"

The creaking of the chair is silenced. "Rumor, we don't have to do this right now."

"I want to." While I'm still numb.

"She did want you. Allison loved you. She passed when you—"

"Were a baby, I know." An eager tear slips from between my lashes and races down my skin. "What happened to her?"

The silence lasts for a long time, and I study the darkness my eyelids project, waiting for either of them to come back.

"She drowned in a lake not too far from here."

My eyes fly open. "What?"

"You'd been with us for five weeks at that point. Your father woke up to you crying and an empty bed. Park rangers found her just as the sun started to come through the clouds."

Oh my God.

"But... why was she out in the dark if she couldn't swim?"

"She knew how to swim, Rumor, she just didn't. Not that night."

"Why wouldn't she swim?"

"Because she wanted to drown."

Low in my gut, a bomb goes off. Bones rattle and muscles strain against the blow. I vibrate and the speed of my teardrops increase. Grasping for the carpet, I panic as it slides between my sweaty fingers.

Don't let me slip.

I don't want to slip.

"Breathe, Rumor!"

His reminder has me wrapping my hand around my neck, expelling an exhale that resembles a wheeze.

"She did it to herself?"

"My only proof is her actions in the days leading up to her death. She battled depression, son. And I think, maybe, in the end, the depression won."

"But you said..." *In the days leading up to her death.* "Is it my fault?"

I slam my eyes shut as if it will shield me from an answer.

The recliner screams in protest as it rocks forward, and I hear Reggie's feet hit the ground. "Oh God, no. Rumor, your mother was diagnosed with depression a decade before she ever met your father. Your presence had absolutely nothing to do with it."

"But I'm broken."

"You're what?"

"Broken." I lift my nub. "My dad swore to me my mother's absence had nothing to do with it but what if he was wrong? What if having a—"

"I'm going to stop you right there."

"It's possible."

"It's not." His tone is tired. "Rumor, if you want me to be perfectly honest—"

"I do."

"She thought it was her fault. Your mother, I mean. When the first scans of you came through, Allison thought that your lack of a hand had something to do with the antidepressants she was taking when she fell pregnant with you. Something about tetragons."

"That's highly unlikely. I've done a lot of research regarding this nub, and the chances that she caused it are like one and five hundred thousand."

"It took a few months and dozens more doctors to get her to believe that, but she did eventually believe it, Rumor. When you were born, there was no doubt in her mind that you were exactly who you were supposed to be. She was smitten with you, kid. Your father had to pry you away just to get his chance with you."

My eyes reopen, and I trace patterns with my eyes using the bumps in his ceiling. The first object I trace is a rose for my mother, and if she were here right now I'd give her a real one, then a dozen more after that.

"Depression is a complicated disease, son. I never knew what was going on in Allison's mind at any given moment but I know her decision that day had nothing to do with you."

"She looks so happy though. In that photo on your mantle. She looks happy."

"She was, I'm sure." He takes a drawn-out breath, and when he speaks again, his voice is a murmur. "Allison used to describe her depression as though she was the television and somebody else had her remote. Channels were always getting switched and she couldn't keep up. Simon was convinced his love would be her savior but depression doesn't work like that. Love isn't a cure-all."

I wish it was.

"She wore an invisible backpack. On the days it was full, she stayed in bed, unable to carry it. On the days it was empty, she gave out laughs like free candy. And you know what, Rumor, I'd never seen her backpack so empty for so many days in a row until you were born."

"You don't have to bullshit me."

"I'm not bullshitting you, kid. It's the truth. She loved you."

I don't want her to be gone.

"I never had the chance to love her back the way she loved me." The tears are hot as they leave my eyes, and I decide those ones are for her. "I wish I could've met her."

"I've got pictures and memories for days, son. It's not the same, but you can get to know her through me. I'd be happy to teach you about her."

"I'd like that." The tremor in my voice is faint but steady, a cause of emotion seeping through the numbness. "I'd like that a whole lot."

"Whenever you're ready though. It can be a gradual thing."

"I've got some questions now, some about my mother and some not."

"Shoot."

"Do I have any cousins? What's my grandmother like? Did you know it was me that first day in the motel? How come you never visited when I was a kid? Does anyone else in this family have congenital amputation or is it just me? How did my parents meet? Did you get along with my father? Do you know why my mother named me Rumor?"

"Whoa, whoa, whoa." He laughs, and I wonder if it sounds like hers. "One at a time, yeah? We can sit here all night and go through them all until you fall asleep with your face in the carpet but let's start with one for now."

Easy. "Did you know it was me when we met?"

"I was fairly certain, yes."

"Why didn't you say anything?"

"It seemed as though my silence was what Simon wanted. Allison's death broke all of us but it ripped your father apart entirely. He was in denial, talking about her as if she were still around and speaking about the future as if she would be in it. When he got offered a job in Chicago, he almost didn't go. He never said but I think he didn't want to leave your mother behind. Eventually, he decided to go. He sent pictures at first, invited us to your first birthday."

"And then what?"

"He began to rebuild his life without her. I think, maybe, he struggled with things that reminded him of her. He shut us out, kid, and back then I was too pissed to argue. I should have fought to see you."

"Do you think that's why he never spoke of her? Or got married?"

"It's possible. Your parents loved each other, Rumor. It was the kind of love I didn't have with my own wife. The kind of love others are jealous of. Your parents weren't married when you were born but that didn't mean Simon didn't want it. It didn't mean he wasn't planning a proposal." His next words are low and come out cracked. "I will never forget the moment your father walked up to your mother, asleep in that casket, and slipped a ring on her finger."

That's why he never dated.

Because he always belonged to her.

And, *God*, I want to be furious with him. Scream curse words at the sky while shaking my fist, demanding to know why he kept her from me. Shout and ask him why he thought I didn't deserve to love her like he did.

But I'm not furious. Because grief changes people. It sculpts you into a person better equipped to handle the pain, and that's what my father spent his life doing.

Handling pain. And though I never witnessed his tears or saw the quiver of his chin, I know they must have existed.

The same as my tears are now, his were for her.

"Next question?" Reggie asks.

Next question. "Do you know why my mother named me Rumor?"

"She named you after herself."

"Huh?"

"Allison's middle name was Rumer. Spelled differently, but she thought spelling your name with an O was manlier. Your grandmother was obsessed with this author named Rumer Godden, and that's how Alise got her middle name. I chose her first name."

"I... I share her name?"

"Yep. Naming you was the first thing she did after finding out you were a boy. She said she wanted you to have a piece of her wherever you went. So I suppose, in a way, you had a piece of her with you all along."

All at once the pain hits. Like a flip was switched, forcing me to feel *everything*. I sit up and gasp, digging at my chest to set my lungs free from whatever has them constricted.

Sobs wrack my body, and the force of them has me coughing and sputtering.

The pain is brutal and familiar.

Grief.

I want to be numb again.

27

BYE BYE BUTTERFLY

ALMA

What I love most about Rumor are the kisses he gave me—
not the ones on the forehead, or the cheek, or the shoulder.
The ones he gave me from a mile away.

The butterfly kisses, gifted to me with his smirk, and his
laugh, and the tips of his fingers when they grazed the edge
of my jaw.

He was my butterfly, and the kisses he granted me with
were exclusive.

But there's this thing about catching butterflies— as
soon as you get close enough, they're gone.

28

THIS IS REAL

RUMOR

With loss comes praise. In the days after my father's death, everyone around me was quick to applaud me for my strength, comment on how tough I was, and congratulate me on my ability to survive after a tragedy.

As if I had a choice.

It's not optional— surviving grief.

It's just something you have to do because, really, there is no alternative.

But what they don't tell you is that survival is painful. It is exhaustion. It is a decrease in appetite and the inability to wash your hair. It is a full body ache after the numbness wears off and an abundance of tears leaves you dry.

Surviving is opening your eyes to a world that took love from you, and finding a way to be grateful for it anyway.

The dark sheets I'm wrapped in are warm, and though they're damp with fresh tears, they're safe. The cocoon I've built myself is free of bad news and pipe dreams. There are no deaths allowed. No liars permitted. No violins to be heard and no feelings to be felt.

It is silent. Surviving is my only expectation.

I plan to stay here forever.

I'm a jackass for letting Reggie limp up the staircase three times a day to feed me and make sure I haven't stroked out. But I'm also too exhausted to vacate this bed. Opening my mouth to bite into the sandwiches he leaves me is a chore in and of itself. The slightest of movement exhausts me.

It's strange. The more I sleep, the more exhausted I become. And I don't get bored or restless. I just become more content. More sated.

The sharp knock on the door is my prompt to pull the sheet over my head. The click of the doorknob sounds and I wait for Reggie's feet shuffling across the carpeting to accompany it. He'll leave a plate on the nightstand like he always does, and then he'll leave. Neither of us speaks because there's nothing left to say. All that needed to be said was said that night in his living room. He kept his promise. He answered every question until my heart could no longer handle answers and I'd fallen asleep on the floor.

I haven't spoken since.

My only companion is the whoosh of the ceiling fan above me, and the sound my tongue makes when I use it to scrape bread from the roof of my mouth.

Reggie clears his throat and I wait for the distinct clank of the plate hitting the wooden surface. It doesn't come. What does come is a dip in my bed when a body settles next to mine. I flinch away from the hand that rests on my back.

This isn't the plan.

This isn't what we do.

"So, do you leave this bed to piss or you got a bucket in here somewhere?"

The sound of his voice is a roundhouse kick to the gut. I gasp and curl in on myself, shielding my heart from any more blows.

I'm covered in bruises, and I can't take anymore. Not from real life and not from lucid dreams that give me my brother and then snatch him away as soon as I emerge from my cocoon.

"Man, your grandpa makes some bomb ass lasagna. Want some? I brought you a plate. Also grabbed you four slices of garlic bread because I know you're a slut for some bread. By the way, are we calling him grandpa now or is he just Reggie?" Something stabs at my solar plexus. "You gonna free yourself from that blanket trap or am I gonna have to come get you?"

He pokes me again and again and again until I reach behind me and capture his wrist through the sheets. His bones don't disintegrate in my palm and the remains don't sprinkle through the cracks in my fingers like they have so many times before.

This is real.

"J... Josh?"

My vocal cords sound like they've been put through a blender but he must've heard my sad attempt at communicating because his hand finds my shoulder and squeezes.

"Hey, brother."

"Hi." I manage to say right before a dry sob rips my throat raw.

"Christ, dude. You sound like a frog giving a blow job. Do they not have water in Michigan?"

I pull the sheet from my wet face. "This whole state is surrounded by water, dipshit." Craning my neck against the pillow is all it takes. Our eyes connect and the relief I feel is imminent. His signature smirk and the small mole beneath his right eye are familiar sights, and nothing feels more like home. "Shit. I thought you were a dream."

"I get that a lot." Pushing his hair back with both hands, he winks at me. "From the ladies, I mean."

"You're an idiot," I say.

Translation: I missed you, and I'm happy you're here.

The mole in his skin moves when he frowns at me. "You smell like roadkill. Seriously, bro, when was the last time you showered?"

"I don't remember."

"That's disgusting.

My shrug is noncommittal and I use my fingernails to file away the dried tears on my cheeks. "Josh, I—"

"Rumor, don't." A lock of hair falls across his forehead with a small shake of his head. "I know everything. You don't need to relive it. I'm not here to break you down, I'm here to put you back together."

I wrap my fingers around the edge of the sheet and pull it up past my nose. The action isn't enough to hide my somber face and I lay here in an attitude of stillness. "What if I don't want to be put back together?"

"Well." Rubbing his hands together, he gives me a pat on the cheek. "That's just too damn bad."

"Josh, I really don—"

"I know, man." His tone is gentle, his gaze steady. He's got his shoulders rolled backward, stretching the T-shirt he put over his head this morning. Determination is chiseled in the lines of his face, piloting the inferno behind his eyelids. The same inferno that'd ignite right before he put his knuckles in a kid's mouth for calling me a retard.

"Rumor, I know getting out of this bed is going to suck

but it needs to happen. You need to shower. Your hair looks like a rat's dumping ground, and I can't imagine the shit that's growing in your armpits."

"It's not that bad." I sit up, and the action fuels a protest from my muscles. With a grimace, I peel the sheet from my body, internally gagging at the line of sweat that keeps my skin and the cotton connected. I drop the fabric into my lap.

Josh recoils. "Dude."

"Okay, so, it's bad." Dragging my hands down my face, I'm not sure if the moisture that meets my palms is tears, sweat, or grease. "What day is it?"

"Saturday. According to Reggie, you haven't left this room in five days."

"That's not true. Believe it or not, I have walked across the hall to use the bathroom. I don't have a piss bucket. I'm not a heathen."

"Yeah? When was the last time you brushed your teeth?"

"You know what, Josh? Piss off!" My jaw pops when I clench it. "Do you know what the last few months have been like for me? Life has literally beaten the shit out of me. Over and over and over again I have been pounded into the ground and thrown into walls, and goddamn it I can't take it anymore, Josh!"

A shadow crosses his face, and I don't know if it's cause of my outburst or the vision I just painted him.

"If you want me to shower, I will. Whatever. I'll wash my damn armpits and brush the fuzz off my teeth. But as soon as it's over, I'm getting right back in this bed."

Our eyes meet, his resolve against mine. Chomping on the inside of his cheek, he shakes his head. Irritation ripples along my spine and I stiffen when he leans close to me.

We're nose to nose and I feel the puff of air when it leaves his nostrils.

"The hell. You. Are." The last word is a snarl that makes his lips curl. With a smack of his lips, he climbs off the bed.

I flash him the deuces and flop backward, properly cocooning myself. "Peace out."

"Oh, you've got to be shitting me." Goosebumps break out across my skin when he rips the sheet away. I reach for it but he grabs it and uses both arms to wad it into a ball and toss it over his shoulder. "Get your ass up."

"Screw you."

He throws a hand over his heart and looks over his shoulder as if there's somebody else standing at the foot of my bed, stripping me of my only comfort.

"Screw. You," I spit, and his reply is to roll his neck and pop all ten of his knuckles.

My temper is rising up my throat like a volcano right before an eruption. "Josh, I'm not—What the hell!"

His hands are wrapped around my ankles and he's tugging. His fingernails dig into my flesh and a grunt leaves his chest with each pull. "Get out of the bed, Rumor! Stop acting like a punk ass bitch!"

A punk ass bitch?

Oh, hell no.

The roar that rips from my damaged chest is animalistic. My eyes feel black inside my head and when he lets go of my feet to pound on his chest, I charge. Rolling off the bed, I free my legs of the throw blanket tangled in them and kick the damn thing across the room. My gaze claws him like a set of talons, but he lifts his chin and closes the distance between us like he doesn't feel the bite of my anger in his skin.

His lips start flapping but I halt his words with a fist in

his shirt. Backing him against a wall, my look of disdain should have him cowering but it only makes his eyes more thunderous.

"You son of a bitch!" His back ricochets off the wall with a thud and I press my forearm across his chest to hold him there. My words are poisonous as they drip from my lips and snake their way to his ears. "What the hell is your problem? Huh? My dad is dead, shitface! My dad is dead. I slept on a mattress that smelled like horse piss before exchanging that for a gas station bathroom all so I could find my mother, who also happens to be dead. I'm living in a house with a grandfather I never knew in a bedroom that belonged to my dead mother. The girl I'm in love with broke my goddamn heart, and I can't stop myself from missing her every time I dare breathe her name. I have no money, no perfect plan for the future, and I think I'm going to fail that stupid ass GED test! I am a mess, Joshua! I am a mess, and I'm scared, and I don't want to hurt anymore."

"Rumor..."

"How dare you?" I'm panting now, choking on my words, and tasting salt on my tongue. "How dare you say that to me?"

"Rumor..."

"Everybody keeps leaving me! My dad, my mom, Ace—"

"Rumor!" He captures my head in his hands, spreading his fingers across my temples. Our foreheads meet the same moment our eyes do and he whispers, "Breathe."

Hot air escapes my chest in a full body shudder. "I'm scared," I tell him, then I drop my arms and let them hang limply by my sides. My shoulders hunch forward and I'd probably collapse if he wasn't holding me up. "You asshole. You baited me with that punk ass bitch comment."

"You're angry, Rum. You're devastated and you're overwhelmed but laying in that bed all day isn't going to make that shit go away. You have to let it out—scream, cry, talk to your girl, go to counseling, visit Allison's grave, get a memorial tattoo. Do what you gotta do, man, however you gotta do it. But I am not going to sit here and watch my brother waste away while smelling like last week's trash."

"So, what are you trying to do here? Offer yourself up as my human punching bag?"

"If that's what I gotta be. Yes."

Christ.

"Josh, I—" *I love you.*

"I know, man." He knocks our foreheads together. "Me too."

I wrap my arms around his shoulders and haul him in for a quick hug, one that won't require him to wear a hazmat suit. "Thank you for being here, J. *Shit.* I guess I didn't realize how badly I needed you until now."

I always missed Josh when he wasn't around. Even as kids and he'd have the audacity to go on vacation without me, I missed him every second he was gone. And not in a sappy, let's have a double wedding and marry sisters so we can live in the same house one day, kind of way. I missed him in a plain, simple way. I missed his existence in my life. I missed the way he was always there. I missed my best friend, and I wasn't willing to admit how brutal the past few weeks have been only talking to him twice a week.

I can admit it now.

"Thanks for not being royally pissed I ran away without telling you."

"Oh, I was pissed." He shoves my shoulder and walks past me, taking up residence on the edge of the bed. "Even more pissed I couldn't tell my parents but I would've been more pissed if you were dead."

I laugh. I can't remember the last time it happened, and it feels good. Like a cold shower after a hot day.

"Do your parents know you're here?"

"Uhm, yes? Dude, they drove me here with a trunk filled with your stuff. They want to see you if you're up for it."

"They do?" I sit beside him, knee to knee. "Well, I'm glad I didn't lose them too."

"Rum, I know how difficult it is for you to see this right now, so I'll keep telling you as long as I have to, okay?" He puts a hand on my shoulder, his fingers contracting in steady pulses. "You've lost some people, but from what I've seen, you've gained some too. Alma, man, she—"

"Is gone."

"Gone? What the hell are you talking about?

Resting my elbows on my knees, I put my face in my hand. "I don't want to talk about her."

I can't even say her name.

"Too bad. Tell me why you think she's gone. Because of your fight? *Dude.*"

"Josh, you don't get it, she—"

"I know what she did, man. She told me."

"She told you?" I find him over my shoulder. "When?"

"Rumor." The asshole chuckles. "Who do you think called me?"

"Uhm, Reggie?"

"Uhm, no. Alma. She is the one who called me, gave me an address to get out here, and spent three hours on the phone with me explaining everything. She told me all the details about your fight. She told me what she did."

"But... why? Why would she call you?"

I screamed at her.

"Man, come on." Josh thumps me. "Get your head out of your ass. I know you've been blinded by grief, and I can't imagine how that feels but you need to wake up and smell the roses where your girl is concerned. She loves you."

I don't allow myself to think about how that last sentence affects me. I've been there, done that with false hope.

Flopping backward on the bed, I throw my arms over my face. "If she loves me, then why did she do that, huh?"

A merciless ache followed her confession that night. I burned as though she ripped my heart from my chest and flipped it upside down before putting it back. It beat, and it kept me alive, but I haven't felt the same since.

"You tell me," Josh says, poking me in the neck. "You know her better than I do. Why'd she do it? I think deep down you know she didn't do it with malicious intent."

Of course not. Alma Underwood isn't capable of doing anything maliciously. When it comes to kindness, Alma gives more than she takes, and finds fulfillment in loving those who probably don't deserve it.

When you're sad, she's sad.

When you cry, she cries.

And it isn't because she's fragile. No. It's because she's made of steel and will carry your burdens on top of her tiny shoulders if it means you get to take a breath. And even just a smile in return means success for her.

"She was giving me the chance to breathe," I tell Josh. "That's what she was doing. Living the life of an insomniac while she thought up the best way to tell me without completely killing me. She was letting me breathe, Josh. It's all she's been doing since she met me, and I told her she was mean."

I push my fingers into my eye sockets. "I told her she was mean. I called her cruel and told her I needed her out of my life. I let her leave, Josh! I watched the door shut behind her, and she hasn't been back."

Please come back...

"Hasn't been back? Bro." He shoves my arms from my face. "Alma has been here every night, sitting on Reggie's couch and staring at the wall while he watches dated soap operas. Just *in case* you come downstairs and decide you need her."

Hope, that bitch, warms my chest.

"She doesn't hate me?"

"No, man. Not at all. You aren't your grief. You aren't your reactions to heartbreak, and she gets that. She's ready for you when you are."

The urge to jump to my feet and run the four miles to her house is fierce. But I don't because— "Can I love her like this?"

"Like what? A little broken? Sometimes moody? Rumor, love isn't just for the happy times. This girl fell in love with you while you were homeless. She knows it's not going to be peaches and crème but she wants it anyway." He lies down beside me. "Real talk? I think this is going to suck for a while. You lost one important person after another, and I can't imagine how hard it is for you to breathe sometimes but you aren't alone in a gas station bathroom anymore. You've got me, your girl, a new grandfather, two dorky friends, and the modern-day Brady Bunch to help you through this."

I grin. "You met her family?"

"Each and every last one of them. They're good people."

"Yeah, they are."

His fingers wrap around my wrist. "Some days are going to try to kill you, man. Some days, you'll probably stay in bed until there's a lint monster in your belly button, but we'll all love you in spite of your lack of personal hygiene."

I flip him off.

Then I think about my girl.

"She's been healing me since I got here, Josh. I felt it in those tiny violins and the way the earth shook each time she smiled at me. She was healing me, and I shoved her away when I couldn't feel that anymore."

He throws his foot into mine. "So, go get her back."

"Is she here?"

"No, she's at her house."

I jump to my feet and move to my bag on auto-pilot, digging for a pair of pants. "I need to go get her."

"Uhm, dude? Maybe take that shower first."

I drop my pants. "Right." Moving past him, purpose in my strides, I tear open the door.

And then I stop.

"How long are you staying?" I ask the door.

Please. Stay.

"Few days," he says. "We're on fall break."

"And then what?"

"Then I go back to Chicago, and you stay here. You enjoy being in love, take time to get to know your grandfather, make memories with your new friends. You have a plan, Rumor. Simon's Space? That's a good ass plan. You're just scared because you don't have your dad here to guide you. But I'll guide you, okay? We got this."

I look over my shoulder. "I am not calling you daddy."

He swoops a sock off the floor and chucks it at me. "Go. Shower and make things right with your girl. When you come back, you're gonna tell me all about your mama."

"And after that?"

"You heal."

29

ON ONE CONDITION

ALMA

The way I found him was serendipitous. But the way I've come to love him is more than just a cheery mishap.

My love for him is a treasure that can't be put in a tub with the lid sealed tight. It's the kind of thing that deserves to be felt, that yearns to be experienced.

And I think maybe I've had it wrong this whole time. Rumor himself isn't the treasure but rather the way he makes me feel. The butterfly kisses and soft touches. The private laughs and exclusive smiles. The times he would look at me, and I'd melt all over his feet. Those were the real gifts, and the vastness of those things wouldn't fit beside drumsticks, Polaroid cameras, costume jewelry, or a maca-roni hat. It merits its own space to breathe, and a box shoved under my bed just isn't good enough. So, I tucked it in its own place, something unshared and personal— my heart.

The whole thing about treasures is that they have to be found, and Rumor was never on a quest to be found. His journey was to find. Perhaps that was my problem. I found a treasure that wasn't supposed to be found.

I wrote a story for someone who wanted to write their own.

Though sometimes I wish I could take it back, I wouldn't dare erase our story. Because doing that would mean expunging all the real treasures from the space in my heart, and though the space feels hollow now, I could never give it up.

My room feels different now that he's gone. The pizza slice is still beside my bed but it's deflated, shriveled up and miserable looking. I feel dejected just looking at it but apparently, I like to suffer because I can't bring myself to get rid of it. Nor can I get rid of the blanket he wrapped himself in and the pillow he laid his head on. They remind me of him and the nights I slept with my arm hanging off the edge of my bed so I wouldn't have to let go of his hand.

I sleep with them now, usually in my arms like a makeshift cuddle buddy. It nowhere near compares to holding his hand but it's the closest thing to a connection I can make. And, yeah, maybe sometimes I like to smell him on the fleece.

Sue me.

Lenox says I'm suffering from a broken heart, and Jackson has diagnosed with me stress-induced cardiomyopathy. Both come with a surge of intense chest pain that knocks the breath right from my lungs.

I don't wish to be suffering from either of them but the soundless tears I shed right before I drift off to sleep at night are proof of my condition.

Broken heart.

Unfortunately for me, the best way to remedy a broken heart is with love, and my love kicked me out of his life.

The staircase outside my door groans as it harbors somebody's weight. Each creak of the wood has me flinching until I roll over and push my face into my pillow. The clouds below my face mock me. I can hear their evil little cackles, see them pointing their creepy cloud fingers at me. I used to fly beside those traitorous clouds. Now, I'm eating dirt.

Stupid clouds.

Heavy footsteps stop outside my door and I sit up, pinching my cheeks to put a little color in them. Folding my hands in my lap, my legs swing back and forth while I wait for one of my family members. It could be any of them. They seem to come in shifts but I can't figure out their rotation.

Since it's a weekend, my money is on Shepherd.

My spine straightens when the doorknob starts to turn. I make quick work of running my fingers through my bangs so he's less likely to guess I've been in bed with my head buried in a blanket Rumor used to breathe on. Fraudulent or not, I struggle to paint a smile on my lips. By the time the door swings open, I've settled for what I think is a look of indifference.

Then he steps through the doorway, and my jaw meets my palms.

"You're not Shepherd."

"Well, that's a damn relief because if I was, it would make what I came to do really awkward."

Did I wake up this morning?

I get a good grip of forearm skin between my thumb and forefinger and squeeze with as much muscle as I can muster.

It hurts, and I smile.

"Are you pinching yourself?" Kicking the door shut, he saunters across my bedroom. I count four steps before he's right in front of me, batting at the fingers giving my arm a watermelon-sized bruise. "Stop it, Ace."

Ace. He called me Ace.

Confusion is a ring around my mind when he starts to lower, bringing himself to a squat directly in front of me. Uncertain eyes watch his movements, and when he reaches for my arm, I give it to him. The tips of his hair whisper across my thigh, provoking goosebumps to form against my skin. Sudden, fiery tears burn the corners of my eyes when his lips, soft and gentle, press against my newly bruised skin.

What is happening right now?

His kisses continue, trailing down my arm in a pattern I think is deliberate. When he reaches my hand, he gifts me with a feather-light kiss in the center of my palm. The hand in question quivers as he takes my fingers, one by one, and curls them into a fist as though he's urging me to hold onto the kiss.

I hiccup.

His head snaps up, hair billowing around him like a curtain. Our eyes meet, but I can't see all that I'd like to with the tears, thick as rain, dripping off my eyelids in a slow sequence.

"Don't cry." The pad of his thumb rids me of my tears, and his next words obliterate me. "I'm sorry, Ace. I'm sorry I called you mean. I'm sorry I told you you were cruel, and I'm so damn sorry for telling you I need you out of my life when all you've ever done is make it better. Your twinkle lights aren't dumb, your treasures aren't stupid, and you have never treated me like an object. I've always been someone to you. Not just the homeless guy, the orphan, or the dude with one hand. I've just been Rumor, and with you around, I really like who he is."

"But I... I lied to you."

"Yeah, and it hurt like hell but I know now why you did it. Hell, baby, I think I understood where your heart was at the moment you confessed. It was my heart I couldn't find. I hurt so bad, Ace."

"Of course you did." With his kiss still in my fist, I use my free hand to run my knuckles down his cheek. The trivial touch sends a warming shiver through me. "I never meant to blindside you. I tried to tell you every day for weeks, Rumor. I didn't know how to hurt you. And I think I was also kind of angry. You came all this way and you didn't even find what you were looking for."

"Yes. I did."

The skin across my forehead pulls tight.

Stretching his neck, he peppers a string of kisses across the wrinkle and moves to sit next to me on the bed. Grabbing the hand that doesn't contain his kiss, he brings it to his chest. "I came here to find my family, Ace. Maybe it wasn't the one I was looking for, but it's a family nonetheless, and it's one I'm lucky to be a part of. I've struggled to remember that these past few days, and I'm sorry. Josh helped remind me."

"Josh? You talked to him?"

"I did. Thank you for calling him, Ace. Thank you for knowing how badly I needed him."

I was a wreck, standing at the phone, stumbling over my words with the tips of my toes tingling, trying to decide if calling Josh would be overstepping. I chewed down all ten of my fingernails and my pupils were the size of saucers before I finally found some nerve.

The second Josh stepped out of his car, I knew I'd made the right choice.

Josh is his solace provider, his guardian angel, his

teammate, his lifeline. He's someone who doesn't have to fill in all the blanks because he's already privy to the inner details of Rumor's life. Their connection is the kind that comes with no conditions. It's honest and it's ruthless, and it's not just a friendship. It's a brotherhood.

Josh is his brother. The same way Lenox is my sister. Blood be damned.

"You're welcome. I'm glad you finally got to see him."

"All thanks to you." The tip of his nose is cold against my hand. "First he was nice to me, then he yelled at me, then he was nice again, then he made me take a shower."

"Uhm, showering is good."

He laughs, and it is beautiful.

"Is he here?"

"Who? Josh? Nah, he's back at Reggie's with his parents."

"Did you see them too?"

"Judy and Scott? Yeah. They brought a ton of my stuff. More clothes, my computer, my skateboard."

"So, you're staying for a while then?"

I press my fist over my expanding chest, my throat thickening with immediate relief. My lips part and I'm light headed as I stare at him, whispering a low prayer of gratitude.

"This is where the people I love are. Josh is going to visit over Christmas break. He also put me in a choke hold until I promised to get my phone turned back on."

I grin, and it's the first one in days. One I wasn't sure I'd feel on my face again because it's one I save for him. "I was worried you might have left already."

"Leaving never crossed my mind. These past few days just kicked my ass. I was crushed and pissed off. At you for lying, my parents for dying, and Reggie for being so damn nice. I've just been in bed... surviving."

I want to thank him for surviving. The act looks good on him. There are some cracks in his lips and dark circles around his eyes but I like the way he's looking through them right now. Gently. Though he's walked through flames and crawled across glass, the makings of a smile are prominent on his cheeks.

I know there are scars I can't see, cuts below the surface that will take longer, if not forever, to heal. But he's here.

He's here.

"Thank you for surviving, Rumor."

"Thank you for reminding me why I needed to."

He brings our hands to his lap, and I happily let him invade my personal space. The tips of our noses touch and I can't see the smile on his lips, but the one in his eyes is spectacular. "I can't stay for long. I promised Josh I'd tell him about my mama. She was wonderful, Ace. She worked at a craft store and ate breakfast food for every meal. You know those paintings Reggie has all over his house? She painted them. How crazy is that? My mom was a painter. Reggie said I could have one."

Desperate to feel his smile, I drag my thumb across his bottom lip. "That's amazing."

"Maybe tomorrow I could come back over and tell you all about her?" He captures the tip of my thumb between his lips and releases it with a kiss.

"Rumor, I'd love that."

"Me too. I'm sorry for the way I treated you. I'll never raise my voice at you like that again."

"I'm sorry too. No more lies. They make me itchy."

He chuckles, and it vibrates against my lips. "Deal."

"Best friends again?" I hold my breath and cross my

fingers, holding them against my heart.

"Best friends but on one condition." Tilting his head, he drags his nose down my cheek, neck, and presses a kiss to my collar bone. "You let me love you."

I stop breathing.

"Because, Alma, I love you. The way I love you has changed the way I see the world and it feels good. It feels good to love you, baby, and I don't want to pretend I don't anymore. I've still got some healing to do, the road ahead of me is rocky, and it might get messy, but I'm done with just surviving. Loving you is living, Ace. I want to live."

The butterflies explode.

I'm tangled in the trail of kisses they left behind, and I have no intention of trying to escape. In their wake they leave behind a current of comfort, flowing through my veins. My cheeks warm, and the heart inside my chest registers an extra beat.

His.

"I love you too."

"Yeah?"

"I've said since the day I found you I've had a feeling. If I would've known back then that feeling was love, I would've tried to find you sooner. You, Rumor Rawlings, are my greatest find."

"Did Alma Underwood just declare me as her favorite lost treasure?"

"Not lost." I cup his face. "You're exactly where you're supposed to be."

Draping my arms around his neck, I kiss him. With all that I have, all that I am, I kiss Rumor, and with it comes the greatest feeling known to man.

An exceptional treasure.

Love.

EPILOGUE
RUMOR

"We are gathered here today to—"

"Jackson!" There's a red rose behind her ear, and it bounces when she shakes her head. "This is a funeral. Not a wedding."

"Alma, please." The sword in Jackson's left hand stabs at the ground as he regards his sister with a pinched expression. "When Rumor asks you to officiate his runaway mother's second funeral, you may write the script. Until then, keep your suggestions to yourself."

Alma nods, pretending to zip her lips. She tosses the key on the ground and stomps on it, digging the heel of her sparkly red shoe into the dirt below us.

I nudge her with my hip. "Behave, would ya? You're gonna get kicked out of my mother's funeral."

"I think that crown on top of his head is getting to him," she says, and then slaps both hands over her mouth like she forgot her lips were under lock and key.

Snaking an arm around her waist, I pull her flush against me and kiss the top of her head. "You should be the one wearing the crown, Ace."

With a soft sigh, she leans into me, wrapping her arms around my middle and squeezing. Smiling against the dress shirt I'm wearing, she gives her attention back to Jackson, and I know she's working hard to keep her giggle inward.

For today's event, Jackson's decided to dress as a medieval king, tights and all. With a surcoat draped over his shoulders and a belt the size of his stomach, he looks fit to the hold sword he drags behind him. Charlevoix matches impeccably, wearing a surcoat of her own, and a tiny crown between her ears.

"We are gathered here today in celebration," Jackson begins, capturing the attention of the small crowd surrounding him.

The thirteen of us have made a horseshoe with our bodies, standing shoulder to shoulder. Between the suits, dresses, and the cape Arthur is wearing, nobody is wearing black today.

I requested color.

Pink, yellow, white, blue, green, purple and red. Color is everywhere—acting as a power that impacts the soul. Not my soul. My mother's.

The color is for her.

"When Rumor asked me to stand before you today and speak on behalf of his mother, I almost said no. Because how do you honor somebody you've never met? Then I realized, I have met Allison. I've met her through Rumor, through Reginald, through paintings that now hang in my parent's motel." With Charlevoix now curled at his feet, he stops pacing and lifts his chin. "My older sister is kind of a kleptomaniac."

Alma groans beside me.

"She has this thing for taking objects people leave behind and making something out of them. She calls them her treasures." Jackson's throat clears and he bites the inside of his cheek, looking at me with a smile that has my lip trembling. "I believe that's what people do when they pass on—leave treasures behind for us to find. Something to remember them by or honor them with. Something for us to give our love to. Allison left lots of treasures behind for us to find but I know I speak for all of us when I say the greatest thing she left behind was you."

Our eyes meet, and a tear rolls down my cheek. It slips off my chin and splashes the tip of my leather shoe. I stare at the puddle it makes, and when another tear joins it, I watch the puddle get bigger. A hand comes down on my shoulder with a strength that belongs to Josh. When he squeezes, giving me a shake, I lift my head and tighten my grip on Alma.

"I'm sorry, Rumor, that the bouquet of roses you showed up with today is next to her resting place instead of in her hands, and I'm sorry you can't remember the woman you share eyes with. I'm sorry we're celebrating her life rather than bearing witness to her living it. And although most of us here never knew her, we'll honor her anyway. Because with her, comes you. Sorry isn't enough to bandage the cuts you wear beneath your skin but I hope knowing what you meant to her is."

Alma's hand is over my heart now, rubbing in slow motion as though she knows I need her to quell some of the pain. The firm grip Josh has on my shoulder tightens with the shudder that moves up my spine.

"Thank you for being here," I want to tell him but he already knows how deeply appreciative I am for the trip he made here this weekend, so I stay silent, the only sounds leaving me the occasional sniff.

It isn't until Jackson asks if anyone would like to share a

few words do I take a shaky step forward. Leaves crunch beneath my feet with each step I take toward my mom. The tombstone is cold beneath my palm when I rest my hand on the curve of it. It's not a replacement for the warmth her touch would bring but it's what I have, so I close my eyes and wait for her to replace the darkness.

When she appears, I find the rose behind her ear has friends now. There are thousands of them, spanning a field that goes on for miles. My mom is standing in the center, her face toward the sun and a hand on her heart. A light wind has them all blowing toward her, and she inhales, smiling as the scent reaches her nostrils.

She looks different now than she ever has before, and I think maybe that has to do with the person standing next to her. Holding her hand tight is a man, he's wearing a shirt with no tie and flashing her a smile that looks just like mine.

"I used to be mad at you," I tell them, and they frown at me. "I was mad at you for leaving me and in some ways I still am. Just a little. I hate that you aren't here to meet my girlfriend or watch me graduate from high school." My dad looks at me, cocking his head as though he doesn't understand. "Reggie he, uh, he helped me enroll at Flat Rock High School and I start in a few days. It's going to be weird without your first day of school waffles, dad. The day I get my cap and gown is going to be bittersweet because it's you that was always supposed to adjust the cap on my head until it sat just right. I feel both of your absences every day, more so now that I'm growing up. I keep trying to make choices that will make you proud, and I can only hope I'm doing okay so far. Turns out, the University of Michigan has a nonprofit management degree. It's the road I'm going to drive down, and I hope somehow, you'll both come with me."

They both nod, smiles etched on their faces. My mother has a hand over her heart, tears in her eyes. My father's lips brush a spot on her forehead that isn't concealed by hair. When their eyes meet, they start to glow and I wonder if it's the violins and the butterflies mixing. I wonder if that's what love looks like when it's the only thing left to feel.

A sob breaks free from my chest, and I let the tears soak the collar of my shirt. They don't burn this time and breathing is less like a chore and more like something that was gifted to me. "It sucks you aren't here but it sucks a little less knowing you're together again. I'll be back with updates as often as life allows and I promise to keep you with me wherever I go." With a kiss to my fingers, I run the pads of my fingers over her name, watching as they wave at me, vanishing into the roses.

My tears dry watching them fade, and I use her headstone to pull myself back to my feet. I look over my shoulder, and like always when I feel as though I might drown, she's right there.

I reach for her, and she dives. Right into the ocean I'm trapped in, wrapping her arms around my neck and tugging me to the surface with a strength she regularly shares with me.

"I love you," she tells me, stretching up on her tiptoes to pepper my jawline with kisses.

"I love you too."

And we stand there, holding each other while the sun goes down and those around us step up to my mother to pay their respects. Josh pats my back when he walks past me, leaving my mother one last rose.

Soon, everyone is gone and it's just my girl and I. Using

my knuckle, I tilt her chin and connect our lips. Gratitude and love pour from my mouth to hers as I kiss her, lifting her off her feet to carry her the way she has me.

"Your love is the real treasure," she told me.

But I disagree.

It's hers.

ALSO BY LACEY DAILEY

Circuit Series

Specter

Mischief

Standalone

Creating Chaos

Devil Side

ACKNOWLEDGMENTS

Tristan, I love you. Thank you for encouraging me to follow my dreams.

Monique, even thousands of miles away I can always count on you to be there for me. As always, you helped this book evolve from an idea to a novel and I'm so thankful for our friendship.

To Keeley, my editor, you help me transform my words and make them shine. Thank you for working your magic on this novel and loving these characters as much as I do.

Thank you to the bloggers and bookstagrammers who have supported me nonstop. The love I feel from you all is profound.

Thank you to all the readers and bloggers who joined my reader group, Lacey's Lounge, on Facebook. I love learning about each and everyone of you, and I'm so grateful I have such a positive group of readers to share my journey with.

As always, thank you to all the readers who continue to read my novels and express their love and interest. It means more to me than you'll ever know. You chose to read my books over the millions of books available, and I'll never take that for granted. If you enjoyed it, please consider leaving a review. Reviews fuel indie authors.

Thank you from the bottom of my heart.

XO, Lacey

ABOUT THE AUTHOR

The best place to find Lacey is with her nose in a book. She's a sucker for a good love story and a happy ending that has her swooning. When she's not obsessing over giving her own characters a happy ending, you can find her in the dance studio empowering young dancers and giving out tons of stickers. Thanks to her mother's pizzeria, Lacey can make a delicious pizza.

When she's not putting on her dance shoes or inhaling a slice of pizza, she's in front of her computer binge watching romantic comedies and penning stories with love so powerful, it'll last a lifetime. As a recent graduate of Central Michigan University, Lacey intends to keep inspiring people through dance and lots and lots of words. She currently lives in Central Michigan surrounded by her family and unpredictable weather.

Connect with Lacey:
www.laceydaileyauthor.com

Printed in Great Britain
by Amazon

16253356R00164